AVERIL, MY ANCHOR

AVERIL, MY ANCHOR

Richard Reynolds

WARREN H. GREEN
8356 Olive Blvd
St. Louis, MO 63132

Published by

Epoch Press

A division of

Warren H. Green, Inc.
8356 Olive Boulevard
St. Louis, Missouri 63132 USA
314.991.1335

All Rights Reserved

©2004 by Warren H. Green, Inc.

ISBN: 0-87527-539-7

For Maureen; my wife, first reader, sanity check, and morning joy.

Acknowledgements

A number of friends, colleagues, and family members have helped me in countless way to write this book.

Thanks to my step-daughter, Liz Mediavilla, for getting me started; to my writing teachers: Miriam Sagan, Jay Udall, and Terry Wilson, for showing me the way and encouraging me to take chances; to Jeri Leibman and Carole Norman for pushing me over the edge and convincing me that I could write a novel.

I'm particularly grateful to members of my first writing group who read the manuscript and offered honest and valued critiques: Stephanie Anagnoson, Freddi Hetler, and Donna Mifflin. Special thanks to friends who also read the manuscript and provided encouragement and advice: George Campbell; Barbara Gray Campbell, keeper of the Queen's English and wise counsel in all matters British; Julie Rubio, and Sharon Stanton.

Beverly A. Clark, Editor and Publisher of *Sweet Annie & Sweet Pea Review,* gave my fiction writing career its jump start when she published two of my earliest short stories. I thank her for her friendship and literary insights. Gershon Siegel, Editor and Publisher of the ELDORADO SUN, published several of my early efforts and continues to give encouragement and support.

My gratitude also goes to members of my current writing group who reviewed the manuscript and showed me how to further polish it: Nancy Evans, Clair Gardner, Frances Lumbers, and Jeanette Woodward.

Finally, a tip of the fedora to Mike Freiermuth, Editor and Publisher of *Timber Creek Review* and *Words of Wisdom,* who also published many of my short stories. In particular, this novel contains material previously seen in "Closure in Cassino," which appeared in the Winter 1999 issue of *Words of Wisdom.*

AVERIL, MY ANCHOR

Chapter One

*A*veril Holloway stood just high enough on the steps of St. Peter's Basilica to be shaded from a June afternoon sun. She looked out over the sea of tourists, anxious for the return of her husband Mark, who was off in search of a public toilet. She was also getting hungry and hoped they wouldn't have to walk far before finding a decent restaurant.

A middle-aged woman, wearing a red baseball cap bearing a large "T" on the front, interrupted Averil's thoughts of food. "Is there anything in there?" the woman asked, pointing to the basilica's interior.

"I beg your pardon?" said Averil.

"I mean, is it worth going inside to have a look around?"

Averil wondered why she would ask. "Why yes, I should think so. You should see Michelangelo's Pieta. Then there's the Confessional Altar where St. Peter is supposed to be buried. And you shouldn't miss the Vatican Museum and the Sistine Chapel."

"Well, I don't know," said the woman. "Seems like an awful lot to see."

A middle-aged man wearing a matching baseball cap walked up to the two women and checked his watch. "C'mon, Darlene, let's get a move on and go inside. We only got an hour before we have to meet Fred and Sarah Jo at the Colosseum." The couple walked inside, leaving an amused Averil shaking her head.

Mark came up beside her. "What's so funny?"

"Those Americans I just talked to—they came all this way, not knowing what they wanted to see. And if they happen to come across something special, they won't even know what they're looking at. Of course they weren't dressed properly so they'll probably be invited to leave."

Mark shrugged and said in a flat Midwestern accent, "What can I say?"

"You could say—let's have lunch."

"OK, let's head in the direction of the Metro station and grab a bite."

"How far do we have to walk?"

"Not far. There's bound to be something on the way."

Both were dressed for summer and wore comfortable shoes, so the walk turned out to be fairly pleasant with the temperature in the high seventies. Averil loved short walks with Mark, but not the longer hikes—"death marches" she called them—the treks he had led when they explored Paris, London, and Cairo.

After walking for a half mile, they found a bustling cafe and bought ready-made ham and cheese sandwiches and cold orange drinks at a long glass-enclosed counter. They found stools nearby and were content to sit, eat, drink, and observe the Roman citizens around them. People watching was their favorite game when they were together in a restaurant or airport terminal. Because of the high noise level in the cafe, they had to practically shout into each other's ear.

A short Italian man in his late thirties standing in front of the lunch counter was first to attract Mark's attention. He wore tight brown trousers and expensive sunglasses perched on an aquiline nose; a yellow cotton sweater was draped over his back with the sweater's arms folded across his chest.

"What do you think of him?"

"He has a lovely butt," she sighed. "Small and tight."

Then it was Averil's turn to point out a woman for Mark's appreciation. A voluptuous blonde entered the cafe, probably in her late thirties, wearing black slacks at least two sizes too small. She wore her hair in a pony tail and sported large sunglasses similar to those worn by Sophia Loren.

"And speaking of butts," said Averil, "how could you possibly miss the one on that woman?"

"No chance of that." Mark grinned. "In fact, if the seams of those pants split, you'd have ass all over this cafe."

Averil erupted in loud whoops of laughter. "Get me out of here," she pleaded, "before I make a fool of myself."

They were soon back on the sidewalk searching for the Metro station. When they found the entrance, the accordion metal gates were closed and locked with a large white sign attached.

"Oh bloody hell," she said. "Can you make out what the sign says?"

"I think the Metro workers are on strike."

"We should have taken a taxi from St. Peter's."

"It's not my fault. I didn't know anything about it."

CHAPTER ONE

Standing on the corner of two major streets they flagged down a passing cab that took them to the Baths of Caracalla. The Baths turned out to be a pleasant surprise because there were only a few people strolling about the tree-filled park. The sun had started to set and a gentle breeze picked up.

They walked hand-in-hand, admiring the three story brick walls and colorful ground mosaics of the ancient public bath's ruins, and came to several posters advertising a production of *Aida*. "It sounds exciting," she said. "You know, we could catch this. After our time on the coast and before we go to Florence."

Mark frowned. "Gee, I don't know. It's a pretty heavy piece of show business. Treason, unrequited love, people buried alive in a tomb. That sort of stuff."

"Mark, I know the story. I just thought it would be worth seeing. If I understand the posters, they're going to have live elephants in the procession."

He had to smile. "You're right. We can't miss the elephants. I'll talk to the concierge when we get back to the hotel and have him order us tickets."

She smiled and brushed his cheek with her hand. "Thank you, luv. I promise you won't regret it."

Mark glanced at his watch, "I think we've seen everything. Ready to move on?"

"Almost. I want to stop at the kiosk we saw at the entrance." Once there, she bought post cards and two newspapers, an *International Herald Tribune* for Mark and *The Sunday Telegraph* from London for herself. They sat on a park bench and read quietly for about five minutes until Averil suddenly cried out, "Oh my God. I don't believe this."

"What's wrong, honey? Did something bite you?"

She shook her head and repeatedly stabbed the paper with her finger. Mark took it from her and began to read:

Terrorist must pay legal fees from prison wages.
A convicted terrorist has been ordered to pay legal costs estimated at £20,000 from his £8-a-week prison earnings after losing a claim for damages against the Prison Service.

> *Sean Flannery, 48, serving 16 years for aggravated assault, battery, and conspiracy to commit murder, lost his case at Peterborough Crown court last week. Flannery had issued a writ against the service in December 1997, eight months after he fell and broke his wrist during a basketball game at Whitemoor Prison, Cambs.*
>
> *He claimed that he had tripped on a football net that had not been put away properly in the prison gymnasium, but witnesses for the service said that the injury happened when he became involved in a violent collision with other inmates.*
>
> *The judge found against Flannery, who conducted the case himself after his legal aid was stopped, and ordered him to pay costs.*
>
> *Flannery was sentenced at the Old Bailey in June 1988 and is now being held at Full Sutton Prison near York. He is due for parole later this year and his earliest release date if parole is refused is in three years.*

"I'll be damned," he said. "Here we are, enjoying our tenth anniversary in Italy, and your ex-husband screws it up."

Averil got up and started pacing back and forth. "This is terrible news," she railed. "He could be released in a few months."

Mark scratched his head as a half-hearted smile appeared. "He really has balls—suing the prison. In the Navy we had a name for guys like him. Sea lawyers."

"Stop it," she said. "Right now."

"He can't hurt you anymore, honey. Not with the Atlantic Ocean between you and him."

She pointed to her side, just above the waist. "Have you forgotten this scar? It's him I have to thank for it."

He looked up at her. "How could I forget? I see it almost every day." She resumed pacing as he looked around. "Please sit down, Av. Everyone's staring."

She relaxed and moved cautiously into his waiting arms. "The man's a murderer, capable of committing the worst possible crimes. He and his mates tried to kill the Prime Minister. Remember?"

He kissed her lightly on her forehead and stroked her cheek with his fingers. "Yes, I remember, but that was a long time ago."

She shivered and said, "Don't underestimate him. Remember that letter he wrote from prison just after you and I married? He felt I'd betrayed him. He was a very bitter man and no doubt still is. He's the type of scum that never forgets."

Mark didn't answer. They held each other in the fading sunlight as Averil wondered how her peaceful world could have changed so dramatically in such a short period of time.

Chapter Two

The next afternoon Mark and Averil left Rome in their small rental car. As he drove through the crowded streets, Averil glanced at him several times and could not suppress a faint smile. She was immensely proud of him, especially in this type of situation. His thirty-four years of experience as a military and commercial airline pilot gave him a quiet confidence and an accurate sense of direction. Even in less-traveled foreign cities, he almost never got lost. But when he did, he was never too proud to stop and ask for directions, a quality Averil admired greatly.

The sun was out, the sky clear, and the temperature in the low seventies, a pleasant day for their drive southeast to the Mediterranean coastal resort town of Formia. After sixty-five miles on the autostrada, Mark found a scenic short cut. They were soon passing through farmland, orchards and picturesque villages, another world altogether. Soon the road ended abruptly at the Mediterranean coast. There was no traffic behind them, so they paused to take in the white beach, softly breaking green surf, and the bright blue sky holding a few white puffball clouds.

Mark turned south and drove along the coast at a leisurely speed. Averil was so entranced by the surroundings that she said little, content to stare out the passenger side window. Without being invited, the newspaper article about Sean Flannery entered her mind and caused her to think of the early days: meeting him, their courtship, and their marriage. *If I had the opportunity to go back and do it all over again, what could I do to make things turn out differently?*

Seventeen years before, thirty-year-old Averil Langford was working in Selfridge's department store on London's Oxford Street, selling women's purses and luggage. One Saturday evening, two other saleswomen, Claire Blackwood and Pauline Templeton, invited her to join them for a drink at the nearby Hogshead pub. All three had just received their annual performance reviews with salary raises so it was an occasion

CHAPTER TWO

to celebrate.

Though the pub was noisy and crowded, the women found a booth and got their gin and tonics right away. They chatted away excitedly and didn't notice a trio of young men sitting nearby, watching them with hungry eyes. Eventually, their waitress brought them three more drinks, causing Averil to protest that they hadn't ordered another round.

"Not to mind, ladies. Compliments of the gents over there." She cocked her head in the direction of the male trio.

The women looked in that direction and smiled a thank you. One of the men rose and headed toward their booth. Averil watched as he ambled forward. She took in his tall frame and broad shoulders, his short red hair and fair complexion, his square jaw, and a wide smile that barely contained a set of large white teeth.

"Good evening, ladies," he started. "Me name is Sean Flannery. I come from Carrickfergus in County Antrim."

He extended his hand toward Averil and, even though she wanted to hide her own hand in her lap, she took his, hypnotized by his intense green eyes. *Good God, why did this handsome man turn out to be Irish?* When he leaned closer, she moved slightly so he could sit down.

Averil's friends chattered amongst themselves while she and Sean began asking trivial questions and giving evasive answers, trying to gain the measure of the other person. Finally, he asked for her telephone number.

"Claire, do you have something to write with?" asked Averil.

Claire produced a pen and small tablet from her purse and Averil jotted down her number on the first page. As she tore the page from the pad and held it out in Sean's direction she tipped her glass, sending her drink pouring into his lap. Both Averil and Sean jumped at the same instant. General chaos followed, both trying to sop up liquid from Sean's trousers and wipe the table.

"You'll be hearing from me," was the last thing he said to a flustered Averil before returning to his own booth. Minutes later, the men emptied their glasses, saluted the three ladies, and left the pub, causing the women to wonder why the other two had not been as aggressive as Flannery.

Flannery eventually called and asked for a date on a coming Saturday when he would again be visiting London. They agreed to meet at the Euston railroad station and have dinner at a nearby restaurant.

Awkward and hesitant at first, they became more at ease and talkative over dinner, their tongues loosened by a bottle of French red wine which they consumed during their dinner salads. As they hungrily set upon their prime rib entree, they started on a second bottle of wine.

"You haven't spoken much about home," said Averil. "Do you have a family back in Ireland?"

"That I do, and a big one at that. Michael is me older brother and the other four are younger."

"I believe you said you came from Carrickfergus."

"That I did. A lovely little village on the north coast. We never had much but me mother always saw to it there was food on the table."

"And you attended school there as well?"

Sean looked away for a moment and then down at his plate. "I've not had much in the way of formal education. Had to take me a job to support the family when times were hard." He looked straight into her eyes and touched her hand lightly with his own. "I was also raised a strict Catholic boy. You being British and all—I hope this won't keep us from having a friendship."

Averil squeezed his hand. "I can assure you that our having different religious views won't be a problem."

Sean took a large gulp of wine and continued, "When me dad passed away last year, the situation at home got much worse. That's when I moved to Manchester and got me this job as a machinist. Pays much better wages than I could get in Ireland. Now I can send some money home to me mum."

Averil became more animated. "My father was a conductor for British Railways and was in a train collision near Basingstoke eight years ago. He died in the crash."

"I'm genuinely sorry to hear that," he said. "Is your mum still alive?"

"Yes, she lives in Southampton, but her health is poor. Like you, I send her a few pounds each week out of my salary. So does my sister, Emma." Averil extended both hands across the table and Sean took them into his own without any hesitation or awkwardness. "Where are you planning to spend the night?"

Sean grinned sheepishly. "Oh, probably on a bench in Hyde Park."

"You'll do nothing of the kind," she shot back. "In fact, I'd be insulted

CHAPTER TWO

if you didn't ask to spend the night in my apartment."

That signaled the end of dinner. Rather than walk to the underground station, Sean splurged on a taxi. Once inside her South Kensington apartment, they couldn't remove each other's clothes fast enough.

As the morning sun streamed through the sheer curtains in her bedroom, she whispered in his ear, "Did you really plan to sleep in Hyde Park?"

He fondled her bare butt and kissed her softly on the lips. "Of course not. I knew all along you'd want your way with me in bed."

She disengaged, jumped out of bed, and said in mock anger, "What a bunch of rubbish." She put on a cotton robe and called out over her shoulder as she left the room, "I'll put the kettle on for tea. Would you like breakfast?"

"I'd fancy another portion of you," he said with a smirk on his face.

After their first weekend together, they established a regular dating pattern. Sean would take the train from Manchester to London on Friday afternoon after work and return late Sunday evening. This went on for several months until Averil suggested that he move in with her and look for employment in London. Sean happily agreed and soon found another machinist job. As time went on, she began to think seriously about making a long term commitment.

Sean, who was not totally impervious to Averil's unsubtle hints, proposed marriage in mid-November. His proposal was not that surprising, but his insistence on a quick wedding did cause considerable chaos in her family.

With many telephone calls and several sudden trips to Southampton, a small private wedding ceremony was arranged for mid-December at her mother's parish church. Averil's sister Emma was the matron of honor while Sean's best man was Padraig Duffy, one of the other two men present at the Hogshead the night Sean and Averil first met. The third member, Malachy O'Brien, was also present at the wedding and simple reception that followed at the Octagon Hotel and managed to become intimately acquainted with Claire Blackwell in a linen closet.

Sean and Averil kept mostly to themselves during the first months of 1984 until O'Brien and Duffy moved to London in April. The men found an apartment uncomfortably close to Averil while Sean helped them find jobs. O'Brien continued his sporadic romance with Claire Blackwell but, in Averil's eyes, a more disturbing trend began. More often than not, Sean would spend his off-duty hours at a local pub with O'Brien and Duffy rather than with her. Many an evening, a drunken Sean would stumble into their apartment, demanding a hot dinner followed by a bit of sex, only to be told in strident terms by Averil that he wouldn't get either one.

She grew more unhappy as the weeks went by and wondered what was happening to their marriage, how long this strife would continue, and what she could do to get things changed back to the way they used to be. In autumn the unpleasant answer came from an unexpected source.

At 2:54 A.M. on Thursday, October 11, while Prime Minister Margaret Thatcher and other Tory leadership were staying at the Grand Hotel in the southern coastal city of Brighton, a bomb exploded near Thatcher's room. She had been working on her speech for the opening of the Conservative Party conference later that morning and was not harmed by the blast. Five people were killed in the attack, however, including Anthony Berry, a member of Parliament, and Roberta Wakeham, wife of the Conservative Party's Chief Whip.

When Averil awoke alone that morning and turned on the television, she became acutely aware of the tragedy and its possible consequences to her life. Sean had not been home for the two previous nights, a situation that was not all that unusual, since by then, he preferred to sleep off his drinking binges elsewhere rather than face Averil's wrath. When she saw the demolished facade of the Grand Hotel and the victims being carried out on stretchers, the seed was planted in her mind that Sean and his pals might somehow be involved in this bombing attack.

For the next two days, Averil slept poorly and worried about many things during her waking hours: her marriage, her ability to keep her job, and the well-being of her wayward husband. About 4:00 A.M. the following Saturday, she was awakened by a telephone call.

"Av, it's me. Have the police been nosing about the place?"

"Where the hell are you? I've been worried sick."

"I'm all right—not too far away."

"When are you coming home?"

"Look. If the police come round, tell them me mum took sick and I had to go home to see her. Will you do that for me?"

CHAPTER TWO

At this point, Averil was crying and, after he promised to call again soon, she agreed to his request.

The weeks passed slowly, punctuated by the occasional call Sean usually made to Averil in the early morning hours. He would not divulge his exact location for fear of her telephone being tapped, which made her suspect that he and his cohorts were part of the conspiracy to kill the prime minister. In mid-December, she received a brief note from him, postmarked Enniskillen in Northern Ireland. From the muddled text of his message, she deduced he was drunk when he wrote his maudlin plea for forgiveness on this, their first wedding anniversary.

Averil's concern about her husband's condition gradually faded until it was replaced with anger for being used by him and then deserted. As his mysterious telephone calls became more infrequent, her anger gave way to a hostile indifference. She stopped feeling sorry for herself and made a concerted effort to communicate more with her family and socialize more with Claire and Pauline.

One night in mid-March of 1985, Averil was wakened shortly after midnight by a loud knocking at the door. She put on a robe and, after looking through the door's peephole, opened it to allow in a dirty, unshaven, and very drunk Sean Flannery. Averil backed away from him and stood erect with her arms folded across her chest. "Look at you," she railed, "you're a bloody mess."

"Aach, don't turn on me now. I need your help."

"I think you've gone way beyond any help I might give you."

"I just need a place to stay for a few days. Do you have any food in the place?"

Averil turned, walked into the kitchen, and sat down at the small table where they had taken their meals in happier times. "You're welcome to look in the fridge and cupboards for something. You know where everything is."

He found a chunk of cheddar cheese in the refrigerator, some crackers in the cupboard, and a paring knife in a drawer for slicing the cheese. Then he sat down facing her and began to eat.

After a long silence, a sullen Averil asked, "What's become of us? Are we ever going to live like a normal couple again?"

"You think too much," he said. "Right now, I just need some time to gain me bearings. Figure out what to do next."

"Tell me something. Did you and your mates have a hand in the Brighton bombing?"

He looked down at the table and said, "You don't want to know about that. For your own good, I'm saying."

"Why did you do it?" She shouted. "What's the point of all this bloodshed?"

He stopped eating and looked at her through bleary eyes. "Do you remember Bobby Sands? No, you wouldn't. He died in Long Kesh prison in May of 1981. Starved himself to death, he did. And what did Mrs. Thatcher do about it? Not a bloody thing. Told the Commons that he chose to take his own life. And nine more of our brothers wasted away in the same prison that summer. So you want to know the why of it now? For them, it is. Bobby and the martyrs of Long Kesh."

Averil stood and moved slightly towards him. "You poor misguided bastards. You haven't accomplished a bloody thing—except to kill more people and turn everyone against you. Will you ever learn?"

He looked up at her and became more agitated. "You've got it all wrong. We're getting more volunteers every day. And someday we'll be the victors."

"You can't stay here tonight. Get out or I'll call the police."

He stood and bellowed, "You can't make me leave. This is me home."

She started to move toward the telephone on the kitchen wall when Sean picked up the paring knife and lashed out at her. She was close enough for the tip of the knife to cut through the right side of her pale blue robe, causing a crimson line to suddenly appear and slowly spread. Averil started screaming and Sean tried to quiet her but she only pushed him away.

When he fully realized what he had done, he panicked and fled the apartment. Averil grabbed a dish towel and, with her left hand, slipped it inside her robe and pressed it against her gushing wound. She was able to dial the telephone with her right hand and eventually woke Claire Blackwell. Claire was her only close friend with a car and, within fifteen minutes, was at her apartment and closely inspecting Averil's wound.

Claire judged that even though Averil had lost considerable blood, the knife had not cut deep. Nevertheless, Claire insisted on taking her to a nearby hospital for treatment. Once inside the emergency room, her wound was cleaned, sutured and she was given a blood transfusion.

While she lay in a recovery area bed, Averil told Claire about Sean's unexpected appearance and their discussion in the kitchen that led to the knife attack. Claire was disturbed, but not totally surprised, to learn of Malachy O'Brien's complicity in the Brighton bombing. She held Averil's hand while they commiserated about their common bonds with these renegade Irishmen.

When Averil finally tired of talking, Claire excused herself to step outside for some fresh air and smoke a cigarette. The sedative given to Averil began taking effect, but not before she came to the conclusion that her marriage had clearly ended and she would have to begin rebuilding her life.

Chapter Three

Mark and Averil were delighted with their Formia hotel. The Grande Albergo Miramare was an old seaside villa with lush gardens, a swimming pool, and private beach. After they checked in, a young man who spoke no English but smiled a lot, escorted them to their third floor room in a creaking elevator.

The room was dark when they entered, the windows hidden behind interior shutters. When the bellman opened the shutters the light streamed in. Then he opened the casement windows and sea breezes billowed the delicate lace curtains. He also opened a large set of louvered doors that led to a balcony overlooking the sea and the villa's private beach.

Averil stepped out on the balcony and Mark followed after the bellman left. She touched the railing with both hands as he came up close behind her, slipping his arms around her waist and planting an exuberant kiss on her neck. "This is even more beautiful than I expected," she sighed. "I want to stay here forever."

"No you don't. You'd get bored and I'd soon run out of money. Could you get by on beans and hot dogs?"

She laughed. "Sure, as long as you were here with me."

They unpacked, showered, and took an exploratory walk around the town. Their first discovery was a large park where a half dozen elderly men were playing bocce on hard-packed dirt. The men were so vocally competitive and enthusiastic that Mark and Averil sat on a nearby bench to follow the game to its conclusion. In the center of town they enjoyed several different sets of entertainers: a mime, a magician who worked with a large and lazy brown dog, and a female puppeteer who charmed the children with her jiggling marionettes.

They eventually moved on and into many little shops that lined both sides of the town's main street. Mark, in an unusually generous mood, bought Averil a pair of silver earrings. In another shop that offered nautical artifacts, she couldn't resist an antique ship's clock in polished

CHAPTER THREE

brass. Mark made arrangements with the saleswoman to have it held for later pickup so he wouldn't have to carry it around town and back to their hotel. Their final purchase was made from an art gallery that specialized in pastel seascapes. She chose a large watercolor, showing a collection of fishing boats in a marina, which the proprietor agreed to ship directly to their home. Averil had furnished their Huntington home with similar treasures, collected during her frequent antique hunting expeditions throughout Long Island.

Averil was enjoying herself so much, and Mark was taking such pleasure in her happiness, that they both lost track of time. Suddenly, each felt hunger pains; it was almost seven o'clock.

They entered the nearby Zi Anna restaurant for dinner and were escorted to a back room with only a few diners. Three of the room's walls were heavy glass panels which gave them a superior view of the sea and the beach in both directions. The sun was setting behind them and the purple and black night sky approaching from the east was softened by three lighted candles at their table.

Over bread and a bottle of chianti, they decided on a first course. For Averil, it was her favorite, insalata caprese, a plate of sliced tomatoes and mozzarella cheese topped with basil and olive oil. Mark ordered an antipasto titled frutti di mare and was taken aback when it arrived. "This stuff is raw," he exclaimed.

"That's the way it should be."

"I don't think I can eat this."

"Just try a couple of bites. If you don't like it, you can send it back."

He took her suggestion and cautiously nibbled a few chunks speared on his fork. "Hmm, not too bad." He proceeded to eat the whole dish, pausing only for an occasional sip of wine and a chunk of bread dipped in olive oil.

After dinner, Averil wanted to walk back to their hotel along the beach and Mark enthusiastically agreed. The temperature was dropping and the off-shore breezes were strengthening so they put on their sweaters. A nearly full moon shone on the cascading surf, making it look like tumbling diamonds.

They started their short hike by removing their shoes and socks and walking on smooth sand just out of the water's reach. Averil was in a playful mood and tried to pull Mark into the surf, but he managed to escape her tugs and grabs. At one point, he decided to retaliate and picked her up, one arm behind her knees and the other around her waist. For a brief moment, she thought he was serious so she kicked and wailed loudly enough to make him loosen his grip. She wriggled free.

Soon, the sand became rock so they moved up to an asphalt sidewalk parallel to the shoreline and put their shoes back on. They continued walking hand-in-hand, their path lighted by strings of Chinese lanterns provided by restaurants bordering the walkway.

After they arrived at the hotel, Mark went into the bathroom to brush his teeth. Averil hung her dress in the closet and opened the louvered doors leading to the balcony. When he came out she was wearing only a black push-up bra and a black thong. She did a pirouette while holding one hand above her head and said teasingly, "What do you think, Mr. Holloway? Do you approve?"

He took her in his arms and gave her a long, tender kiss. "You never wear things like that at home. Where did you get that outfit?"

"In New York, just before we left."

He kissed her again and let his hands slide downward. As he caressed her smooth butt he whispered, "Have I ever mentioned that you have the most gorgeous ass I've ever seen."

"Many times, luv, but I never tire of hearing it."

Mark hurriedly undressed and slid into bed while Averil turned out all the lights except for a small table lamp on her side of the bed. As they moved closer together, he undressed her slowly while kissing her breasts and a long flat scar on her right side just above her waist. Their passionate lovemaking was slow and deliberate, a familiar and comfortably intimate journey. Later they were content to rest silently in each other's arms.

He was the first to speak. "That was very nice, Mrs. Holloway."

"Yes indeed. Perhaps I should thank the raw seafood."

He laughed and kissed her again. "It wasn't the sushi, you fruitcake."

"We're in Italy, luv, not Japan."

"Whatever. I think it was your sexy underwear."

"And not my luscious body?"

After a few more minutes of talk, he rolled over onto his left side. She turned off the light and pressed her breasts up against his back, her knees curled up into the space behind his knees.

He was the first to fall asleep and, as she listened to his soft snoring, she first stroked his face and then his hairy chest. She felt secure, cherished and fulfilled, yet there was also a lingering doubt, a realization that all of this was so fragile. *What other outside forces are waiting to threaten this loving union?*

Chapter Four

Over breakfast in the hotel's ground floor restaurant, Mark and Averil planned their activities for the rest of their stay in Formia. "Here are the places we talked about at home," he said, pointing to an illustrated map of Italy's Lazio and Campania regions. "We can head south toward Naples and check out Pompeii or Herculaneum. Or both if you're up to it."

"I think one should be enough. They're similar, aren't they?"

"You're right. Let's do Herculaneum. The guidebook says it's well preserved and more interesting than Pompeii."

"I really want to see Sorrento and take the Amalfi drive. The pictures I've seen are so beautiful. And romantic too."

"Here's something I've always wanted to see," he said, pointing to a spot on the map. "The Abbey of Monte Cassino."

"Another church, is it?"

"It's more than that, Av. It was a famous battle site in World War II. They made a movie with John Hodiak. Remember?"

"No, I don't. Definitely not my cup of tea."

Mark slumped in his chair and sipped his coffee in silence. Finally, she reached over and touched his hand. "Now luv, don't pout. Why don't you go see it by yourself? I'll just relax here on the beach with my book."

"Are you sure? Will you be all right?"

"Not to worry. We'll see those other places tomorrow and the next day."

They finished breakfast and were leaving the restaurant when Mark had a sudden question. "Say, are you going topless?"

She stopped and met his eyes with a puzzled look. "I may. And then again, I may not. Would it bother you?"

"Well, not exactly," he stammered. "I was just thinking. Be sure to use plenty of oil. I wouldn't want those beautiful breasts to get burned."

"You just let me worry about that," she giggled.

"Hey, I've got an idea. Why don't I hang out with you at the beach. I could rub them with oil myself. Wouldn't that be fun?"

CHAPTER FOUR

She laughed and pushed his chest with her palms. "You need to go to that Abbey and do some praying. It will help you get your mind off my chest."

Mark's rental car struggled valiantly up the winding road to the Abbey of Monte Cassino, a seven story building perched on top of a hill at 1700 feet above sea level. He downshifted numerous times before reaching the summit, prompting him to vow he would never again lease the cheapest car on the lot.

After buying a ticket and guidebook at the Abbey's entrance, Mark strolled through well-tended rose gardens and worked his way through several cloisters, climbing stone staircases towards the main basilica. Upon entering, he was overcome by the beauty of multicolored marble pillars and gold filigree that outlined every seam of the ceiling. He stared upward at the side windows when a young man bumped into him, almost knocking him down.

"Oh pardon me. Did I hurt you?"

Mark grabbed him by an arm and steadied himself. "That's quite all right Father, I was in the wrong. I wasn't looking where I was going." The priest looked to be in his late twenties and Mark felt uncomfortable calling him "Father."

The priest smiled. "Well, I really wasn't paying attention either."

They disengaged and continued on separate paths. Mark had been impressed by his rugged good looks and tall athletic build. Mark also thought that this young man's vocation would be severely tested by the romantic advances of various women he would encounter during his priesthood.

Mark took a seat in front of the chapel while a dozen Benedictine monks filed into the sanctuary from a side door, taking their places on individual wooden kneelers, and singing Gregorian chant. Though he had intended to stay just a few minutes, he lost all sense of time during this unexpected glimpse of heaven, the echoes of the monks' holy unselfish dedication to the service of God.

After the monks left, Mark retraced his steps out of the chapel onto an elevated stone walkway named the Loggia of Paradise. He stopped at the rear railing and looked down on the red tile roofs of white stucco houses surrounded by farms and orchards. He could see for miles in almost every direction and appreciated the value of this summit as a military observation post. Directly below was a military cemetery containing the remains of 1100 Polish infantrymen who died in the final assault of the mount in May 1944. And there, amid the white marble headstones and alabaster walkways between the graves, walked the young priest. Conspicuous in his black shirt and trousers, Mark had no trouble following his movements. He seemed to be searching for something, stopping periodically to read a headstone's inscription.

Mark continued his tour of the Abbey, conscientiously viewing everything suggested by the guidebook. He stopped in the gift shop to buy silver crosses for each of his three daughters and two grandsons, walked to his car, and began the trip back to Formia. A few hundred yards down the mountain, he came upon the young priest walking briskly.

"Hello there, Father. Can I offer you a ride?"

"That would be great."

"I'm Mark Holloway." He held out a hand.

"A pleasure to meet you, Mark." The young priest offered a firm right hand. "The name's Jerome Soric, but please call me Jerry."

"Where are you from, Jerry?"

"St. Louis. I've been in Rome for the past year doing postgraduate study."

"Isn't this a small world? St. Louis is my home town too, although I haven't lived there since I was in college. Why did you come to Monte Cassino?"

"I came with some friends to see the Abbey and take a few days off. But more than that, the pope who reestablished the Jesuit order, Pius VII, was a Benedictine monk. Since I'm a Jesuit, it's a big attraction."

"So, how long will you be in Italy?"

"I have to be back home by the end of July."

"Will you be assigned to a parish when you go back to St. Louis?"

"No, I'm going to teach religion and history at our high school."

"I went to an all-boys high school myself. We had the Brothers of Mary but there weren't enough to go around, so they brought in a few Jesuits to keep us guys in line. You know something, Jerry? I never really knew how good an education I got until years after I graduated."

Jerry grinned and said, "Then you already know that education and

CHAPTER FOUR

scholarship are our strong suits."

By this time, they had reached the town of Cassino at the base of the mountain. "Where can I drop you?" asked Mark.

Jerry stared straight ahead for a few moments before turning his head toward Mark. "Have you got time for a cup of coffee? I'm buying."

There was something vaguely familiar about this young man that made Mark want to learn more. "Sure, I've got time."

They found a cafe near Cassino's main square and picked up sandwiches and cappuccinos from the lunch counter. They took a corner table with a view of the Abbey, its looming presence impossible to escape even inside the restaurant.

"I assume you're here on vacation, Mark. What do you do for a living?"

"I'm a pilot for Trans-Global Airlines, flying between New York and Paris. This is really my second career. My first career was the Navy for twenty-four years. After two years of college, I went to aviation cadet training in Pensacola, then to a fighter squadron operating off a carrier. When I got older, I switched to transports, the big fat uglies. So how about you, Jerry. You come from a big family?"

"No, not really. I'm an only child. Dad's a commodity buyer for a brewery and Mom's a cartographer. She's been with the same company since she graduated from college. Except for taking time off to stay home and look after me."

"They must be pretty proud of you, a Jesuit studying in Rome, about to become a high school teacher."

A dejected look came over his face while he stared into his cup. "Sorry Mark, you're not even close. Both my parents are Protestant. They've been pretty negative ever since I entered the seminary. I think Dad has finally accepted the fact that he'll never have any grandchildren, but Mom probably never will. She didn't even come to my ordination."

"Raised Protestant and now you're a Jesuit? How did that happen?"

"I was a student at Washington U. and a trio of bridge players needed a fourth. When I became a regular, I discovered the other three were members of a Catholic group called the Newman Club. They invited me to one of their meetings and, shortly after that, I had a feeling that I needed to change the direction of my life. To make a long story short, here I am today wearing a Roman collar."

"That's the most bizarre story I've ever heard." Mark paused briefly and continued, "Did you have any girl friends?" After a second, he added, "That's none of my business. Forget I asked."

"No, that's all right. There was a girl that I went steady with in high school and college. Stephanie was pretty upset when I broke it off, but she recovered pretty quickly. She's been married now for a couple of years."

"I don't mean to be pushy, but here you are, a handsome young man, who's going to remain celibate for the rest of his life. I've always had a problem with the church's view on this."

Jerry drew his shoulders back and replied crisply, "I didn't say it was going to be easy. I expect it will probably be very difficult. I'll just have to deal with it."

An awkward pause followed. Mark felt embarrassed and decided to change the subject. "I saw you down in the military cemetery, looking around for something. What was the attraction there?"

"Oh, I had a great-uncle who fought in the Polish army. He died in the big battle. I found his grave and said a prayer at his headstone."

"Good for you. Soric doesn't sound Polish though."

"His name wasn't Soric. It was Krenowicz, from Mom's side of the family."

Mark dropped his cup on the saucer and knocked his spoon to the floor. When the noisy clatter subsided, he had just enough breath to say, "What's your mother's first name?"

"It's Joan. Why do you ask?"

Mark stared out the window but neither his eyes nor his brain were functioning. He had been transported back thirty-six years to a small college in St. Louis, powerless to stop the pain from returning that he had buried so many years ago.

Chapter Five

On a day in March 1964, just as Mark was leaving a morning physics class, Joan Krenowicz stopped him in the hallway. She stood out from the other girls at Harris Junior College mainly because of her height, only two inches shorter than Mark who was six feet tall. She was on the quiet side, shy around boys, but able to make her presence felt when she chose with mischievous chocolate-colored eyes, a fully expressive mouth, and a subtle but sharp sense of humor.

"Hi, Mark. Can I talk with you a second?"

"Sure. Let's get out of the traffic first."

They walked up the hallway to a small alcove next to a trophy display case where they could talk privately, each standing and holding a load of books.

"What's on your mind?"

"Well, my sorority is having its annual spring prom in May. Would you be my date? Oh yes, it's formal."

Mark was stunned, in a pleasant sort of way, feeling flattered that this pretty girl had not only noticed him, but was attracted to him enough to ask for a date. And a very special date it was.

Joan sensed she was about to be rejected. The disappointed look on her face prompted Mark to blurt out, "Wow, you want me to be your date? Sure, I'd love to. Tell me all about it."

She immediately relaxed and smiled. "The details are not worked out yet, but it's going to be on the first Saturday in May. So be sure and put it on your calendar. I have to go to my next class now, but I'll let you know."

Mark watched her walk away, feeling very warm inside. Ten years later, when a certain song became popular, he would recall this day, just like the guy standing on a corner in Winslow, Arizona, who was amazed that a girl in a flatbed truck would slow down to have a look at him.

Later in the day, Mark began to think of more practical matters concerning the big date, such as renting a tuxedo and making a fool of himself on the dance floor. He knew he was not a good dancer and hoped that she would be just as bad or that he could fake it somehow. The prom would be a big deal and all her sorority sisters would be watching him closely, mentally comparing notes. Disappointing Joan that evening would not be an option.

After thinking about it for a couple of days, Mark decided to ask Joan for a date before the prom so they could get to know each other better. When Mark suggested a movie, she eagerly accepted. They agreed on a Sunday matinee at a downtown theater followed by an early dinner since both had classes at eight o'clock the next morning. The only detail to be resolved was the choice of movies. He was interested in seeing *Goldfinger*, the newest James Bond thriller. He also suggested *Seven Days in May*, the tale of a group of high ranking American military officers taking control of the government.

Months later, Mark learned that Joan was secretly horrified at his suggestions but had the presence of mind to tactfully offer several alternatives. *A Hard Day's Night* was being shown and coincided with the Beatles' ongoing U.S. tour. Joan also suggested *The Americanization of Emily* or *The Pink Panther*, but Mark hesitated long enough so that she knew these were not quite right either. Finally, they found a good compromise in *My Fair Lady* so all the arrangements were set.

Mark talked his dad into loaning him the family car, a black 1958 Chevrolet sedan, for his movie date. When he arrived at her home in south St. Louis, she introduced him to her parents. He noticed two unusual things about them right away. First, they appeared to be much older than his own parents, which meant that their only child, Joan, was conceived rather late in the couple's lives and was obviously very special to them. Second, both parents were Polish immigrants and spoke very little English. Making small talk was impossible.

Even though the movie was longer than usual, it seemed to pass quickly. Afterwards, they found a nearby grill and had cheeseburgers with French fries and shared a pitcher of draft beer. Conversation centered first around the movie, then teachers, classes, fellow students, and tentative plans for the future. Mark was a member of the local Naval Air Reserve unit and thought he would have to spend some active duty time after graduation to avoid the draft. Joan planned to transfer to the

CHAPTER FIVE

University of Missouri in Columbia and get a degree in geography.

When they finished their meal, Mark suggested a quick drive to the river, telling her only that he wanted to show her something special. They drove toward the Eads Bridge and stopped in a large construction area on the west bank of the Mississippi, next to the giant arch that was nearing completion. Its formal name was the Jefferson National Expansion Memorial, but almost everyone in the city called it the St. Louis Arch. Joan had only seen pictures of it in the newspapers so she was awe-struck by its size. They walked hand in hand beneath the floodlit structure. "This thing is an engineering marvel," Mark observed. "I'd like to be involved in a project like this someday."

"I thought you wanted to be a chemical engineer."

"Maybe I could design an oil refinery. Something like that."

She smiled at him. "I'm sure you'll do well, whatever you decide to do."

When they returned to her home, Joan left the car quickly and Mark followed her up to her small front porch. Without hesitation, she surprised him by putting her arms around his neck and stepped fully into his tentative embrace, kissing him long and hard on the lips. Then she broke away and, as she opened the front door, thanked him for a lovely evening and promised to see him tomorrow at school.

On the long drive back to his home in north St. Louis, Mark was so aroused that he had a difficult time keeping his mind on traffic. He had an even more difficult time going to sleep that night. Everything replayed in his mind. The physical attraction was powerful, but there were two things holding him back. First, his Catholic education had emphasized that sex before marriage was not allowed. And, at this stage in his life, he believed that was a good policy. But even if he had been able to toss his religious scruples aside, there was another point to consider; the respect he felt for Joan. He knew enough about girls to realize that she was something special and probably wouldn't take kindly to a groping in the back seat of the family sedan. He decided he would remain on his best behavior and see what developed.

Mark and Joan had many more dates in the months following their first outing, including a Cardinals' baseball game. When Joan's spring prom came around in early May, it was almost an anti-climax. She turned out to be a natural dancer, not at all concerned about Mark's dance floor moves, but helpful in making him feel at ease and improve his technique.

In early June, Mark's kid brother Matthew graduated from high school and their parents decided to throw a big party for him in their backyard. Mark thought this would be an auspicious moment to introduce Joan to his family and friends, so he invited her to be his guest. As expected, she was a hit with everyone.

Joan made a concerted effort to meet and talk with each person at the party. She danced several fast numbers with Matthew and his dad, made up a dinner plate for Mark's mom, but saved all the slow dances for Mark. Her natural charm and obvious affection for him was so well received that his aunt Lorraine later told his mother privately, "I do believe that she's the one for Mark."

Mark and Joan were looking forward to spending a lot of time together that summer, but events conspired against them. In the last half of June, he had to spend two weeks on active duty with his reserve unit at the Naval Air Station in Miramar, California. Later, Joan's mother shipped her off to Kenosha, Wisconsin, for all of July and August to look after an ailing grandmother. That was the story he was told but he wondered if this was some kind of parental strategy designed to keep them from getting too close to each other.

When school started again in September, they spent as much time together as possible, every school day and almost every weekend. Lack of privacy was one of their biggest problems because her parents watched them closely. But they found ways to evade their prying eyes with hayrides, long walks in the red and gold hills of an autumn Missouri countryside, and study halls where they kissed much more than they studied. By then, each had stopped dating others and it was pretty clear that they were both deeply in love.

The affectionate couple always appeared together on campus and enjoyed many private conversations during their final semester at Harris. They found they could talk freely with each other about almost any topic except religion. Joan had been raised a Lutheran and attended Sunday services regularly with her parents. Mark learned quickly during one of their early dialogues that their religious differences would best be avoided if he wanted the date to have a pleasantly romantic ending.

Their last date was another sorority-sponsored dance held on the

CHAPTER FIVE 37

Saturday before Christmas and they decided to give each other their gifts just before it started. Joan gave Mark a handsome fountain pen with his name engraved on the barrel. She joked he would use it to someday write the great American novel. He gave her a gold chain with a small heart pendant attached; she loved it and seemed thrilled to wear it.

After the dance, they stood in her doorway, holding each other tight, shielding each other from an icy winter wind. They were having a most serious conversation about marriage, children, and commitment.

"Yes, Mark, I do love you with all my heart. There isn't anybody else."

"Then why won't you marry me? I just don't get it."

"We've been through all this before. You're Catholic and I'm Protestant. If we got married in your church, I'd have to agree to raise our kids in the Catholic faith. I just can't do that."

"I love you so much, Joan, that I promise you right now we wouldn't have to do that. We'll raise our kids Buddhists, Muslims, whatever you want."

"You say that now, but I know you. You'll feel different when the time comes. And if our children were raised as Protestants, you'd never forgive me. You'd hold it against me for the rest of our lives." He continued to plead his case, but she only cried. He kissed her tears while they held each other close, wishing that fate had been kinder.

Classes started up again in early January. They were so busy, preparing for final exams and graduation, that they didn't spend much time together. Of course, they could have found the time if they really wanted to, but the disappointing end to their Christmas dance date gave each one a convenient excuse to avoid the other while pondering what to do next.

One cold and overcast afternoon, Mark had an hour to kill between classes, so he went into the college's library to do some studying. He found an empty seat in front of the hall at one of the long wooden tables, directly in front of another male student. All the overhead lights in the hall were lit, giving the place a warm and friendly glow on this otherwise gloomy winter day.

After fifteen minutes passed, the man opposite him decided to pack it in and left. Mark looked straight ahead across six similar tables that coincidentally had vacant spots in the same position as his own, on both sides of every table. But at the seventh table, in the same spot as Mark's but facing him, sat Joan, hunched over a book and a note pad, writing hurriedly while lost in concentration.

The sudden sight of her nearly took his breath away and he continued to stare hard, wanting to engrave her image in his mind forever. She had pulled her long auburn hair back into a pony tail and still managed to look gorgeous with little makeup. She wore a long-sleeve white silk blouse with a high collar and, around her neck, was the gold chain and heart pendant that he'd given her for Christmas.

She must have felt his eyes burning holes in her head for she eventually looked up. Her moist brown eyes looked straight into his, across the expanse of tables and chairs, holding that gaze for what seemed like hours. During this interminable period of staring at one another, an encyclopedia of silent words and airborne feelings passed between them. While he was telling her that he would love her forever, she was saying that she understood and would never forget him. The spell was finally broken when another girl passed Joan's table and accidentally dropped an armful of books.

Joan reached into her purse, pulled out a hanky, and wiped the tears spilling over her cheeks. She rapidly chucked all her belongings into a canvas book bag, stood up, and gave him a small wave of her hand. She turned and left the library by its rear entrance and that was the last time he saw her.

Joan graduated at the end of January, but Mark left for Pensacola, Florida and Navy flight training two days before the ceremony. He wrote her a half dozen letters, but she didn't answer any of them. As for the handsome fountain pen, he threw it overboard one night, off a carrier's fantail into a churning black ocean.

Chapter Six

Mark stared out the window at the Abbey's facade. Jerry's hand lightly touched his wrist. "Are you all right? Did I say something wrong?"

Mark drained the cappuccino from his cup. "I don't know any good way to say this, so I'm just going to say it straight out and hope you understand. I dated your mother a long time ago when we were in college together. I loved her very much and I've never forgotten her."

Mark expected some type of negative reaction but was surprised when Jerry's face showed a wide grin. "You and my mom were college sweethearts? That's absolutely amazing. How come you two didn't get married?"

"We wanted to but just couldn't figure out a way to make it happen."

"What do you mean?"

"I was a pretty staunch Catholic in those days. More so than I am now, sorry to say. You already know how dogmatic your mother can be about religion. We couldn't find any middle ground and the big sticking point was the business about raising our kids Catholic." Jerry nodded, still wearing the Cheshire Cat's smile, and looking much wiser than his twenty-seven years would suggest. "How is she? Is she all right? I mean, how does she look?"

"Well, let me see. She's definitely in good health. Plays tennis twice a week and bowls on the weekend sometimes with dad. Works full time for a mapping systems company. Been with them, oh, since I was ten years old."

Mark smiled. "She loved geography in college and always talked about getting into the map-making business."

"She's done very well. Got promoted to department manager a year ago." Mark squirmed in his seat and slid his cup and saucer to one side, then back again. "How does she look? I'm not sure how to answer that one. Maybe a bit heavier than she looks in her college pictures. But she dresses like a model. Used to drive Dad nuts, seeing all that money go out for her wardrobe. But she made it clear that it was her paycheck she was spending—not his."

Mark laughed. "She wasn't that fashion conscious in college, but the rest of it sounds like Joan, all right." He shifted in his chair and fiddled some more with his cup. "Has she ever mentioned me?"

"No, I'm sure I've never heard your name before today." Jerry looked up at the ceiling for a few moments and rubbed his chin with his thumb and forefinger. "Think about the irony here. Mom won't marry you because she can't agree to raise any children you might have in the Catholic faith. Then her only son converts to Catholicism and becomes a priest. God sure works in mysterious ways."

"I'll drink to that." Mark walked back to the lunch counter and returned with a tray holding two espressos and two small glasses of grappa.

As they sipped their grappa, Jerry said, "I'm really happy I ran into you—no pun intended. Your story helps put lots of things into perspective. And I don't think for a minute what happened today was accidental."

"How so?"

"It's part of God's plan. More of his mysterious ways."

"When you get back home, are you going to tell your parents about this?"

"Not Dad, but I will have a talk with Mom. I have no idea how she's going to react, but I hope it will bring us closer. I just can't let this breach in our relationship continue, especially now that I understand her better."

They continued sharing their fondest memories. Mark spoke of the good times they'd had in college and Jerry recalled his boyhood. "Today you have soccer moms. But when I was growing up, soccer wasn't very popular in our neighborhood so I played Little League baseball. First base. And Mom would be up there in the bleachers for every game, cheering me on. And on Halloween, she made a different costume for me each year and took me out trick-or-treating. Then there were my birthday parties. She went all out with the cake, the gifts, and the entertainment. Later on, when I was in high school, she made sure there was a girl for every boy at my parties—well chaperoned, of course—and everyone had to dance. No wallflowers allowed in our rec room."

"Fill me in on something," asked Mark. "How did your parents meet?"

"As I understand it, they met on a blind date. And this was two years after she graduated from the university and moved back to St. Louis. Her sorority buddy, Rosemary, fixed her up."

CHAPTER SIX

"Did they get married right away?"

"No, they didn't. Mom first thought he was too old—he's got seven years on her. But he was persistent and finally wore her down, I guess."

"That sounds a bit cynical."

Jerry smiled and said, "Oh, I don't mean it to be. They're still very devoted to each other after all this time. Thirty years together this summer. Rather unusual these days, don't you think?"

Mark finished his espresso. "In my case, you're right on the money. I'm on my second marriage. Ten years now and it's a good one. My first one lasted almost twenty years but it was a disaster right from the start. She was very Catholic, and I sometimes thought she was working for sainthood while she was still alive."

"Is your present wife Catholic too?"

"No, she's not. But she's a wonderful woman and very tolerant of my faith and religious views. In fact, she urged me to visit the Abbey today. She's back at the beach in Formia, catching up on her reading."

Jerry glanced at his watch. "I hate to break this up, but I'd better get moving."

"Good idea. My wife is probably starting to worry about me right now."

They both rose from the table, and Jerry offered his hand. Instead of a handshake, Mark embraced him with a fatherly hug and Jerry returned the affection without embarrassment. "Remember me in your prayers, Jerry. Please?"

"I will. Any message you'd like me to give to mom?"

"Just say . . . tell her I wish her every happiness in the world."

They went outside into fading sunlight and, as Mark started walking toward his car, he noticed Jerry lagging behind and apparently deep in thought. *Maybe there's something else he wants to share.*

"You know, Mom and Dad never argued in front of me, but one time they did have a big fight. I guess they thought I wouldn't hear them. Something about a piece of jewelry, a small heart on a gold chain. Dad wanted her to throw it away—wear a diamond that he bought her. She told him it was a gift, something she got long before he came into the picture. She still wears it. Often, too."

With a familiar twinkle in his eye—Joan's eyes—he added, "You wouldn't know anything about that, would you Mark?"

Chapter Seven

Mark drove from Cassino back to Formia in a mental haze, reviewing the afternoon spent with Father Jerome. He struggled with his emotions, trying to determine just how he felt. On the one hand, he was pleased to receive information about Joan, her husband, her Catholic son, and her own well-being after all these years. But on the other hand, he was disturbed and felt a nagging at his nerves, something he couldn't name. Perhaps it was sympathy for the pain Joan must be feeling about the way her son's life and religious beliefs diverged from her own. Or maybe it was his own feeling of helplessness, knowing that now there was too much time and space between them to achieve any type of satisfaction. Surely, he reasoned, she must regret their failure to resolve the bitter ending to their relationship thirty-six years ago.

Mark also thought about Averil and what she might say about all this. He wanted to tell her everything that had transpired at Cassino. He also hoped that she would be patient and understanding while listening to his story about another woman, ask probing questions, and tell him what she thought, all in the spirit of helping him sort out his feelings and emotions. In short, he was disturbed and hoped that she could somehow make him feel better.

When he arrived at the hotel, the desk clerk handed him an envelope with his room key. The note inside from Averil said that she had walked into town to do some shopping and would return before dinner.

Mark went up to their room, poured himself a shot glass portion of Scotch, and took a leisurely shower. While he was getting dressed, Averil entered the room with two shopping bags filled with clothes.

"Hello, luv. Did you have a pleasant time at the Abbey?"

"Yes, I did. A very interesting day. Care for a drink?"

"Not right now, thanks. I want to show you what I just bought." She reached into one of the bags, pulled out a dark blue dress with spaghetti straps, and held it up to her body. "Do you like it? I couldn't resist it."

CHAPTER SEVEN

Mark sat down on the edge of the bed and looked up at her with a serious face. "Yes, it's nice. Are you going to wear it to dinner?"

She frowned. "I thought I might. Is something wrong?"

"No, nothing's wrong. How was the beach?"

"You're wondering about the cost of all these clothes, aren't you? Well, don't worry. The dress was only several million lira."

"You're kidding—right?"

She flashed a teasing smile as she turned toward the bathroom. "Give me a few minutes to change. I won't be long."

Within half an hour, they were walking hand-in-hand along Formia's bustling main street. Averil attracted considerable attention during their stroll; outright lustful stares and whistles by men and politely jealous looks from women. This secretly pleased Mark because he was proud to have such a beautiful wife.

They eventually found a small restaurant in the town's center, were promptly seated, and placed their order. The waiter soon returned with a bottle of white wine, a bottle of mineral water, and a mound of heavily crusted bread. After the waiter left, Averil said, "You're rather quiet, luv. Is something wrong?"

He took advantage of this opportunity by telling her of his meeting with Father Jerome at the Abbey and their subsequent conversation in the cafe. He covered almost everything, omitting only a few details that he thought might be misconstrued, such as the gold chain and heart that Joan still wore. The news that she still wore them inflated his ego but he also wondered about her motivation. Why didn't she just throw them away?

Averil sipped her wine and listened intently without once interrupting his story. When he had told her everything, she said, "That's quite a remarkable coincidence. Meeting a priest who happens to be the son of your first love."

"I guess I should have told you about her a long time ago."

"Not necessarily. Why should you have done that?"

"I'm not sure. Full disclosure, maybe. Does it bother you at all?"

"No, of course not. All this happened a very long time ago. Even before you were married to Margie."

Mark relaxed slightly and took another sip of wine. "This whole business is unsettling. Jerry even made a comment about our meeting not being an accident."

"Does that mean you're going to follow up on this in some way?"

"Oh, no. I'm just trying to understand what it all means."

"It probably doesn't mean much of anything."

Mark stiffened as a serious look came over his face. "You're being a bit cavalier about all this, don't you think?"

Averil's eyes flashed and her voice became sharper. "Because I refuse to make a mountain out of a mole hill? The point is, we're happily married and so is she. The only problem is her relationship with her son, but I should expect that to be resolved when he gets back home."

Quickly sensing that he had overreacted, he smiled nervously and said, "I'd like to be a mouse in the corner when he tells her about meeting me."

"Yes, I'm sure you would."

Their conversation moved on to other topics: her relaxing interlude at the beach, her afternoon nap, mutual opinions of the book she had just finished, and her impressions of the town formed during her afternoon shopping spree. Mark was not totally satisfied with her reaction to his Cassino story, but thought that, for now, it was the best he could hope for. If he pursued it any further, he feared they might get into territory better left unexplored.

After dinner and a second bottle of wine, they were once again in a relaxed and cheerful mood. Their waiter turned out to have a pleasant baritone voice and serenaded the dining room with selections from Puccini's *La Boheme*.

As they left the restaurant, Averil suggested they make a stop on their way back to the hotel. "There's a kiosk that sells beautiful post cards. I won't be long."

"Just don't buy another London newspaper, OK?" Averil stopped and stared at him, her mouth drawn tight. Mark smiled nervously. "I mean, it would be a shame to spoil our vacation by reading any more news about your ex-husband."

Averil didn't answer and remained silent until they reached the kiosk. "Be back in a jiffy," she said as she dashed inside.

"Take your time. There's no hurry."

A few minutes later, Averil came back outside with two magazines, six post cards in a brown bag, and a copy of the *International Herald Tribune*.

CHAPTER SEVEN 45

She thrust the newspaper at Mark and said, "I believe it's safe to read. I've scanned the headlines and saw no mention of—what's her name again?—Joan Sorehead?"

Mark chuckled nervously. "Very funny, Av. Now can we call a truce? No more talk about our former loves for the rest of our trip?"

She took his hand as they resumed walking to their hotel. "The rest of our lives is long enough for me."

Once in their hotel room, Averil browsed through one of her magazines for a few minutes but decided she wasn't sleepy. Mark read only about half the newspaper before turning off his lamp, rolling over, and falling asleep.

After turning out her bed lamp, she stepped out on the balcony and immersed herself in the seaside darkness and cool breezes. The only visible lights came from the resort city of Gaeta, seven miles north along the curving Mediterranean coast.

I know something's still bothering Mark, something about his meeting with the young priest. But the problem is surely not with the priest—it's his mother. There are some loose ends that he feels should be tidied up but he doesn't know how to go about it. He'll worry constantly about this, over and over in his mind, like a dog gnawing on a bone. And I won't have a bloody clue on how to help him. But why should I help him?

She crawled back into bed without waking Mark and eventually fell into a light and fitful sleep. At one time during the night, she had a disturbing dream. Sean Flannery appeared at the door of her Huntington, New York home with a beautiful woman in tow. Flannery introduced the woman as Joan Soric and they barged right into the house without so much as a by-your-leave.

"Tis a fine thing seeing you again, Averil. Me lady and me were in the neighborhood and thought you'd want to have us staying over for a week or so. Now would you be knowing about any machinist jobs available in Huntington? Me parole just came through."

The woman stood motionless, looking at Averil with a wide loopy grin. Flannery turned toward the kitchen and called out over his shoulder, "Would you be having any cold beer in the house for a thirsty man and his lady?"

Chapter Eight

Ten days after his return from Cassino, Jerry Soric was playing bridge with three other men in the kitchen they shared as part of their living quarters. Jerry's partner was forty-two-year-old Ryan Mahoney, also a student at Rome's Gregorian Pontifical University.

Jerry and Ryan complemented each other well. As the virtual 'older brother' with a previous career, Ryan provided Jerry with the benefits of his secular experience. Jerry, on the other hand, was further along in his priestly vocation than Ryan and helped him often, not only with his studies, but as a wise sounding board in their frequent theological discussions.

Tonight, Jerry and Ryan were partners against two Italian priests who spoke little English. Their opponents often erupted in long, explosive diatribes which Jerry and Ryan were sure contained 'table talk,' a euphemism for improper communications.

The hour was late and the foursome decided to play one last rubber. That is, whichever team won two games first would be the winner. On the next deal, Ryan successfully played a Three No Trump game and even scored an extra trick. The second hand was a little more difficult. Father Paolo, the priest on Jerry's left, played a Four Spades contract and won only because Jerry made an error.

In the third game, both Jerry and Ryan had strong hands which escalated the bidding to the highest level, a grand slam. Jerry played the hand carelessly, allowing Father Paolo to take one trick and defeat the contract.

As they were shuffling the cards, Jerry looked over at his grim-faced partner. "Sorry about that. Guess I could have played it better."

"Right you are." Ryan's voice was clearly strained.

Jerry looked to his left. "Father Paolo, if it's all right with you, I'd like to stop playing now. We'll concede the rubber to you and Father Umberto."

After a lot of self congratulations, the Italian priests left the table in a jovial mood and headed for the pantry, looking for a bottle of Chianti.

Ryan looked at his dejected partner. "Seems like you've been riding an emotional roller coaster lately. When you came back from Cassino, you

CHAPTER EIGHT 47

were happy and peaceful. The last few days, you've been irritable and jumpy. What's wrong?"

"You know what happened at the Abbey. I told you about meeting the man who dated my mother in college. I felt very good about that. Like a mystery had been solved. It was a missing piece to a jigsaw puzzle, something that helped me see my mother in a whole new light."

"I remember that," said Ryan. "So why the troubled mood now?"

"I got a letter from her three days ago."

"You told her about meeting this man?"

"No, not at all. I'm saving that for later, when I go home next month. I want to tell her the whole story, face to face."

"So, what was in the letter?"

Jerry went to his bedroom and came back with a letter which he handed to Ryan. "Here, read it for yourself."

Ryan opened the envelope and removed a single page of computer-generated text.

Friday, June 16

Dear Jerry,

Thanks so much for your letter of May 22nd. Your dad and I enjoyed reading about your classroom activities and your explorations of Rome. I can just picture you jogging in the early morning around the Vatican, whizzing through traffic and trying to dodge all the locals on their motor scooters.

Your dad is wondering about your golf game and whether you've had any opportunities to play this summer. He's been playing every weekend since the courses opened up this spring and even goes out to the driving range once in a while to hit balls. I think he's trying to get his game in shape so you don't embarrass him too much when you get back home.

And speaking of that, I want you to plan to stay with us, at least until you have a definite housing assignment from your superiors. We've turned the guest bedroom back into your old bedroom. Well, not quite that far. Your dad wanted to hang up your Little League pictures and pennants, but I thought that was a bit much. So the room looks fine for a young man and not a teenager.

In your last letter, you mentioned that you were going to visit the Abbey of Monte Cassino. Did you get to make the trip? If so, did you find Uncle Tadeusz's grave in the Polish cemetery? I'm anxious to hear what it looked like. I did some checking with Bill Lottman in our European department and he gave me a very nice tourist map of Italy. I guess I should have thought of this sooner. I could have sent it before your trip.

Now I have some news for you. It's not the most pleasant thing to report but I feel you should know about it before you come home. Last Sunday at church I saw Stephanie. She was alone so I took the opportunity to say hello. She seemed so troubled that I asked her to have coffee with me at the after-service social in the parish hall. Shortly after she started talking to me, she broke down and cried hard. Her marriage to Justin has collapsed and they are talking about divorce. They are still living together but she didn't know how long this would last. Probably not much longer unless I miss my guess.

She made the point several times that she should never have married him. She said it was a terrible mistake on her part and—please forgive me for throwing this in your face again—it was done only to spite you for having rejected her when you decided to become a priest. She is a miserable woman, Jerry, and there is not much I could do for her except give her my love and offer to talk to her whenever she feels the need.

You may wonder why I'm telling you all this and ask why it should be any of your concern. Well, it is apparent to me that Stephanie has still not gotten over you. She may still be in love with you. So at the very least, she has some strong feelings and emotions to work out and she needs help. Specifically, she feels she needs your help, although I couldn't speak for you and tell her what kind of help you would be free to give.

Anyway, she wants to see you again when you come back to St. Louis, and she wants to have a long talk with you. I don't know how you'll react to this but I urge you, when she does contact you, please don't reject her again. Do this as a favor to me. Try to

CHAPTER EIGHT

imagine her as a member of your own parish, a woman with serious emotional problems, and extend to her the Christian love that I know you have.

Please let us know your travel plans and flight schedules so that we can meet you at Lambert Field. Oh yes, is there any special music you'd like the brass band to play when you get off the plane? Just kidding!

Love you,
Mom

Ryan chuckled to himself as he folded the letter and returned it to the envelope. "My, my, what a tangled web we weave."

"What's so funny?" asked Jerry.

"It looks like you're about to be reunited with your long lost love. Hearts and flowers and all that romantic malarkey."

"Stop clowning around, Ryan, this is serious business."

"It's only serious if you choose to make it. It's been seven years since you've seen this woman, right?"

"That's true," said Jerry. "But this whole thing is unsettling for a number of reasons. Steph is also Protestant and used to attend services with her parents at mom's church, but she joined a different one when she got married and moved away. And now, all of a sudden, she's back in the same church as Mom. How convenient, running into Mom and crying on her shoulder."

"And isn't your mom a sensitive, caring and compassionate woman?"

"Normally, yes. But there may be more here than meets the eye. I have a suspicion that she may just be the frustrated matchmaker, wanting to make that last ditch effort to get us back together again."

"Point of law, Father Soric," interrupted Ryan with a raised forefinger. "Remember that the defendant is presumed innocent until proven guilty."

Jerry looked at his good friend and briefly pondered his comment. Previously a successful attorney in Santa Fe, New Mexico, Ryan was respected by everyone in the largely Hispanic community, not only because of his personal integrity and willingness to work extra hours for his clients, but also because of his high profile in his parish church, St. Francis Cathedral, and his fluency in Spanish. He was not yet a priest, but would be ordained upon returning home.

Jerry got up and helped himself to a bottle of beer from the refrigerator. "Ah, but the evidence speaks for itself, counselor. Remember that I've known my mother for almost twenty-eight years. Even today, she doesn't accept my vocation."

Ryan helped himself to a large glass of Chianti from the bottle left on the kitchen counter by Fathers Paolo and Umberto.

"You mentioned that there were a number of reasons why this bothered you. Tell me honestly, do you still have some feelings for this Stephanie woman?"

Jerry twirled the bottle on the table. "Until I got this letter, I thought I was safe. Oh, I still think of her. You know, when you're celibate, the intimate times you've had with a woman come to haunt your dreams at all hours of the night."

"Oh, I know the problem well. And I can tell you that even at my advanced age, the sensual part of the brain still remembers those earlier carnal pleasures. That's the way God made us and it's also one way the devil tempts us. The combined blessing and curse of our humanity."

"I suppose I'll have to see Stephanie again, if only to get Mom off my back."

"But you'd rather not," said Ryan. "Is that the sum of it?"

"Part of me does and another part doesn't. So much has happened to both of us since we broke up. We're not the same people anymore. I'm not sure how I should act when I see her again. What do you think?"

"Just be yourself," said Ryan. "You're an ordained priest now and this woman can't be anything more than a good friend. Listen to her story, try to be as objective as possible, and give her the benefit of your wisdom. And it probably wouldn't hurt to pray for a wee bit of spiritual strength and divine guidance."

"I think a lot of prayer will be needed for this one."

"Another thing to consider," added Ryan, "You may be faced with similar situations throughout your life that involve women. Face it, Jerry, you're a good looking fellow and the ladies can't help being interested in you. Sort of a trophy for them, you know, getting a Jesuit into their bed."

Jerry frowned. "That sounds a bit far fetched."

"My point is that you've got to learn how to deal with this kind of problem. Your meeting with Stephanie will be excellent training."

"Good grief." Jerry threw his hands in the air. "Let's take a walk. I need some fresh air."

Chapter Nine

After their stay in Formia, Mark and Averil returned to Rome for two more nights so they could attend the performance of *Aida* at the Baths of Caracalla. The opera surpassed their expectations and even Mark reluctantly admitted that he enjoyed the music, the costumes, and the elaborate pageantry.

The next morning, they boarded a train to Florence. When they emerged from the station, they tried to hail a taxi for transport to their hotel. Much to their confusion, each cab driver erupted in a loud voice and spirited hand gestures when Mark showed him a brochure listing the name and address of the hotel. The fourth driver knew enough English to point out their hotel across the piazza, less than a hundred meters from where they stood. Mark and Averil took it all in stride and it became a running joke during their four days in Florence.

They were constantly on the go, visiting museums and churches. They spent a full day browsing through the boisterous street market surrounding the Mercado Centrale as well as the more expensive shops near the Ponte Vecchio.

One day, Mark surprised Averil by renting a motor scooter and making arrangements with the hotel's concierge for an elaborate picnic basket containing meat, cheese, bread, fruit, and wine. They made a comical scene riding together, trying to balance themselves and the elaborate basket on the scooter while touring the old roads of Tuscany.

After a long relaxing lunch, they lay side by side on a black and red plaid blanket next to a tranquil lake. Averil rolled over, stroked his cheek with her palm, and kissed him. "This is so lovely, so romantic. It's a wonderful idea you had."

He smiled and said, "You inspire me to do romantic things."

She swung one leg across his body and lightly straddled him just below the waist. "You've been such a dear. Now I'm going to do something for you."

Averil first unbuttoned the front of her pale blue sweater, followed by the release of her bra, allowing her breasts to spill free. Mark watched in rapt silence as she bent forward, rubbing her nipples across his nose and mouth. He reached up and caressed her back, gently pulling her closer while he licked her breasts.

Mark asked, "How far are we going with this?"

"As far as you like, luv."

"You mean doing it in broad daylight? Right out here in the open?"

"Why not? Haven't you ever heard that ditty?
Hooray, Hooray,
the first of May.
Outdoor fucking
starts today."

Suddenly they were joined by an unwelcome visitor, a large black shaggy dog. Averil squealed and jumped up, quickly fastening her bra and buttoning her sweater. The dog figured he wanted to play and became even friendlier, licking Mark's face and pawing his chest.

The dog's owner, an old man wearing a black beret and a threadbare blue suit, arrived and put an end to the chaos. He shouted several short commands to the dog and peace was restored. After making his apologies for interrupting an intimate moment, the old man and his dog resumed their stroll along the lake shore.

As they were packing up the blanket and picnic food, Averil giggled. "I've always wondered what a ménage à trois would be like."

Mark managed a weak grin and swatted her playfully with a napkin. "Sometimes you say the craziest things."

Averil stared dreamily out the Trans-Global 767 window while Mark fondly recalled the last days of their Italian holiday. She interrupted his reverie with a sigh. "I don't want to go home."

He took her hand and said, "I feel the same way, sweetheart. But we've had our fun and now it's time to pay the piper."

She leaned toward him and put her head on his shoulder. "I think I should visit the loo before they start serving."

"Good idea," he said, getting up and letting her out into the aisle.

When lunch was finally served, Mark and Averil were treated to a delicious meal, better than the other passengers had, thanks to his status

CHAPTER NINE 53

as an employed pilot. Averil also enjoyed a French white wine while Mark had only iced tea, a long standing tradition of not drinking alcohol while in an aircraft, whether he was flying or just a passenger.

After lunch, Captain Clay Parcel emerged from the cockpit for his customary stroll about the passenger cabins, something the crew referred to as "showing the flag." He stopped when he reached Mark's seat, shook his hand, and called out a jovial hello. Clay and Mark had flown together many times on the same New York-to-Paris route. He had thinning dark brown hair and a dark brown mustache, unlike Mark's light brown crew cut and clean shaven face. He was several years older than Mark and it was common knowledge that he colored his hair, trying to look more youthful. Mark replied in a soft voice, pointing to Averil who was taking a nap beside him.

"The flight attendants told me that you and Averil were on board today. Where have you folks been?"

"We've spent the last two weeks in Italy. Doing the tourist bit. Rome, Florence and a beach resort near Naples. It was wonderful."

"I just may have to do it myself. Barbara has been wanting to take another European vacation. Do our part to prop up the Italian economy."

"So, how's everything back at the ranch? Anything new and exciting happening in the Trans-Global family?"

"Not a whole lot, except for the new plane coming along. They awarded a contract to a company that makes flight simulators and they're looking for a pilot to work with the contractor. You know, help review the software specs and operate the simulator when they get it running. Get all the bugs out."

"That doesn't sound like much fun to me," said Mark. "Did you sign up?"

"Hell no. I'm too old. They're looking for guys that have a few years of flying left. Pilots they can assign to fly the new plane. Maybe you should think about it."

"Who, me? Why would I want to do something like that?"

"For starters, it would give you a break from the same old routine. And when the new aircraft becomes operational, it may be just the ticket that gets you promoted to captain. Think about it."

"I don't know," said Mark. "Do I really want to be a captain?"

"Sure you do. And here's the kicker. The contractor's facility is in St.

Louis, right next to the airport. That's your home town, isn't it?"

Mark quickly looked over at Averil. He said a short silent prayer of thanksgiving that she was sleeping soundly. Several scenarios flashed through his mind, all involving some kind of meeting with Joan Krenowicz Soric.

"Uh, yeah, it's my home town," he finally replied. "Maybe I shouldn't dismiss your idea out of hand."

"Attaboy, Mark. It doesn't cost anything to think about it. Now you'll have to excuse me. I need to finish my public relations gig before they show the movie."

When the flight attendants darkened the cabin and started the movie, Mark was too agitated to concentrate on the film. *Do I really want to see Joan again and run the risk of opening all those old wounds? Maybe I should and get all this emotional turmoil resolved, once and for all. Would she even agree to see me, let me back into her life, and possibly disrupt her marriage and peace of mind? And what would Averil's reaction be? Would she even stand still for me spending time back in St. Louis? The last thing I'd do is jeopardize my own marriage, just to see Joan one more time. On the other hand, if it was a path to captain, the financial rewards would be considerable. My Trans-Global pension would be more, something we'll need when I retire.*

After their flight landed at JFK, Mark and Averil retrieved their luggage, cleared customs, and boarded a mini-bus that took them to the large parking lot where they had left their car. Mark guided them expertly through the bustling Saturday afternoon traffic and, an hour later, they pulled into their driveway in Huntington on Long Island.

Averil went about the musty smelling interior of the house, opening the windows and sliding glass door to the rear patio deck while Mark brought in the luggage and took it upstairs to their bedroom.

"Hey Av. I'm going across the street to pick up our mail. I won't be long."

"Good idea. I'll be in the shower."

Their friend and neighbor, Laura Carnahan, had spotted the homecoming. She was in a chatty mood and wanted to hear all about Italy. Mark gave her an abbreviated summary and promised that Averil would give her the unabridged version when they next got together. Finally, Laura went to her front entryway and produced a white plastic basket, overflow-

CHAPTER NINE

ing with two week's worth of mail. Mark had to use both hands and some muscle power to take it all back to his house.

He went directly outside to the patio and made a first pass through the mail, sorting it into his and her stacks. Averil got the lion's share and it was mostly catalogs. There was also a letter from her sister Emma in Portsmouth and a yellow slip from an international delivery service that Mark assumed was for the painting they bought in Formia. Mark's mail consisted of monthly bills, financial statements, and a letter from the airline regarding his health plan.

Averil came out to the patio with wet hair, wearing a long sheer white cover-up that revealed the faint outline of her white panties and bare breasts. She handed Mark a remote handset and said, "I've reconnected the telephone. After I dry my hair, I think I'll fix a bite to eat. Would you like something?"

Mark leaned back and thought for a moment. "You know what would hit the spot right now? A big bowl of popcorn."

"You've got it," she said. "Just give me a few minutes."

He went into the kitchen, opened a bottle of Heineken beer, and resumed his mail browsing on the patio.

Averil eventually returned with two large bowls of popcorn and a gin and tonic for herself. In addition to butter and salt, she had added slivers of sharp cheddar cheese and apple slices to each bowl. Then she sat down in a chaise lounge next to Mark and started flipping through her stack of mail. Her first choice was the envelope from England, which she tore open and began to read.

"What's the news from Emma?"

"Just the usual. She read about Sean in the newspaper but she doesn't seem too concerned. Then again, she doesn't know him like I do."

The sun dropped below the horizon and daylight began to fade. Presently, a string of low voltage accent lights placed around the backyard came on, illuminating the blooming lilac and rose bushes at the rear and side of the yard. Averil folded the letter and returned it to the envelope. "Mum's health is failing. It's only a question of time before she has to get help or go into a home. She's also mad at me because we didn't stop in London and come down to visit."

"Why did you even tell her that we were going to Italy?"

"I didn't. It was Emma what spilled the beans. You know my sister doesn't know how to keep a secret. Now I'll have to grovel for the next six months until Mum stops pouting and feeling sorry for herself."

The quiet and peaceful setting was interrupted by the telephone. Averil answered and only said hello before passing it to Mark and silently mouthing the words, "It's your ex-wife."

When Mark responded, Margie assaulted him with a barrage of angry words. "Where have you been? I've been trying to reach you for over a week. Your answering machine never even came on. You should buy a good one—they're not very expensive, you know."

"I unplugged it. I always do when we're going to be out of town for more than a few days. What's on your mind?"

"I just spent three horrible days with Karen in San Francisco. She's dating some black musician and he's about to move in with her. I think they might be doing drugs. Then she's got a ring in her nose and another one in her navel. And she's talking about getting sunrise tattoos on her breasts." Mark laughed softly, prompting another angry outburst from the other end. "What's so damn funny?"

"She sure knows all your hot buttons. Hey, she's an adult now. She can do whatever she wants."

"Mark, she's barely twenty-four. She's still a child in so many ways."

"So, what do you want *me* to do?"

"Talk to her. You're her father. Maybe she'll listen to you. Try to get her straightened out before it's too late."

"I'll call her tomorrow. I'll try, but I'm not making any promises."

After he disconnected, Mark slammed the handset loudly on the glass table top and stared out into the twilight. Averil sipped her drink and looked over at him. "What say you, Dad? Trouble with one of your girls, I presume."

Mark told her the other half of his conversation, the part she hadn't heard. "I don't get it. We never went through any of that crap with Karen's sisters."

"How old was she when you and Margie separated? Thirteen, I believe? Your other girls were a bit older then. I think the youngest sibling always suffers the most when parents divorce."

"Good point. Any suggestions on how I should handle this?"

CHAPTER NINE

"Just do what you feel is the right thing. Bear in mind that she's craving attention and all her actions may be her strategy to get it. She probably feels quite justified in laying huge amounts of guilt on both of you."

"Maybe I should fly out there and spend some time with her."

"Right. After coming back from a two week vacation. Do you think the airline would let you do it?"

"Probably not. Maybe I should invite her to come visit us."

"That would be fine, except you'd be flying and I'd be at work some of the time. She'd get bored rather quickly and probably resent us for not being here."

"Sounds like loving fatherly concern is the best approach," said Mark.

"I should think so," agreed Averil.

Mark reached out and squeezed her bare foot. "I am so glad that I married such a wise woman."

She smiled back at him and said, "And your marrying me confirms that you are indeed the wisest of men." Mark continued massaging her foot with more pressure while she moaned. "Oh yes. This is better than sex."

"No it isn't," he said, "Nothing's better than sex."

Their mutual admiration society was again interrupted by the telephone. This time it was Averil's boss, Harry Turner, owner of the largest marine supply company located in Huntington's marina. After exchanging a few pleasantries about her vacation, Harry came to the point. "We've got a little problem and I need your help. Shirley's gone for a couple of weeks. Her mother died so I had to rearrange everybody's schedule. Can you come in Monday morning and work the full week?"

Averil groaned audibly. "I thought you wouldn't be needing me until Tuesday afternoon. I was hoping to have some personal time to get myself organized before starting back to work."

"I know. I wouldn't ask unless I was really stuck. And I'm in a real pickle here. Will you do it? For me?" The income from Averil's part-time job was relatively insignificant compared with Mark's flying salary and his Navy retired pay. She only worked because it gave her the opportunity to collect nautical antiques.

"All right, but I'll be expecting some comp time when Shirley gets back."

"You're a doll. See you bright and early Monday."

After Averil hung up, it was her turn to pout. And when she told Mark the disappointing news, he laughed, cupped his hands around his mouth, and said in a god-like voice, "Welcome back to the real world, Mr. and Mrs. Holloway."

Chapter Ten

While Mark and Averil readjusted to their usual routine, and Father Soric made preparations for returning to St. Louis, Sean Flannery passed his time in England's Full Sutton Prison near York, counting the days until his parole hearing.

One evening, the guard on Flannery's cellblock, Tommy Godwin, was making a routine check before the lights were turned out. When he got to Flannery's cell, he stopped and looked in. Flannery was lying on the top bunk and staring at the ceiling. The bottom bunk was empty because its previous inhabitant had been released a few days before. Flannery enjoyed being alone in the cell and hoped that another cellmate would not be assigned soon. It relieved him of any need to take part in conversation and gave him more time to think.

Tommy ran his baton across several bars to make a rippling, clanging noise. "Are you in there, Flannery?"

"Yes Tommy, I'm dreaming about how I'd like to bugger your queen."

Tommy appeared unfazed by Flannery's remark and even allowed a faint smile. "I thought a chap like Prince Philip might be more to your liking."

Flannery laughed. "I'm Irish, you rotter. Not Greek."

"So, would you have her royal highness smuggled into your cell or would you be sneaking into her apartment at Buckingham Palace?"

"You know I could never get her past the likes of you," said Flannery with a chuckle. "I'll just have to have me way with her after I get paroled."

"Ah yes, your parole. That's a real fine dream you have there, mate. But a bit of a fantasy, wouldn't you say?"

Flannery became serious as he sat up. "Now listen here, Tommy. You know I've been behaving meself for the last two years, slaving away in that machine shop and learning me trade. I do believe that I've got a good shot at it the first time I go up before the board."

"Have you really changed, Flannery? Or are you just so clever that we haven't been able to catch you red-handed doing something wrong?"

Flannery leaned back against his pillow. "Well, you and your blackguard mates should keep trying. Maybe you'll get lucky one day."

Tommy crossed his arms in front of his chest, his baton dangling from his right hand. "There's just one fly in the ointment, I believe. Don't you owe the prison authorities some large sum? A few thousand quid, as I recall."

"You guards make bushels of money. How about advancing me a loan?"

"Ha!" Tommy barked. "Fat chance of that."

"I'll just take me chances then. Something will surely come up."

Tommy shook his head from side to side, ran his baton across a few more steel bars, and continued walking slowly down the cellblock corridor.

Flannery placed his hands behind his head, resumed his staring at the ceiling, and let his mind wander, something he often did when alone.

Tommy's not such a bad sort, but he is a screw, and he'd sooner beat the bejeezus out of you than have a few pints at the pub. After all, this is a British prison and living conditions here, if you can call them that, are barely tolerable. I've just finished another rotten dinner of cabbage and potatoes and I'm thinking once again of gaining me parole and what I'll do when it comes through. I'm trying to be on me best behavior, so when the parole board meets later this year, they will smile kindly on me and grant me an immediate release.

Me mind is filled with other concerns these days: the daily monotony of prison life, the tension, the worry that I won't be murdered in me sleep at night, and the devious means one must pursue to get marijuana or cocaine. Thanks be to God for the dope. How else could a person cope with this madness?

Yes, I should have used better judgment when the boys came to me in 1981 and filled me head with all that patriotic nonsense about dying for Ireland. But they spoke so fine and offered so much more than I was having in England then. The wages were poor and the conditions in the factories were terrible.

The best thing that ever happened to me was on that London holiday with Padraig, God rest his black Irish soul. It was there in 1983 that I met Averil, the love of me life, in a pub near the Marble Arch. We hit it off right

CHAPTER TEN

away and later, at the end of our first date, we couldn't keep our hands off each other.

Flannery reached into his shorts and stroked himself. He had a full erection, something that happened whenever he fantasized about Averil. He continued massaging himself until he came. After wiping his hand on the leg of his prison uniform, he rolled over and was soon dreaming about the events that brought him to Full Sutton.

In March of 1987, Flannery and his two pals, Malachy O'Brien and Padraig Duffy, were hiding in the countryside, just outside the village of Ballygawley in Northern Ireland's County Tyrone. Flannery had persuaded an elderly widow to allow them to stay several nights in her barn.

On March 17, the rogue trio came out of hiding to join in the local celebration of St. Patrick's Day. They were spotted by an informer, however, and two days later their barnyard home was surrounded by a British Army patrol. In the ensuing gun battle, Duffy was killed and O'Brien seriously wounded, but an unharmed Flannery surrendered meekly.

That June, Flannery was moved to Brixton prison near London where Scotland Yard and the government's prosecutors began their investigations and preparation for his eventual trial in a Crown Court. O'Brien was transported to the same prison; however, he was kept in a separate area and not allowed any contact with Flannery. After considerable maneuvering, the Crown prosecutors convinced O'Brien to testify against Flannery in exchange for a more lenient prison sentence.

During his imprisonment, Flannery wrote often to Averil, pleading for her forgiveness and begging her to come and visit him. She ignored his letters and when he went to trial in the spring of 1988, she didn't even go to the courtroom. Flannery was tried, found guilty of multiple high crimes, and sentenced to a sixteen year prison term.

On a cold and blustery December Sunday in 1988, a guard came to Flannery's cell and called out, "You've got a visitor. Make yourself presentable."

"Who would be coming out to see the likes of me on a day like this?"

"A pretty woman, I'm told. Someone you probably don't deserve."

Flannery jumped out of his bunk. "It's Averil—it's me wife. She hasn't deserted me after all these years."

He was escorted by the guard into the visitors area, a long cavernous hall with individual tables lined up along the room's long dimension and spaced about ten feet apart. Inmates dressed in dull green uniforms sat on one side of a table with each individual visitor on the other side, separated only by the table's width. There were numerous prison guards stationed throughout the hall, most of them slightly to the rear of the visitors' tables. Their primary concerns were to keep order and make sure that prisoners did not receive any contraband.

When Averil saw him come through the door, handcuffed with shackles around his ankles, she sucked in her breath and covered her mouth with her hand. After he sat down at the table opposite her, the guard stepped back a few paces and started a conversation with another guard.

At first, neither Averil nor Flannery spoke. Each had considerable difficulty even looking the other person in the eyes. He was first to break the silence.

"Thanks for coming. You look fabulous."

"What happened to your hair? Your head looks like a snooker ball."

"It was me own idea. Makes the head lice look elsewhere for a home."

"And that scar on your cheek?"

"Just a little row with one of the boys. Nothing to be concerned about."

Their conversation was interrupted by moans and groans coming from an inmate at the next table. His visitor was a young, long-legged blond woman in a black mini-skirt, low cut gold top, and black fishnet hose. She had taken off her right shoe and fully extended her leg while she wiggled her toes, her foot firmly nestled in the man's crotch.

"How utterly disgusting," was all Averil could say.

Sean leered at her. "I wouldn't mind if you'd be doing the same for me."

"That's not the reason I'm here."

Sean's face fell. "Ah yes, you're a woman with a mission. And not a mission of mercy."

"I've some news for you, things I didn't want you to read in a letter. The truth of the matter is that I've retained a solicitor and filed for a divorce." She paused and relaxed, apparently relieved on how calmly he was taking her news.

"I've really made a mess of it. But we're still husband and wife. And

CHAPTER TEN

there's always the chance I'll be released early if they look kindly on me appeal. I'll make it up to you, Av, I promise. Just give me a chance."

"We haven't been husband and wife for a long time. And you're going to be locked up for many more years. You're only deluding yourself if you think otherwise. And what about me? I'm still young and have my whole life ahead of me. I'll not grow old waiting for the likes of you."

Sean leaned forward as his eyes narrowed to slits. "You've got it all set up now, don't you? Dumping me so you can be cozy with your Yank."

"What are you talking about?"

"Don't play games with me. I know all about the two of you. What was it that attracted you to him, his uniform or his money?"

"How do you know about him?"

"The boys have been watching you for months and they keep me informed. You with that cushy job at Selfridge Hotel. They've seen you all lovey-dovey with that American naval officer. Holloway's his name, is it?"

"I don't believe this," she said. "Your brain's gone all barmy."

"Well, you'd better take heed because I'm not letting you off the hook that easy. There's a name for what you're doing and it's called adultery. That should put a stop to all this foolish talk about a divorce."

Averil stood up. "You can rot in prison for all I care," she said. "You're a bloody fool if you think we could ever be together again."

He rose quickly and lunged forward, sliding across the table top on his stomach. He would have caught her with his handcuffs but she had pushed back her chair and stepped backwards. "You're still me wife, Averil Flannery," he shouted, "and you'll be mine again someday, I promise you. And I'll find you, no matter where you are."

A half dozen guards rushed their table, grabbing a yelling and flailing Flannery by the arms and legs. Averil watched him being dragged away, too stunned to move or speak.

Somewhere in the darkness before dawn, Flannery awoke and crawled out of his bunk. He walked to the front of his cell, placed both hands on the vertical bars and stared out at the dimly lit corridor. He recounted the number of days until he would have his parole hearing and resumed thinking about himself.

Sure, our married life was troublesome, mainly because of my consorting with the boys, and of course all the drinking. And yes, I'm sorry to say, I treated her shabbily and knocked her around a wee bit. But that was no excuse for her deserting me, not even lifting her pinkie finger when I was hauled off and sentenced at the Old Bailey for a good portion of me adult life.

Averil's married again, this time to a rich American pilot. They have a very cushy life together on New York's Long Island. The boys have told me so. They haven't given up on me like she did. They know what loyalty is all about.

The way I see it, the boys will come through again for me when I win me parole. They've been holding several thousand pounds for me in safekeeping and they'll help me get a new identity with passports and the like.

After me release, I'll do a bit of detective work and track Averil down in New York. It shouldn't be too hard. Her mum still lives in Southampton and her sister in Portsmouth. So I'll just cruise down to Southampton and shake up the old lady a bit until she comes around and tells me what I need to know.

I'll give Averil one more chance to come to her senses and be me wife again. And if she doesn't? Then I'll finally have me satisfaction and Averil will regret the day she deserted me for that Yank.

Chapter Eleven

On a warm Friday morning in mid-July, Jerry Soric and Ryan Mahoney departed Rome's Fiumicino airport on a flight for New York. It was a bittersweet occasion for them because, on the positive side, their academic lives were successfully concluded and they eagerly looked forward to the excitement and spiritual satisfaction of beginning their priestly careers. The downside was that these two very close friends would now be geographically separated by a thousand miles. Only God knew when they would see each other again.

They were seat mates in economy class on a fully packed 747 and had a barely tolerable, but uneventful flight to JFK. Once they arrived, cleared customs, and consulted the departure TV screens in the bustling and noisy terminal, they said their final goodbyes.

"Well, Jerry, I guess this is it. Remember me when you say mass."

"You know I will. I wish I could come to your ordination."

"Me too. It should be a grand occasion. The archbishop with all his minions, combined choirs and even a mariachi group. My parents are coming down from Seattle and my sisters will be there with their families—great gobs of nieces and nephews."

"Let me know when you find out which parish you'll be assigned to. I'd like to stay in touch."

"No problem there. You'll be one of the first to know. Maybe we can e-mail each other. Good luck to you, riding herd on those teenage hooligans at the high school. And all the best dealing with your mom and Stephanie. I wish I could be a mouse in the corner when you have your talks with those ladies."

They gave each other a long hug and mutual pats on the back. Ryan began the long walk to his departure gate in the domestic part of the terminal, while Jerry had to take a bus to another terminal for his flight.

By the time Jerry's St. Louis flight reached cruising altitude, it was almost 7:00 P.M. He was very tired, having risen at 5:00 A.M. in Rome to make his flight to New York. But he was too nervous and excited to nap; excited about being home again where he could speak the language and enjoy familiar creature comforts such as English language newspapers, a ready supply of books, and occasionally, U.S. television. His nervousness was centered around his mother; what kind of mood would she be in, how insistent would she be about his contacting Stephanie, and what would her reaction be to his news about Mark Holloway. To occupy his time on this relatively short flight, he indulged in one of his favorite pastimes, completing a crossword puzzle. He usually excelled at this, but the one he chose was from that day's *New York Times* and he couldn't complete it. *I'm just out of practice. I'll have to get my edge back by doing the ones in the Post-Dispatch.*

Jerry dressed casually for his journey in a dark blue polo shirt, tan slacks, and tennis shoes instead of his black priestly garb. He wanted mainly to be comfortable, but he also wanted to give a distinctly nonreligious appearance to his parents when they met him at the airport and resume his relationship with them on a happy note. His sporty secular appearance also attracted some admiring looks from several flight attendants and the one who served him peanuts and a soft drink openly flirted with him. This appealed to his male vanity and his capricious sense of humor so he did nothing to discourage the female attention.

It was just after 9:00 P.M. when his flight taxied to the arrival gate at Lambert-St. Louis International Airport. In that short space between the plane and the terminal, he could feel the oppressive heat and humidity that was characteristic of the city's summer weather. He easily found his parents standing near the arrival gate and, after he dropped his piece of carryon luggage, gave them both warm hugs. Frank Soric was a stocky man and gave his son a strong fatherly embrace while Joan's hug was warm and tender but somewhat tentative. In the instant when he first recognized them but before he spoke, Jerry thought his father had shrunk and put on some weight since he had seen him a year ago. Frank Soric wore glasses, was clean shaven, and his short wavy hair was almost completely white. On the other hand, it seemed that his mother had become prettier and grown taller, but he dismissed the latter idea when he

CHAPTER ELEVEN

noticed that she was wearing high heels.

"Welcome home, son. We sure have missed you. Did you have a good flight?"

"I've missed you too, Dad. Yes, the flight from Rome was OK, but it was packed and took forever to reach New York. My friend Ryan sat next to me but we parted company at JFK."

After Joan hugged her son, she looked him up and down. "You look pretty much the same. All that Italian food and wine didn't stick to your waist, I see."

Jerry laughed. "No problem there, Mom. As long as I worked out every day, the pasta never had a chance to hang around very long."

Frank took charge of Jerry's carryon bag and Joan took Jerry's right arm in her left, leading him to the baggage claim area while Frank followed them. Joan wore a light blue sleeveless one-piece dress whose hem stopped just above the knees. It fit loosely, but could not disguise her well-tanned limbs and attractive frame. Her dark brown hair fell onto her shoulders in soft curls, accented by a broad-band silver necklace, the only jewelry she wore except for her wedding ring. As they walked along, she peppered him with questions. "How long can you stay with us? When do you have to start work at the high school? Are you still assigned to be a teacher there? In what subjects? And what's your schedule going to be for the summer?"

Jerry let her chatter as they walked and answered her questions whenever she paused to catch her breath. "Tomorrow, I have to call Father Cecil over at Holy Family Church and see if I can help him out with his Sunday mass schedule. I know he's short-handed. Then on Monday, I need to check in with Father Burke. He should be able to tell me about vacancies at Jesuit Hall. Then I'll have a meeting with him to review the academic program at the high school and see how I fit into things. So, as you can see, there's a lot I have to do."

Jerry's two large black suitcases were almost the last ones to appear on the baggage carousel. Both bags had handles and wheels so Jerry took one, Frank the other, and Joan took the carryon bag. Frank drove their dark red Blazer while Jerry rode in the right front seat and Joan sat directly behind Jerry. "I hope you don't have to spend the whole Sunday over at that church," she said. "I've invited some of your friends over to the house for dinner." Jerry turned his head and torso around sharply so that his mother got a good look at a quietly alarmed face. "Don't worry," she added. "Stephanie's not coming. I wouldn't do that to you."

Jerry turned his head back to the front. "But I didn't say a thing," he protested.

"You didn't have to," she said as she reached over the seat and handed him a small slip of paper. "Here's her number. Call her when you get a free minute."

Frank took them initially west on I-70, turned south on the I-270 beltway, and finally drove in a northwesterly direction on I-55 to the suburb of Wilbur Park. The Soric residence was a modest three bedroom single story house on a quiet street. Similar homes could be found in virtually any large mid-western residential community. The oak and elm trees lining the street were over thirty years old, tall and stately, and every house had a large well-tended lawn with abundant rose bushes and various types of juniper bushes and trees.

Frank parked in their driveway and took one of Jerry's suitcases inside while Jerry followed him with the other one. They wound up in Jerry's bedroom, followed by Joan who started opening the windows. "It's cool enough outside now," she said. "We can probably turn the air conditioner off."

Frank went back outside to get Jerry's carryon bag and park the vehicle in the garage while Joan went about the house opening the rest of the windows. Alone in his bedroom, Jerry moved about slowly, taking in the aura of the room and the various objects associated with his youth. The bookcase was filled with many of his own books, going all the way back to his early childhood and included some of his college textbooks, boyhood mystery novels, and adventure classics such as Jules Verne's *20,000 Leagues Under the Sea*. He fondly caressed a gold baseball trophy on the top of the bookcase that he had won in Little League and gazed wistfully at a red and white St. Louis Cardinal's baseball pennant, a souvenir of his first major league baseball game.

But the item that meant the most to him was a six string guitar standing on a corner chair. He had taught himself to play in high school and often sang and played folk songs to entertain friends or just himself when he was alone. He picked it up gently and quietly strummed a few strings. He had not been able to take the guitar to Italy because of the airline's baggage limits. He was afraid to have it shipped, fearing that it would be damaged or 'disappear' in transit, so he had left it at home for safekeeping.

He sat down on the chair and starting singing and playing a John Denver folk song. Frank and Joan reappeared in the doorway and lovingly watched their son get reacquainted with his musical friend. At the first break, Frank said, "That's the best sound I've heard in quite a long time. Hey son, we're both beat so we're going to hit the hay. We'll get caught up tomorrow morning at breakfast. OK?"

Jerry got up, put the guitar back on the chair and gave each parent a hug. "I'm exhausted myself," he said. "Let's see. It's about 5:00 A.M. in Rome right now, so I've been awake for twenty-four hours. No wonder I'm so spaced out."

After they left, Jerry hung his clothes in the closet, turned out the lamp on his desk, and was sleeping soundly in less than five minutes.

Chapter Twelve

Around 2:30 A.M., Jerry awoke suddenly and sat up, momentarily disoriented to the extent that he forgot where he was. A short time later, he was comfortable enough to pad down the hallway to the guest bathroom, his way shown by a night light fronted by purple and gold glass tennis rackets. After emptying his bladder, his next stop was the kitchen. He turned on a light over the breakfast table which sat next to a bay window looking out at the back yard, found a half gallon container of chocolate ice cream in the refrigerator, and filled a cereal bowl with his frozen treasure. He sat down at the breakfast table and ate slowly, savoring each bite of a treat that he seldom had in Italy, when he heard footsteps coming from his parents' bedroom. It was Joan, wearing cloth slippers and a white cotton robe covered with black oriental characters.

In mock anger but with a smile on her face and hands on her hips, she scolded him. "What are you doing out here? You're supposed to be sleeping."

"That's the problem with jet lag. My body clock is still on Italian time. It'll take me a couple of days to get adjusted, I guess."

Joan poured some water in a tea kettle and placed it over a burner. "I guess I'll just have to keep you company for a while. You want some hot chocolate? I'm having a cup."

"No thanks, Mom. I'm fine with the ice cream."

The water came to a boil and she poured it into a cup of cocoa and stirred several times. She brought her cup over to the table and sat down next to Jerry, pushing a plate towards him. "Try some of these cookies. They should go well with your ice cream. I made them myself."

Jerry devoured one. "They're great. Hmm, extra chocolate chips, too."

Their conversation initially consisted of small talk, mother and son getting reacquainted with each other after a year's separation. When there was a lull, Jerry thought this would be a good opportunity to introduce one

CHAPTER TWELVE

of several potentially sensitive topics. "Remember me writing to you about my trip south to Cassino? And searching for Uncle Tadeusz's grave at the Abbey?"

"I certainly do. You were very sweet to do that for me."

"Well, Mom, I didn't tell you the whole story. I bumped into somebody at the Abbey. Literally. A man. Someone you used to know a long time ago."

Joan lowered her cup and looked at him quizzically. "You met a man in Italy that I used to know? I don't think I know any Italian men. That sounds very mysterious, Jerry. Who could it be?"

"Mark Holloway."

Joan's eyes widened, her mouth opened, and her empty cup fell onto the nearly empty cookie plate making a loud clatter. Jerry erupted in a hearty laughter, prompting her eyes to narrow and a low voice ask angrily, "What's so funny?"

"You. The two of you. You both have the 'dropsy.' When I told him you were my mother, he dropped his coffee cup into his saucer and almost broke it."

Joan grabbed a paper towel to wipe up the cocoa spill. "What? How? I don't understand this. Why was he there? I mean, how did you connect him with me? Or me with him? Oh, I don't know what the hell I'm talking about."

Jerry placed his hand over hers. "Relax, Mom. It was all quite innocent. He gave me a ride down the mountain to the village of Cassino. That's when we found out that we were both from St. Louis. So we decided to have a coffee at a small cafe. He had seen me walking around the Polish cemetery and I mentioned that my great uncle was buried there. When I told him Uncle Tadeusz's last name—your maiden name—he put two and two together."

By now, Joan was simultaneously laughing and on the verge of crying, a condition that prompted her to pull a tissue out of her pocket and blow her nose loudly. "Dear God. Oh my dear God," she kept repeating.

Jerry was silent while she composed herself and could speak again. "After all these years, it's hard to believe that Mark has surfaced again. How is he? What does he look like? You say he was there alone?"

"He looks great and he's a pilot for Trans-Global Airlines. Has short brown hair but it's graying at the temples. He's married—for the second time—but his wife stayed back at their beach hotel on the coast. She's Protestant and doesn't seem to share his interest in visiting ancient Catholic churches." Jerry ate a large spoonful of ice cream while munching on another cookie. "These are really good cookies."

"Never mind that. Tell me more about Mark."

"Well, he made a career of the Navy and retired as a captain. Then he divorced his first wife after being married for twenty years. She was a very devout Catholic, as I recall him saying. His present wife is British and they've been married about ten years."

Joan paused momentarily to contemplate the irony of Mark's marital experience and continued, "Does he have children?"

"Yep. Three daughters by his first wife and two grandsons."

"This is all so bizarre. I imagine you talked a good deal about me."

Jerry grinned widely. "You? No, Mom, we never talked about you at all. Why would we talk about you?"

"Don't be cute with me, Jerome Soric. I want to know everything."

"OK, he told me all about meeting you in college, the dates you had, and how you broke up just before graduation."

"Did he tell you the reason we broke up?"

"Yes, he did. He wanted to marry you and said that you two couldn't resolve your religious differences. And for what it's worth, Mom, he thinks very highly of you. In fact, I think he still loves you in some small way."

"No, no, no. That's entirely out of the question. It's been over thirty years since I've had any contact with him."

"Hey, Mom. I'm just telling you what I heard and saw. Don't shoot the messenger."

"What did you tell him about me?"

"Just the good stuff. How well you've done in the map making business, your awesome tennis serve, and all the times you beat me when I was a kid."

Joan passed over the last item, assuming that her son was trying to lighten the moment with humor. "Did he mention anything about contacting me?"

"No, he didn't. But he did want me to give you a message. Said he

CHAPTER TWELVE

wishes you all the happiness in the world, or something close to that."

Joan got up, washed out her cup at the sink, and sat down again at the breakfast table. "Jerry, please don't mention any of this to your Dad. He doesn't know anything about Mark and I'd like to tell him the whole story myself. At the right time."

"All right, Mom. My lips are sealed. But what do you think it all means? He and I meeting each other like that."

"It's just an amazing coincidence. A very unlikely and improbable event that somehow happened. It's nothing more than that as far as I'm concerned."

Jerry rinsed out his ice cream bowl, placed it in the dishwasher, and returned to his chair at the table. "I have to be honest, Mom, and tell you it does mean something to me. I feel I understand you much better now. Why you've been so negative about my conversion to Catholicism and becoming a priest. Don't you think that your breakup with Mark is part of this tension between us?"

Tears began forming in Joan's eyes as she took both his hands in hers. "How did you get to be such a wise man?" She paused in the ensuing silence and continued, "I'm sorry, son. Please be patient with me and let me try to work through all of this. I need some time alone to give it some serious thought."

"Sure thing, Mom. And I'll always be available if you want to talk some more about it."

Joan blew her nose again and Jerry stood up to leave. "I think my body's ready for another couple of hours sleep." Then he bent over and kissed her. "I love you, Mom. See you in the morning."

Joan turned out the lights and returned to her bed, quietly sliding under the sheet next to her snoring husband. She felt lonely and wanted desperately to be held, caressed, and cherished, but she knew that Frank wouldn't appreciate being wakened to ease her longing. She was so agitated that she just lay on her back for a long time, staring at the ceiling, running Jerry's news through her mind. Before she was finally able to drop off into a light and fitful sleep, the image of Mark in the college library on that January day in 1965 burned brightly in her mind's eye.

Chapter Thirteen

Mark resumed his usual flying schedule three days after returning home from Italy. Averil also kept busy, working full time at the marine equipment store while her co-worker, Shirley, extended her absence to settle her late mother's estate.

Mark flew the New York-to-Paris and Paris-to-New York routes almost mechanically for the next three weeks. He had little free time since it was the height of the tourist season and the airline was trying to squeeze as much profit from its operations as possible by using crews and equipment to their maximum availability—consistent with FAA regulations, of course.

On the Friday evening of his third week, Mark was flying co-pilot again with Clay Parcel. They had not seen each other since the time when Mark and Averil were returning from Italy. Their initial conversation this evening was all business: discussion of en route weather, cycling through preflight checklists, departing the terminal, taxiing to their takeoff position, and finally, reaching their cruising altitude of 35,000 feet.

Clay switched on the automatic pilot, leaned back in his seat, and turned to Mark. "I don't know about you, podner, but this job is getting to be a real hassle."

"I know what you mean," said Mark. "Maybe you need some time off."

"Yeah, right. Fat chance of that, right at the peak of the European season. Maybe Barbara and I can get to Italy in September or October. Visit that beach town where you and Averil went."

"Don't wait too long. You don't want to get caught by an early winter."

Clay interrupted the conversation to respond to a radio transmission and then changed the subject. "Hey, Mark. Have you thought any more about that tech job in St. Louis I told you about?"

"Yes, I have. I still don't know if it's right for me. I haven't decided yet."

"What's to decide? It can only help your career."

CHAPTER THIRTEEN

"How come you're pushing me into this? What's in it for you?"

"Just looking out for your best interests, old buddy. And the airline, too. Down the road, I want all my stock to be worth a lot more." What Clay had conveniently forgot to mention was that he had already been interviewed once for the job. By his reckoning, if nobody else volunteered, Clay would be stuck with a job that he didn't want.

"What a bunch of B.S.," said Mark. "If I took that job, the flight schedules would get even tighter and you'd be bitching from here to kingdom come."

Clay grinned widely and threw his hands in the air. "What can I say?" Then he and Mark both laughed loudly.

After ten minutes had passed with only a little more talk, Clay looked at his watch and noted it was 7:30 P.M. in New York. He got up from his seat, patted Mark on the shoulder and said, "Time to show the flag. You're in control."

Mark lapsed into a piece of Navy jargon and replied, "I have the con, aye."

Mark scanned the glowing instrument panel to make sure all systems were operating correctly and then looked out the cockpit windows into the night, two time zones later than New York. The Boeing 767 was cruising in a cloudless moonlit sky with no clear air turbulence so far. There was little noise in the cockpit since the engines were far back and away, along the plane's swept wings. The lack of engine noise and the apparent absence of forward motion gave Mark a feeling of being suspended somewhere between heaven and an ocean resembling an unending slab of dull obsidian. This phenomenon unsettled him when he started flying passenger jets, mainly because of his experience flying military aircraft where the pilot was usually next to the engines. But now, he was so accustomed to this feeling that he actually enjoyed it. This period was his favorite part of each transatlantic flight but, although he loved it dearly, he also felt an acute loneliness, feeling isolated in this small cabin and so far away from Averil.

He recalled his conversation with Clay and agreed that the temporary assignment would probably be a good career move and give him a break from his hectic flight schedule. But it also presented both a predicament and an opportunity.

After getting settled in St. Louis, he would probably call Joan and suggest some kind of lunch or dinner meeting, somewhere convenient to her office. Would she insist on bringing her husband along? He hoped not. It wouldn't be much fun for him anyway. He wanted it to be just the two of them, talking about their college days and possibly her relationship with Jerry.

He wondered why he wanted to see her again. He did feel a need for resolution of some kind, to reminisce and possibly get his ego stroked in the process. On the other hand, why should he tempt fate? He didn't want to damage his relationship with Averil but he did have a strong desire to see Joan one more time. For a brief moment, he thought he would enjoy rubbing her nose in it, pointing out that since her son was now a Catholic priest, she had made a gigantic mistake by not marrying him in the first place. If she had married Mark, she would also have been able to travel the world and experience foreign countries first hand instead of merely looking at them on a map. *What about the possibility of a romantic interlude? No way.* He was happily married and assured himself that Joan was too. The last thing he wanted to do was embarrass himself by making a pass at her and then being rejected. *But what if she . . . ?*

When Mark returned to New York, he made an appointment to meet with Patrick Keating, one of Trans-Global's senior pilots who now worked in the airline's personnel department. Keating's office was located in the Trans-Global terminal at JFK, the same departure terminal used for Mark's flight, so the meeting was arranged for an afternoon when Mark would be later flying to Paris.

Keating was a tall, lanky Oklahoman with gray bushy hair, and a long bespectacled face. He welcomed Mark, poured him a cup of coffee from a decanter, and invited him to sit next to his large wooden desk.

After some pilot chit-chat, Keating got down to business. "So you're interested in this temporary job in St. Louis. Why?"

Mark was initially taken aback by Keating's directness but eventually found his voice. "Why? Several reasons, I guess. First of all, I have at least five more years of flying left. Ten at the most. And with the new aircraft coming on line, I figure I can become more valuable to Trans-Global by getting this kind of experience. And maybe—just maybe—I might get a

CHAPTER THIRTEEN

captaincy out of it."

Keating smiled, "Can't argue with that. What else?"

"Oh, variety. Something different—a change of pace. Flying that same route over and over can get kind of boring. You know what I mean?"

"Yes, I do. I flew the Seattle-Tokyo route many times."

Feeling more at ease, Mark volunteered some personal information. "I was raised in St. Louis and still have some family there. A brother, some cousins, and a few friends. So it would be a good opportunity to catch up with them."

Keating opened a brown cardboard folder on his desk and said, "I've been looking at your personnel jacket and you have some interesting qualifications. Granted, you've got one helluva bunch of flight time in the Navy and with us. I see you received B. S. and M. S. degrees from the Navy Postgraduate School."

"That's correct. Both in aeronautical engineering. The Navy sent me to Monterey for three years and then I served in a technical billet as a payback."

"And that was your next assignment?"

"Right. I worked in a contractor's plant as the Navy's technical representative, making sure the airplanes being built met the contract specs. But that was no vacation. All this time, and while I was in school, I had to keep my flight qualifications current."

Keating's eyes widened as he smiled, "Looks to me like you have the perfect background. But I'm curious about something. Is your wife OK with this?"

Mark shifted his eyes and nervously answered, "Uh, well, I haven't told her about it yet. Thought I'd see if I got the job first." *Damn. Fifty-four years old and I still can't tell a good lie.*

"The job is yours if you want it."

"If you don't mind, I'd like to hear some more about it."

"Fair enough. First thing is that we have to juggle flight schedules around and get someone plugged into your slot. This will take about a month so I see you going to St. Louis in early September. You already know that Tri-Star is building the plane. They've contracted with a company near the airport called SIMFLIGHT to build the flight simulator. Your job is to advise the SIMFLIGHT engineers about the operational realism, safety factors, and whatever—all about the simulator. And make recommendations about the specs for the software being written for the simulator's computer."

"Why go to the expense of putting a pilot there?"

"Tri-Star wanted a real pilot looking over SIMFLIGHT's shoulders. It turns out the expense was factored into the purchase order. We're getting a break on the price of the planes in exchange for your services."

"The job sounds pretty complicated. How can I get up to speed on this?"

"I know it sounds overwhelming right now. But I'll assemble a package of documentation for you, stuff to review in your spare time."

"So who would I report to while I'm there?"

"Good question. Your point of contact will be Kent Waldorf in our contracts section. Now one thing that you should keep in mind is that Tri-Star's contract is with SIMFLIGHT. You're there to advise and not get caught in any crossfire between those two companies."

Mark smiled. "I understand completely. How long will I be there?"

Keating frowned. "That's kind of hard to say at this point. If all goes well, your part should be wrapped up by the end of this year. Now you're free to go home for the weekends during this job. Just book yourself on one of our flights. You may even want your wife there with you. On your nickel, of course."

Mark glanced at his watch and saw that his flight's check-in time was rapidly approaching. As he rose to excuse himself, Keating stood and shook his hand. "I'll be in touch, Mark. Thanks for coming forward and volunteering for this job. You won't regret it."

The last words echoed in Mark's ears as he wheeled his black luggage through the terminal. He certainly hoped it would turn out that way. Then he started mentally rehearsing the scenario he would follow when presenting this *fait accompli* to Averil.

Mark returned from Paris the following Saturday afternoon and had Sunday off. Since the marine equipment store was also closed, Averil was free as well.

They both slept late and spent the morning lounging in their king-size bed, reading the Sunday *New York Times* and enjoying a breakfast of coffee, orange juice, croissants with jelly, and juicy cantaloupe slices.

CHAPTER THIRTEEN

At one point, after they had finished eating and were just about through with the newspaper, Mark turned to her and said, "Oh, I almost forgot to tell you. I'll be getting a new assignment in about a month."

"Really? Will you still be flying to Europe?"

"No, I won't be flying at all. It's completely different. A desk job in a contractor's plant." Mark continued to purposely ramble, telling her mostly about the technical aspects of the work, alluding to his earlier meeting with Keating.

"I don't know if I like this," she pouted. "How long is it going to last?"

"Just about four months, I believe. But I'll be coming home every weekend so we'll have that time together for ourselves."

"Why in the world did they pick you? Out of all the pilots in Trans-Global."

"I guess they went through all the personnel records. I think it had to do with my engineering degrees and that tech rep job I had in the Navy. It's pretty unique when you stop and think about it."

"Pardon me if I seem a bit mercenary here, but what's in it for you?"

"Ah, that's the good part. It will give me a leg up on all the other pilots when this airplane comes into the fleet. I should be able to make captain out of it."

"Did Keating promise you that?"

"No, not in so many words. But the opportunity is there."

Averil got out of bed and looked out the window into their back yard and stretched her arms high in the air. "Well, I suppose I can tolerate it for four months. I've endured longer privations."

"That's my girl," enthused Mark. "There's no reason why you can't spend some time during the week with me. Just hop one of our flights and boom—You're there."

"That's if I can get the time off. Harry does owe me some comp time."

Averil went into the bathroom, intending to take a shower, when she had a sudden thought and turned around. Standing in the doorway, looking at Mark in bed, she asked, "Where is this job? You didn't say."

Mark cleared his throat and put on his most innocent and sincere face. "I didn't? It's at the St. Louis airport. Both contractors are located there."

"St. Louis? How interesting." Averil turned and went back into the bathroom and stood at her sink while brushing her teeth.

Mark quickly got out of bed and went to the bathroom doorway. "Yeah, that's a lucky break for me. I'll be able to spend some time with my brother and his family. My cousins, too. I haven't seen them in years."

"Sounds like you'll be very busy. Are you sure you want me there?"

"Of course I do. You've never met my cousins. And I can show you all kinds of things. Where I grew up, where I went to school. All the neat stuff."

Averil said nothing more. She took off her night shirt and panties and stepped into the shower. Mark, sensing the conversation was over, turned back into the bedroom, picked up the breakfast dishes and the newspaper, and went downstairs to the kitchen. His stomach was churning and an uneasy feeling came over him. He felt that the conversation had not gone well and he had handled the breaking of his news poorly. He now suspected that there would be a dark cloud of suspicion hanging over their activities for the rest of the day and again wondered if he was doing the right thing.

Meanwhile, Averil stood in the shower and let the hot water run through her hair and over her body. This latest news would have been only mildly upsetting had it not been for one particular detail: St. Louis. *Of course he would see his brother and his cousins, but what about the person he didn't mention? Is he thinking about contacting Joan and doesn't want to tell me about it? And if he does happen to see her, would anything happen between them? And what if I did fly there and stay with him? Would he resent me for being there or does he really want me to come? And what would I do with myself while he's working during the day?*

After she shampooed and showered, she stepped out of the stall and toweled off. She then looked in the mirror and continued the short conversation with herself. *We've been married for ten years and I'm positive he's been faithful the entire time. Why should I doubt him now? And if he wants to ring up his old college flame—well, just let him scratch that itch. He should get her out of his system, once and for all. Nothing will happen because we have a good marriage. And isn't that what it's all about? Trusting one another?*

Chapter Fourteen

A week after Jerry returned from Italy, he moved into Jesuit Hall, a hotel-like building on St. Louis University's Frost Campus. The living quarters were neither Spartan nor luxurious but they were, in Jerry's opinion, more comfortable than his digs in Rome.

Jerry was assigned to share a room on the second floor with thirty-two year old Leo Byrne, originally from Denver, Colorado. Father Leo was an almost saintly individual, soft-spoken and extremely intelligent. He seemed to be constantly in a good mood, eyes bright and a wide grin all over his face. Jerry admired his subtle sense of humor, and his unbridled optimism at being able to see the positive side of everything, no matter how disastrous it might look to the casual observer. Father Leo taught English grammar, English composition, and American and English Literature courses to undergraduates. He even found time to write and publish several short stories. Jerry and Leo took an instant liking to one another and each was grateful for drawing a compatible roommate.

On the first Saturday of August, Jerry awoke at 5:30 A.M., dressed in Bermuda shorts and a polo shirt, and drove out to his parents' house. He had a quick cereal breakfast with his dad, after which they took Frank's Blazer and their golf clubs out to the Piney Hills Municipal Golf Course in nearby Bella Villa. They checked in at the pro shop just before 7:00 A.M. for their 7:18 tee time and were teamed up with two male college students.

After playing the first five holes, it became apparent that Frank was playing much better than his golf handicap would suggest. Conversely, Jerry was playing much worse than normal, a situation that put Frank in a jovial mood.

The sixth hole was a short, par three and the men ahead of the Sorics were still on the green lining up their putts. Frank and Jerry talked while standing next to a ball washer, each with a club in his hands. The two students were on the far side of the tee box, practicing their violent, loopy swings.

Frank asked, "How are things shaping up for you at the university? Are you getting settled in OK?"

"Pretty much. The living quarters are kind of tight, but I've got a pretty congenial roommate, so it shouldn't be too bad."

"You have a roommate? I thought you'd be living by yourself."

"A couple of years ago I would have been alone. But the order had to close one of the residence halls. Too expensive to keep them both going, I guess. So they have all of us in one building—high school and college teachers alike. Anyway, Leo's a good guy. You'll have to meet him one of these days."

"Sounds like a plan. Maybe we can have you both over for dinner."

Jerry was going to make a flippant comment about his mother joyfully cooking dinner for two Jesuits, but he decided instead to bring up another topic. "Hey Dad, before I forget. I met with Father Burke last week and got my teaching schedule. You wouldn't believe the load he gave me."

"Really? You mean it didn't turn out like you thought it would?"

"Nope. I'm teaching algebra to a freshman class, plane geometry to sophomores, and religion to several freshmen and sophomore sections."

"Good grief, that does sound like a heavy load. How come?"

"In a few words, they're short-handed. It's going to take a lot of preparation on my part, but I figure that after I teach a class all the way through one time, it will be a lot easier the second and third time around."

The foursome ahead putted out and moved off the green. Jerry turned to his dad and said, "OK, par shooter, you're up. Put it in the cup."

The Soric foursome completed the eighteenth hole shortly after noon. When the scores were tallied, Jerry had an 85, some eight strokes higher than his usual round. Frank beamed when he saw his final score of 96, a good ten strokes lower than his average outing. If not a numerical win, Jerry considered his dad's score both a virtual and moral victory and offered to buy lunch at the club house.

Frank and Jerry sat in the corner of the club house restaurant, having a Polish sausage in a hot dog bun and a cold drink, watching a women's golf tournament on a large screen television set. After eating their sandwiches, Frank turned to Jerry and said, "That's quite a story. You bumping into your mother's college boyfriend in Italy."

CHAPTER FOURTEEN

"Oh, she told you about that, huh?"

"Yep, the other night over dinner. So this guy's an airline pilot. And he's been married twice?"

"That's what he said. Twenty years to his first wife, a devout Catholic. And ten years to a British woman."

"What does he look like?"

"He's a couple inches taller than you, I'd say. Kind of an average build."

"Where does he live now?"

"New York, I think. Somewhere on Long Island."

"That would make sense. He'd want to be close to the airport."

Jerry looked into his dad's eyes and asked, "Does this bother you? Hearing about a guy that Mom dated before she married you?"

Frank laughed. "Not at all. That's the way things work. Your mother isn't the first woman I ever dated either. But since we've been married, she's been the only woman in my life. And you can take that to the bank."

Jerry smiled. "I'm sure that his golf handicap is higher than yours."

Frank continued, "The way I understood your mother, this guy didn't seem too interested in making contact with her."

"That's right. I thought he might like to call her up and talk about the good old days."

"I guess it's all for the best. I'm not sure I'd want to check up on any of my old girl friends. I'd like to remember them the way they were—young and pretty. Their husbands probably wouldn't think much of me poking around either."

Jerry glanced at his watch. "If you don't mind, Dad, I'd like to move on."

"OK, I'm ready. You've got some things to do?"

"Yes, I want to spend some time in the library this afternoon. I need to polish up the homily I'm giving tomorrow at mass."

"Oh, really? What are you going to talk about?"

"Faith. Trying to relate it to our everyday lives and put it into practice."

"That's an interesting topic."

"I'm going to start by mentioning St. Paul and his letter to the Corinthians. The one about faith, hope, and charity. Then I want to give an extreme example. Testing Abraham's faith when God asked him to sacrifice his son, Isaac."

"It's extreme, all right. Are you going to draw any moral from all this?"

"That's the part I need to work on. It's a bit fuzzy in my mind right now."

"Are you doing anything tonight?"

Jerry looked away and answered nervously, "I'm having dinner with Stephanie."

Frank almost shouted, "You have a date with Stephanie?"

"It's not a date, Dad. It's more of a counseling session."

"Yeah, right. Where are you having dinner?"

"At a restaurant. A very public place with lots of people around. She wanted to cook dinner at her apartment, but I didn't think that was such a good idea."

"I'm with you on that. But why are you doing this? Is it because of your mother?"

"Well, partially. But Stephanie's having a rough time now because of her divorce from Justin. I'd still like to think of her as a friend and, if I can help her get on with her life—well, isn't that what friends are for?"

As they were leaving the club house, Frank admonished his son, "Just be very careful. You don't know these women like I do. They're dangerous creatures and they have their own agendas."

Chapter Fifteen

Jerry arrived at Lampara's restaurant just before seven o'clock and found a parking place in their crowded lot. Located in a predominantly Italian South St. Louis neighborhood, it was a popular dining spot for the locals.

When he walked into the air conditioned lobby, he immediately saw Stephanie on the right, sitting on an upholstered bench. He took a few seconds to look at her profile before walking over to greet her. He was momentarily stunned by her appearance, no longer the scrubbed twenty year old college student, but a beautifully mature twenty-seven year old woman.

Tall and slender, just a few inches shorter than Jerry, she had pulled her long sandy hair back into a pony tail. She must have sensed him moving in her direction because she turned to look at him and then stood.

She wore a cotton trellis garden dress the color of butter with short sleeves and a scooped neck. The hem stopped just short of her brown ankle-strap thongs. Her dress had fifteen brown buttons down the center from neckline to hem, the last five unbuttoned to reveal her bare tan legs from the ankles to her knees.

Jerry, upon getting close to her, extended his hand and said, "Hello, Steph. So good to see you again." *In another time and place, we would need privacy after dinner and both enjoy my unbuttoning that dress.*

Stephanie smiled and her blue eyes twinkled, but both faded in quick disappointment when she saw how he was dressed. Jerry had chosen all black this evening: black shoes, black socks, black shirt, black jacket and, of course, the white Roman collar. He wanted to be sure that there would be no misunderstanding about the nature of their meeting.

Stephanie resigned herself to Jerry's handshake instead of the hug she had hoped for. As she stretched out her right hand, her purse slipped off her shoulder. She picked it up from the floor and said, "Hi,

Jerry. Excuse me for being such a klutz, but you look so . . . holy. I guess I was expecting you to look different. So what do I call you? Reverend? Father?"

Jerry gave her his most sincere smile. "You'd better call me Jerry or I'm heading right back out that door."

Stephanie had made reservations in her own name and, after some nervous small talk, the hostess invited them to follow her to their table. They attracted many curious stares as they walked the dining room's full length.

Jerry was unnerved by the watching eyes and felt them boring holes in his body. He sensed the ambient noise level had subsided and imagined the minds of all the patrons, grinding their speculative wheels, wondering what he was doing with this statuesque blond. He prayed silently that everyone would think Stephanie was his sister.

When they came to their table, Jerry pulled Stephanie's chair out and invited her to sit down. After she was seated and closer to the table, he caught a whiff of her perfume. *Wasn't this the same perfume she wore when we were dating?*

Jerry walked around the table and sat down opposite her. The bus boy had lit a candle inside a dark red vase that reminded him of an altar votive candle. Stephanie moved the candle aside, remarking that she could now get a better view of his face.

"Before we go any further," she began, "I'd like to say how much I appreciate your meeting me. This situation must be very awkward for you. Especially because of what you and I had together."

Jerry put his napkin on his lap and rested his joined hands on the table. "That was a long time ago, Steph. So much has happened since then. We're both different people now."

Their waiter appeared and took their drink orders. Jerry opted for a glass of Chianti and Stephanie asked for Chenin Blanc.

She continued, "Yes, I know we've changed. For one thing, I'd like to believe that we're both much more mature. I think we can be honest with each other and speak our minds freely. What do you think?"

"Yes, I can go along with that."

"OK, then. So can we be friends?"

Jerry looked puzzled. "Sure, we can be friends. But nothing more than

CHAPTER FIFTEEN

that, I'm afraid. We can never be the way we were in college."

Stephanie blushed and said, "Don't worry, Jerry. I won't hit on you. Unless you give me just cause, of course."

The waiter returned with their wine and took their dinner orders; beef ravioli for Jerry and shrimp with angel hair pasta for Stephanie.

Jerry decided to change the subject. "Where do you stand with your marriage? Since you have your own apartment, I guess the chances of reconciliation are slim."

"That's right," she said. "I've already filed for divorce and it's moving along quite well." Stephanie was employed as a paralegal in a downtown law office and one of the firm's attorneys was representing her in the uncontested legal action.

"Justin's being extremely cooperative in the property settlement so I should come out of this with a nice chunk of money."

Jerry's eyes widened. "No kidding. How did you manage that?"

"He started up a software company three years ago selling virus protection programs and it's been a very lucrative venture. But that's also the root of the problem. He got so damned busy—pardon my French—that he forgot he had a wife. What good is being rich if your marriage is a flop?"

"Do you still love him?"

"Now that's an interesting question. I think the answer has to be no. Did I ever love him? Right now, I'm not so sure. Maybe at the start I did, but our relationship changed. I guess I was only fooling myself, thinking that we would get closer as time went on. But we drifted farther apart instead. And these last couple of years have been pure hell."

"I'm curious," said Jerry. "Why did you marry him in the first place?"

"Oh, you poor man. You really don't know?"

"No, I don't."

"Because I couldn't have you, dummy. Justin was available, attentive, good looking, and said all the right things. So why shouldn't we get married?"

Jerry took a sip of wine. "That sounds pretty cynical to me."

"I'm just being honest now. Telling you how I feel. I'm tired of holding things back."

"Just before I left Rome, I received a letter from my mom. She painted a very dark picture of your situation."

Stephanie blushed slightly. "I guess I really dumped on her with all my problems. She helped me get over the really rough spots."

Jerry nodded his head in silent agreement. *Yes, Mom laid it on extra thick in that letter, making sure that Steph and I would see each other one more time.*

Over dinner, they talked about less sensitive subjects. Jerry was interested in everything that had happened in her life since they broke off their relationship. Stephanie and Justin married a year after that traumatic event, their wedding coinciding with both their graduations from Washington University. Justin's degree was in computer science and he easily found a well-paying job with a large software company in St. Louis. He held this position for three years until he quit to develop his Internet venture. Stephanie was initially a stay-at-home housewife but she quickly became bored and found a job at the law firm where she was now employed. The partners were so impressed with her intelligence, enthusiasm and capacity for work that they paid for her to attend a paralegal course.

Stephanie was curious about Italy and Jerry's experiences living in a foreign country. He told her of his Monte Cassino meeting with Mark Holloway, a story that she found both romantic and entertaining; but over coffee and gelato, the conversation turned personal again.

"Tell me something—and be honest," she said. "Are you happy?"

"No question about that. I hope I don't sound too pompous, but I'm doing the work that God put me on this earth to do. It's taken a long time to get to this point. I thought I had turned into a professional student."

"So you made the right decision? To become a priest?"

"I believe I did. And I'm excited about starting my teaching career next month. It will certainly be a challenge but I expect the satisfaction to be immense."

"Do you ever think about me? About us?"

Jerry shifted nervously in his chair and broke eye contact with her. The silence hung in the air like a guillotine blade until he answered. "Sure, I've thought about you. Did you think I could just forget what we had?"

"One more question. Do you remember the last time we made love?"

Jerry replied sharply, "Steph, there's no point in resurrecting all this ancient history. It doesn't help either of us get on with our lives."

CHAPTER FIFTEEN

She smiled and said, "Never mind. You answered my question."

Jerry drained his coffee cup and changed the subject. "So what about you? Looks like you'll be able to do most anything you want with your life."

"I'm thinking of law school. I love the profession and I know I'd be good at it. When the divorce is final, I'll be able to go back to school and support myself without having to work part-time. And when I get my degree, I'd like to set up my own practice."

"What kind of law?"

"Believe it or not, family law. Looking after battered wives, chasing down child support payments from deadbeat dads. That sort of thing."

"I'm sure you'll do well. You'd be fantastic at anything you pursue."

"Thanks for the vote of confidence. And who knows? Maybe someday Prince Charming will ride up on his white horse and sweep me off my feet. And if I'm really lucky, he'll turn out to be like you."

Jerry glanced at his watch. "Sorry to be a party pooper, but I'm saying an early mass tomorrow."

Stephanie insisted on paying for dinner and Jerry graciously accepted her treat. While walking to her car, she asked, "Where are you saying mass?"

"At Holy Family Church. Looks like I'll be a part-timer there for a while. Father Cecil convinced my superior that this should be one of my additional duties. He thinks I'm particularly effective with the parish youth."

"I'll bet," she said. "Especially with the girls. Maybe someday I'll sneak into a back pew and catch your sermon."

When they arrived at her car, Jerry again offered his right hand but she had something different in mind. She first grabbed his coat lapels and pulled him close. Then she put both arms around his neck and kissed him on the lips.

At first, her action startled him, but since that section of the lot was dark and there were no other people around, he brought his arms around her back and returned the embrace. This time, she was the one to break contact and step back.

"Just friends, now," she said, smiling and wagging her finger at him. "Remember what you said."

As he watched her drive out of the lot, he muttered, "Right. Just friends."

Before going to his room, Jerry walked across the university campus to St. Francis Xavier Church. He entered a side door and went immediately to a small chapel at the rear and knelt in front of a three foot statue, stylized to show Jesus and his bleeding sacred heart crowned with thorns.

His mind was a jumbled jungle of emotions as he prayed for strength, guidance, and forgiveness. Clearly, he had been tempted this evening, particularly while kissing Stephanie in the restaurant's parking lot. The distinct pleasure of holding her close, feeling her warm supple body pressing against his, savoring her familiar scents; they were all powerful temptations. He also had to admit that he lusted for her body, feelings that he thought were buried seven years ago.

On the plus side, however, he felt morally elevated since he had successfully resisted the carnal urge to pursue her. True, Stephanie deserved some of the credit because she had the good sense to deflect his all-too-willing affection. He also reasoned that she was indeed a good friend who still loved him but now in a different way. She was affectionate, but unwilling to tempt this priest into bed because she knew that the long term consequences would be far worse, especially in Jerry's case, than the pleasure brought on by a brief sexual interlude.

His mind wandered to the earlier afternoon when he was in the library, working on tomorrow's homily about faith. He could now see and appreciate that this evening's dinner with Stephanie was a test of his own faith—and he had not been found wanting. He would rejoice in his faith and thank God for helping him confirm it. He concluded his chapel visit by making a mental note to add a brief postscript to his homily; he would give the congregation a well-disguised but personal example of faith in action.

Chapter Sixteen

On the second Friday of August, Sean Flannery was escorted from his cell to the parole hearing room in the same general area as the warden's office. He had a fresh haircut, was clean-shaven, and wore his best prison-green uniform, freshly washed and pressed by fellow inmates in the prison laundry.

Flannery sat outside the hearing room with five other men on a simple wooden bench while two uniformed armed guards stood nearby. The prisoners were not shackled or handcuffed because prison policy assumed that these inmates, wanting to appear favorable to the parole board, would not cause trouble.

Flannery was eventually summoned into the room, the third inmate to be interviewed that morning. He was directed to a wooden chair facing a long table being used by the parole examiners, two men and a woman. Two armed guards flanked the chair and stood at a short distance from the parole applicant. Flannery sat erect, arms folded across his stomach, looking earnestly at each board member.

Since it was a warm and humid morning, all the room's windows were open, but no breezes passed through the steel bars. The only air moving about the room was pushed by two large pedestal fans, one in each front corner, facing the members of the parole board.

The woman on the board, sitting at the center of the table directly in front of Flannery and between the two men, spoke first. "Good morning, Mr. Flannery. I am Mrs. Aldershot and these gentlemen are Mr. Ashmore on my left and Mr. Fairgrieves on my right. I'm sure that you are fully aware of the hearing process and the conditions for parole should it be granted. Now before we begin, do you have an opening statement that you would care to make?"

Flannery cleared his throat before speaking. "Yes, I do, your honor. I would like to say—"

She interrupted, "We are not judges or magistrates, Mr. Flannery."

"Begging your pardon, missus," he continued, "I would like to say that after serving thirteen years in prison, I have seen the error of me ways and I am truly sorry for all the pain I've caused. I have tried hard to be a good prisoner and stay out of trouble. I believe that I'm ready for parole and confident that I can live as an honorable and productive member of society after I'm released."

Mrs. Aldershot, a frumpish woman in her mid-fifties with brownish-gray hair tied up in a bun, opened a dark brown folder on the table. She looked through reading glasses that hung around her neck with a chain and, with the other hand, riffled through a few papers in the folder. "Mr. Flannery, I see in your personnel file that you've been involved in several altercations with other prisoners. Would you care to comment on that?"

"I was only defending meself, missus. Every one of those little tiffs was started by the other person."

"Perhaps you did something to provoke an attack. A remark or gesture?"

"Oh no, missus. I wouldn't be doing that now. You can ask all those boys if you like." He instantly regretted his last remark because it sounded foolish. "I would like to say," he continued, "that I've kept me nose clean for almost two years now. Not a single row."

"Yes, quite so," noted Mrs. Aldershot.

Mr. Fairgrieves, a short frail man in his early forties who wore glasses, leaned forward and spoke, "Mr. Flannery, I'm curious about something. Earlier this year, the Peterborough Crown Court made a judgment against you for legal costs in connection with your lawsuit against the prison service. I see that you still owe a sum in excess of 20,000 pounds. What do you intend to do about that?"

"Ah yes, I'm happy that you brought that up. It's me intention, you see, to pay the amount in full. I'm a machinist by trade and that's how I hope to earn me living once I'm released. I've worked in the prison shop and kept current with all the new technology. It will take a few years, but I'd be making payment every week from me wages."

The answer seemed to satisfy Fairgrieves who leaned back in his chair, prompting Flannery to smugly grin and add, "I couldn't have paid off that debt by me normal release date with me prison wages. It would be in the

CHAPTER SIXTEEN

Crown's best interests to see me hold down a steady well-paying position."

Fairgrieves looked at the other board members and then addressed Flannery. "You've made a valid point. Thank you."

Mr. Ashmore, a sixty-two year old silver-haired man in a black pin-striped suit, had a question. "Mr. Flannery, are you currently in contact with any member of the IRA?"

This unexpected query jolted Flannery momentarily but he had the presence of mind to answer quickly, "No sir, I am not." This was a bold-faced lie but he hoped it sounded convincing.

"You realize, of course," continued Ashmore, "that any IRA contact whatsoever would be a violation of your parole. And you would be returned to prison straight away."

"Yes, governor, I understand that completely. I would not be taking that kind of risk." Flannery could feel the sweat dripping from his armpits as he recalled a recent talk with his IRA link on the possibility of bribing or extorting one of the parole board's members. *Did Ashmore know anything about this?*

The remaining questions concentrated on the period before his arrest. The board wanted to know about his family in Ireland, where he would live if paroled, his marriage to Averil, and even his role in the Brighton bombing. Flannery gave short general answers to these queries, repeating his intention to be a model citizen.

Forty-five minutes after Flannery had entered the hearing room, Mrs. Aldershot concluded the proceedings. "I think that will be all, Mr. Flannery. The board thanks you for your cooperation and also your patience while we deliberate on your application for parole. You will be informed of our decision in the matter. Good day."

On Monday afternoon, ten days later, Tommy Godwin made an unscheduled visit to the machine shop, looking for Flannery. Tommy was to begin his watch in Flannery's cell block at 4:00 P.M. and wanted to give him some news before his duty tour began.

Flannery was monitoring a job that was under the control of a small computer next to the machine. When he saw Tommy enter the shop, Flannery smiled and walked over to him. "Now isn't this a surprise. What brings you down into this grimy pit?"

"I've some news for you, Flannery." He handed him a single sheet of paper.

Flannery read the short letter several times. His face turned red as he shouted, "They've turned me down. The bloody bastards have turned me down. And they didn't even give a reason. They just said no."

"Sorry to be the bearer of bad news," said Tommy, "but you can apply again next year. Maybe that board will be a more generous lot."

Flannery crumpled the paper and threw it into a waste basket. He walked away from Tommy and paced nervously up and down the shop, staring at the floor in deep thought. Without any warning, he picked up a six foot section of steel tubing and began smashing things: the computer, the machinery, and anything that could be broken.

Tommy did not attempt to subdue Flannery but instead ran from the shop and quickly returned with two other guards. Before they could tackle Flannery and get him handcuffed, he had swung the tube at Tommy and hit him across his left forearm. They dragged a kicking and screaming Flannery back to his cell.

Tommy stayed outside and spoke through the bars, "You stupid Mick. What you did just proved they were right all along. You're not ready for parole. You'll be lucky if they don't add more time to your sentence."

Flannery sat on the edge of his bunk looking away. "Sod you," he said, his angry mind searching for solutions to his present turmoil.

By now, Tommy's arm was throbbing with pain. He reported to the prison dispensary for treatment and, when it was diagnosed that his arm was broken, another guard was assigned as a replacement while Tommy's arm was wrapped in a plaster cast.

Around midnight, while patrolling the cell block area, Tommy's replacement smelled smoke and determined it was coming from Flannery's area. He shone his flashlight into the cell and witnessed a most peculiar sight.

Flannery had folded his mattress on the floor and set it on fire. After the fire had a good start, he added his prison uniforms to the small blaze. Flannery had taken off all his clothes and now stood on a small table, urinating into the fire while yowling and cackling a demonic laugh.

The guard first set off the fire alarm and then called for help that arrived momentarily. They opened the cell and took Flannery out forcibly while the others doused the fire with two portable fire extinguishers. The guards dragged Flannery to another part of the prison where they placed him in

CHAPTER SIXTEEN

a much smaller cell, one that was equipped with thick padding on all sides, from floor to ceiling, to prevent the prisoner from doing any further harm to himself or the prison.

Flannery crawled on the cold cement floor to a far corner and curled up into a fetal position whimpering like a baby.

Three days after his entry into solitary confinement, Flannery was again visited by Tommy. He spoke through a small window in the cell door, a window that opened only from the outside. "Are you having a good time in there?"

Flannery came to the door and pressed his face against the window. "When do I get the hell out of here?"

"Whenever the warden says so. Another couple of days and I think you'll be ready to toe the line."

Flannery noted the cast on Tommy's arm. "Is it broken?"

"Yes, it is, but it didn't break the skin."

"I'm sorry about that, Tommy, I am. Didn't mean to hurt you. I just lost me head when I read that letter. I still can't believe the bastards turned me down."

"Listen here, Flannery. This attitude of yours—the violent behavior when things don't go your way—it's a non-starter."

"Yeah, I know. But that's the way of it."

"Think about getting out of here in three years, in case you've queered your chances for parole. You don't want them tacking more time to your sentence, do you?"

"I'll be out of here before then. You can bet your mum's knickers on it."

Tommy looked at Flannery's intense angry eyes, framed by the small window in the door, and instinctively stepped backward. "I don't know why I waste my breath on you."

As Tommy retreated down the dimly lit corridor, he recalled seeing that same look two years before. A man had killed another inmate and Tommy had witnessed the entire event. Tommy attended the murderer's trial and was in the courtroom while he testified. When the convict told of stabbing the man with a switchblade for simply stealing his cigarettes, his eyes betrayed inner emotions of joy, anger, and revenge, the same look that Tommy had just seen in Flannery's eyes.

Chapter Seventeen

On a mid-August Sunday, Stephanie went to the 10:30 A.M. services at Christ Immanuel Church, the same one attended regularly by Joan Soric. After the service concluded, Stephanie waited on the sidewalk in front of the church. When Joan spotted her, she smiled warmly. "I'm so glad to see you. I was hoping you'd be here today."

"Nice to see you too, Joan. Do you have time for coffee? I'd like to talk."

"I've got a better idea. Let me buy us brunch. I know a nice air conditioned restaurant close by."

"Sounds good to me," said Stephanie. "Where's Frank today?"

Joan chuckled. "Playing golf with his buddies. Ever since he played that last round with Jerry, he's thinks he's a threat to Tiger Woods."

"You mean he actually beat Jerry?"

"No, but he came pretty close. I guess if you subtracted their handicaps from their actual scores, it would be nearly a tie."

The women took Joan's car to a nearby restaurant called Kathy's Kountry Kitchen, a large structure designed to look like a New England cottage, painted white with green shutters at every window. The ladies attracted many admiring glances from the male diners as they were escorted to their table at the back of the restaurant. They were served a large carafe of coffee and a young waiter immediately took their food orders.

Joan wasted no time quizzing her young friend. "I heard that you and Jerry had dinner together a week ago. How did it go?"

"It went very well, although it got off to a rocky start. He wore his priest clothes and that threw me off at first, but I got used to it." She paused for a moment and added, "Well, I'd better get used to it because that's the way it's going to be—from now to kingdom come."

Joan frowned. "That man. He has other clothes he could have worn."

"No, I think he did the right thing. He's made a life-long commitment to God and he was making sure that I saw it first hand. He also wanted me

CHAPTER SEVENTEEN

to understand that there are new boundaries on our relationship. I was thinking about this all during the service this morning. Seeing him again has given me a whole new perspective on my life."

Joan took a sip of coffee. "I guess this means there's little chance of you two getting back together again."

"I think that's true. We can be only friends now. But that has to be tempered as well. A Jesuit priest can't be buddy-buddy with his divorced college sweetheart. It just wouldn't look good."

"You have a point."

"There's something else that occurred to me. What if Jerry and I had married after graduation? If his religious calling was as strong as I believe it is, we might have wound up getting a divorce just so he could pursue his vocation. And what if we had children? God only knows what might have happened then."

Joan sat up straighter and spoke in a stern voice, "I think you're getting carried away with all these 'what ifs.' I can't see Jerry backing out of a marriage with you. He'd stick with it—and you."

"Well, maybe he would. But he'd be very unhappy and I'm sure I'd be miserable right along with him."

Joan decided to probe further. "If it's not too personal, I'd like to know something. Do you still love him?"

Stephanie smiled widely, a reaction that Joan had not expected. "That's the crazy part. I do still love him, but it's different now. He's happy and fulfilled, something that's evident when you hear him talk and see the fire in his eyes. I'm happy for him, that his spiritual hunger is satisfied, something that I could never have given him. Is this making any sense?"

Joan patted her on the hand. "Yes, dear, it makes sense. Not what I was hoping to hear, but I can respect your feelings about it."

The waiter interrupted their conversation with breakfast plates; a mushroom omelet for Stephanie and eggs Benedict for Joan. The women were silent for a few minutes while they ate a large portion of their meal. The pause also gave Stephanie a chance to change the subject. "Jerry told me an interesting story the other night. About meeting Mark, your college sweetheart, at an Italian abbey."

Joan blushed slightly. "He told you about that? With all the catching up you two had to do, I'm surprised that even entered the conversation."

"I wanted to hear about his travels in Italy and meeting Mark was a big event for him."

"Well, it was an amazing coincidence. After all these years, it's hard to believe him popping up like that."

"Jerry seemed to think it was once pretty serious between you and Mark. Did you consider marrying him?"

Joan was not entirely comfortable talking about herself and Mark, but since she had made Jerry and Stephanie's relationship her business, she resigned herself to divulging the details of her college love affair. "Yes, he asked me to marry him many times, but I always turned him down."

"Why was that? Didn't you love him?"

"Oh, I loved him all right. It was so strong. So real. I used to wake up in the middle of the night, thinking about him, so happy that he was a part of my life. Oh yes, I've never loved anybody like I loved him. Not even Frank."

Joan's last statement mildly shocked Stephanie. "Not even your husband? That's a funny thing to say."

"Your first love always has a special place in your heart, whether or not you marry him." Joan smiled as she added, "I would think that you, above all the women I know, would surely appreciate that."

"Touché," said Stephanie. "So why did you keep turning him down?"

"Believe it or not, it was a religious problem. He was Catholic and I just couldn't agree on raising our kids in the Catholic Church."

"That was it?"

"Isn't that enough? You can't imagine the pressure my parents—and my minister—put on me in those days. To marry a man of my own faith so we didn't have those basic conflicts working against our marriage from the start."

"But interfaith marriages happen all the time."

"Yes, now they do. But you have to remember that I was dating him back in 1964, zillions of years ago."

"I understand the whole dating thing was different then."

"Oh yes, much stricter. Very few couples had sex before marriage in those days. And if they did, the girl either got a bad reputation or got pregnant, and that was a very traumatic event that ruined many lives just trying to deal with it."

CHAPTER SEVENTEEN

"With such different religious backgrounds, how did you two meet?"

"I needed a date for a big sorority dance and I didn't have a steady boyfriend. I'd been watching Mark for a while, hoping he would ask me out, but he was pretty shy. So I just bit the bullet and asked him to take me to the dance."

"That's so cool."

"And we got along so well. After we went out a few times, we wondered why it took so long for us to get together. At the beginning, I didn't even know he was Catholic. It just sort of came out as time went by."

"Any regrets?" asked Stephanie.

Joan paused again, searching her own psyche for clues about how much to say. Finally, since she didn't have any close women friends in which she could confide, she chose total honesty. "Yes, there have been regrets and I want you to keep this to yourself. If I'd married him, it wouldn't have been all sweetness and light. I would have been moving all about the country as a Navy wife and would have been separated from him while he was overseas or on a ship in some ocean. But in the long run, we could probably have come up with some arrangement on our kids' religious education. I'm sure we would have had lots of children, too. Surely, all of them wouldn't have turned out to be nuns and priests."

"Jerry told me that Mark's been married twice. His first wife was Catholic but his present wife is Protestant."

"Yes, that's pretty ironic, isn't it?"

"He has three daughters by his first wife and several grandsons. That might have happened to you if you had married him. A divorce, that is."

"Well, I'm not going to think about it. It's all water under the bridge."

"Would you like to see him again?"

"I don't think so. What would be the point of it? Besides, he's not interested in seeing me. At least that's the way he left it with Jerry at Cassino." Joan paused for a few moments before continuing. "I don't want you to get the wrong idea here. What I said about having regrets and not marrying my first love. I love Frank very much. He's been a good husband, father, and provider. He's also given me a lot of support and my independence so that I can enjoy a successful career. It's not perfect, but then, what marriage is?"

Joan became silent and sensed that perhaps she had said too much, but there was much more that she wanted to say. She wanted to tell Stephanie about her unhappy love life—that she and Frank had not enjoyed sexual relations during the last five years, primarily due to his impotence and apparent lack of interest. At one point about three years ago, Joan had urged him to see a doctor and ask if he was a candidate for Viagra. Frank dismissed the idea out of hand, telling her that the drug was still unproven and potentially dangerous. It might even give him a heart attack or cause some other health problems.

"I understand perfectly," said Stephanie, breaking Joan's reverie.

Joan took Stephanie's hand in hers and said, "I'm so happy we had this talk. Even though you'll never be my daughter-in-law, I'd still prefer to think of you that way. And a very dear friend as well."

Stephanie squeezed Joan's hand and tears welled up in Stephanie's eyes. "I like that. I would like us to always be close friends."

Joan paid the bill with her credit card. They were about to leave when Stephanie had an idea. "You know, Jerry is saying mass at Holy Family Church. I've decided to attend one of his masses some Sunday. I told him that the other night at dinner. How would you like to come with me? I'm sure our presence would mean a great deal to him."

The invitation caught Joan off guard, but after looking into Stephanie's eyes for a moment she consented. "Well now, that would be a huge surprise for him, wouldn't it? OK, I'll do it. Just let me know which Sunday is good for you and what time. And say a prayer the ceiling doesn't fall in when we get inside that Catholic church."

Chapter Eighteen

On Labor Day evening, Mark flew to St. Louis and checked into a Drury Inn near the airport. He had made arrangements earlier for a discounted rate on a small suite, anticipating living there many five-day weeks while he worked on the simulator project. He wanted not only the comfort of a suite but plenty of room in case Averil decided to come over and spend some time with him. Neither Mark nor Averil had a large physique; like most well-traveled people, each craved a large living space when away from home.

Mark was anxiously looking forward to the new job but also had a nagging uneasiness about taking this assignment. He felt some small measure of guilt, knowing full well that he was not being one hundred percent forthcoming with Averil about all the things he might be doing during his time away from home.

He awoke early the next morning after spending an uneasy night with a series of short naps. He arrived at the hotel's coffee shop just after it opened and ate only small samples from the elaborate breakfast buffet. Since he had plenty of time to kill, he sat at a corner table with a full carafe of fresh coffee, thoughtfully reading the *Post-Dispatch,* one of his favorite newspapers, from front to back.

He returned to his room and thought for a moment about what to wear on his first working day. He was well aware of the informal dress code at many of the Seattle software companies and also the electronics firms in California's Silicon Valley, but he decided that he would not go down that sartorial path. His choice boiled down to either a suit or his pilot's uniform. He chose the latter, reasoning that it would set just the right tone with SIMFLIGHT's management; he was a pilot and he was there to do a pilot's job.

He easily found the single-story SIMFLIGHT facility in an industrial park midway between the hotel and the airport. As he cruised slowly through the crowded parking lot in his rental car, he was pleasantly surprised to see a parking space near the building's entrance with a blue and white sign attached to a metal stand that announced: RESERVED FOR M. HOLLOWAY. As he turned off the car's engine he had a thought. *This outfit has class. I'm impressed.*

He introduced himself to the receptionist and she telephoned someone to report his arrival. Within a few minutes, a tall, lanky and nearly balding man came walking briskly from a double set of doors near the receptionist's desk. He smiled and extended his right hand. "Hello, Mark and welcome to SIMFLIGHT. I'm Tom Campbell, project manager for the Tri-Star simulator. Did you have any problems finding our place?"

"No, the directions were fine. And thanks for the special parking place."

"Come on in and we'll meet some of the guys you'll be working with."

They walked down several long corridors, past individual offices and several large open areas that were populated with cubicles containing young men and women in casual clothes, chatting in small groups or staring intensely at their computer screens. They finally arrived at a conference room containing a large oval table surrounded by a dozen upholstered chairs on rollers. The room was flanked on one side by large picture windows that provided excellent views of the employee eating and recreation areas.

Campbell introduced Mark to two other men in the room who were standing next to a counter that held a silver coffee urn and a plate of Danish pastry. "Mark, this is Dick Hightower, our project's Technical Director, and Fritz Delano, our Quality Manager. You'll be seeing an awful lot of these guys over the next couple of months." Mark shook their hands and was invited to have coffee and a pastry but politely declined, citing his earlier breakfast.

Mark, Dick and Fritz took seats near the head of the table while Tom gave an overhead projector briefing on SIMFLIGHT's organization and product lines. During the briefing, Mark reflected that Campbell's spiel was similar to other contractor presentations, also known as "dog and pony shows," that he had heard many times before as an in-plant technical representative for the Navy. Campbell then gave a detailed presentation on the project and ended on a cautionary note. "This is only the tip of the iceberg. I'm sure you'll be getting into the guts of it before too long—more than you ever wanted to know."

CHAPTER EIGHTEEN

Dick and Fritz excused themselves so Tom took Mark further along the same corridor where he pointed to a large office. "This is where I hang out, Mark. My door is always open for you." They walked a short distance further and Mark was introduced to a buxom middle-aged blonde woman in a bright red dress. "This is Nancy, Mark. She's my secretary but she'll also be taking care of all your typing and administrative needs."

Nancy shook his hand and moved closer, flashing a large white smile. "Oh Captain, I'm so happy to meet you," she gushed. "Anything you want—just ask."

I'll bet, Mark thought to himself. He made a mental note to be careful with this woman and keep a healthy professional distance from her.

Tom showed Mark to the office he'd be using, just on the other side of Nancy's cubicle. It wasn't as large as Campbell's, but was comfortably appointed and had several large picture windows with views of the parking lot and surrounding office buildings of other companies. Tom pointed to a stack of documents on Mark's otherwise clean desk. "I've assembled a data package for you—something you'll want to dig into first. The contract, the statement of work, the system spec—that sort of gudge."

After Tom left, Mark hung up his hat and coat, opened his black brief case, and populated the desktop with personal mementos including a framed photograph of Averil talking on the phone, his favorite snapshot. Then he sat down in the well-padded leather chair, swiveled to the right and gazed out the window, letting his mind ramble freely. He then turned back around to face his desk and picked up the first document on the stack. *Let's go to work.*

Because of the Labor Day holiday, Mark's first week was shortened to only four days. But they were busy days, crammed with meetings, one-on-one discussions, informal design reviews, and the pressing need to read every scrap of pertinent documentation about the project. On Tuesday evening, after a light dinner at a restaurant near the hotel, he spent the evening in his room pouring over papers and manuals, generating a list of questions for which he would try to get answers.

There was little time for socializing with family members but he did manage to connect with his younger brother, Matt, on Wednesday evening. Matt had been divorced for eight years and had no children—at least none that he knew about, a joke he told frequently to the annoyance of his friends. By his own count, he was currently dating four different women, each of whom wanted to stabilize him with "the old ball and chain." Because of their respectively busy schedules, Mark and Matt could only manage a meeting at a sports bar in North St. Louis for several beers and expensive hamburgers, content to catch up with each other while watching the Cardinals play baseball on a large screen TV.

Later in the week, he talked with his cousin, Donna, who lived just across the Mississippi River in Belleville, Illinois. She was a year younger than Mark and had been married for thirty-two years to Charlie Clark. They had established a heating and air conditioning business early in their marriage and it had grown steadily into a financially successful operation. It was now operated and managed by their four adult children, two sons and two daughters. Six grandchildren had also appeared on the scene, much to the delight of the semi-retired and doting grandparents. Due to their own individual schedules, Mark and Donna were not able to find an evening when they were both free, but Mark did agree to come to their home for dinner on the following Tuesday.

Mark checked out of the Drury Inn on Friday morning. He was hoping to get away early that afternoon and catch a flight to JFK, but Tom Campbell called an informal gathering just after lunch in the facility's manufacturing and modeling area. It was for the unveiling of a full scale mockup of the cockpit for the new aircraft, the same compartment that would form the flight simulator's interior cabin. Mark was so intrigued by the new electronic devices and flight controls pictured that he almost lost track of time. He asked many questions and was given detailed explanations by the engineers, resulting in appointments next week with several individuals to pursue some ideas he had.

Dick Hightower tapped Mark on the shoulder and looked at his watch. "Don't you have a plane to catch?"

Mark looked at his own watch and almost shouted, "Oh my god, you're right. I'll see you guys bright and early Monday morning."

On his flight to JFK, Mark leaned back and sipped a diet cola, feeling the most relaxed he'd been all week long. He was tired and anxious to get

CHAPTER EIGHTEEN

back home again, but he was also exhilarated, genuinely excited about the project and the contribution that he could make to ensure its success. He was also impressed with the technical expertise and creativity of the SIMFLIGHT engineering team as well as their attention to detail. *If the simulator works as well as the mockup looks, it's sure to be a winner.*

Somewhere over the state of Ohio, another thought popped into his mind; he had not called Joan Soric. In all the rush surrounding the project and the time spent with his brother and talking with his cousin, the idea of contacting her had slipped his mind. Had he just forgotten or was there some other reason for not calling her? He smiled to himself while thinking about it. *I did the right thing for the wrong reason. Oh well, there's always next week.*

Mark took a shuttle van from JFK and arrived at his home shortly before 8:00 P.M. He had called Averil from the St. Louis airport just before takeoff and had given her a pretty accurate estimate about when he would arrive.

He called out her name when he entered the front door and she responded faintly from the kitchen. He dropped his luggage in the entry hall, hung his hat and coat in the hall closet, and walked toward the kitchen at the rear of the house. As he passed through the dining room, he noticed five things: the tantalizing aroma of veal piccata cooking in the kitchen; the dining room table with candles, miniature pink roses in a bud vase, and an open bottle of French red wine; and soft orchestral music coming from stereo speakers in a corner cabinet.

Averil greeted him with a quick kiss when he sauntered into the kitchen. "Are you hungry, luv? We should be ready to sit down straight away."

"I'm starving," he said. "I haven't had anything since lunch."

She turned back to the stove to check on their meal which gave time for Mark to get a better look at her. She was barefoot, wore a tight pair of black Capri pants, and a sleeveless gold top that hung loosely over her waist. Mark was so taken by her appearance that he moved next to her back, rubbed his groin against her butt, placed his arms around her waist and kissed her noisily on the neck which prompted her to squirm and giggle. "You smell good enough to eat," he whispered in her ear. He became more aggressive and moved his hands under her top, first rubbing her tummy and then attempting to work his fingers under her bra.

Averil turned her head sharply and kissed him hard on the mouth. "Oh dear," she wondered out loud, "is the dashing airline pilot a wee bit horny?"

"Ooh, yes," he moaned. "Can you put the meal on hold for an hour while we dash into the bedroom?"

Averil broke out of his embrace and backed away. With her hands on her hips and her head cocked to one side, she smiled with a coquettish look on her face. "And pray tell, kind sir, how you propose to make it last that long?"

Mark laughed, "You sure do know how to hurt a guy. OK, thirty minutes then."

"No, we're not going to ruin this lovely dinner that I've been slaving over the entire afternoon. You'll just have to be patient. All good things come to he who waits." Mark munched a celery stick stuffed with cream cheese while helping her carry food from the kitchen to the dining room.

The meal was delicious and both ate hungrily. The conversation was lively and, even though they had talked on the phone several times during the week, they still found much to talk about. Shirley had finally returned to the marine equipment store and resumed her normal work schedule. This, in turn, allowed Averil to go back to working part time, giving her hope that she might be able to join Mark in St. Louis.

He did most of the talking during dinner, giving her more details about SIMFLIGHT and the project than she really wanted to know, but she remained alert and feigned interest. He also told her about having dinner with his brother and his plans to visit his cousin, Donna, during the following week.

After draining the bottle of wine, Mark easily convinced Averil to leave the dishes until later and move quickly to their bedroom. Even though he was burning with desire, Mark took pains to be a tender and thoughtfully passionate lover. For her part, Averil was so aroused by his romantic overtures that she had a difficult time holding back and not rush into an orgasm before him.

As they later lay side-by-side, satisfied and stroking each other tenderly, Averil whispered, "Now wasn't that worth waiting for?"

"I'll say it was. You know what? I missed you terribly this past week."

Averil punched him on the shoulder. "No you didn't. You were too

CHAPTER EIGHTEEN

busy to even notice that I wasn't there."

"Not true. It would have been so perfect if you were with me."

"Will it be as frantic for you next week?" She asked.

"I suspect it will be like that for several more weeks. At least until I get on top of it and really understand what's going on."

"Then I shouldn't be getting in your way. You're having a good time with this. I can see the excitement in your eyes and hear it in your voice. Go ahead and enjoy yourself."

Mark became drowsy and made a final insightful comment before dropping off to sleep. "You are so clever, reading me like a book. I could never fool you."

Averil rested in his arms for a few more minutes before nodding off, thinking about something that had not surfaced during their conversation. *Yes, my love, I do know you so very well. In fact, I'm now certain that you had no contact whatsoever with Joan Soric last week and it gives me great peace of mind.*

Chapter Nineteen

Mark's second week at SIMFLIGHT was just as busy as the first, except that he spent more time in meetings and dealing with other individuals than reading documents. Tom Campbell introduced him to Andy Thompson, SIMFLIGHT's point-of-contact with Tri-Star. Thompson, in turn, invited Mark to their nearby manufacturing plant for a look at the new aircraft's prototype. Mark accepted the invitation eagerly and spent the entire Wednesday inspecting the plane and discussing its advanced control features with their aeronautical engineers.

But all was not work. He visited his cousin, Donna, and part of her large family on Tuesday evening. Donna's husband, Charlie, cooked a standing rib roast on his new grill while Mark was entertained by their grandchildren; nine year old Emily beat him in a heated chess game, and seven year old Alex won a loud session of Frisbee golf in the Clarks' spacious back yard.

On Friday, Mark placed a call to his Trans-Global point-of-contact, Kent Waldorf. Mark summarized his activities during the first two weeks which seemed to please Waldorf. At the end of the conversation, Waldorf informed Mark that he had heard some favorable comments from the SIMFLIGHT management and exhorted him to keep up the good work. As Mark flew back to New York, he thought it was a nice way to end the week.

Mark and Averil spent a pleasant weekend together. On Saturday morning, they drove out to the Hamptons at the end of Long Island, walked along an almost deserted beach, and had lunch at a small seaside cafe. Mark rambled on about his work week, his dinner with the Clark cousins, and the complement from Kent Waldorf, all to Averil's patient amusement. On the way home, they visited several antique markets. She didn't see any treasures that she couldn't live without so they went home empty handed.

CHAPTER NINETEEN 109

Mark's third week at SIMFLIGHT was noticeably slower and quieter than the previous two. He was caught up with his reading and there were only a few meetings scheduled for that week. It was probably natural that this sudden period of relative inactivity would cause him to indulge his curiosity about Joan.

On Tuesday afternoon, he borrowed a telephone directory from Nancy and found a listing for Frank and Joan Soric, the only family by that name in the book. He jotted down their number in his notebook, intending to call her later that evening, but then had second thoughts. *What if Frank answered the phone? What would he do? But what if Joan answered and found it awkward to speak?*

He perused the phone book's Yellow Pages and found seven companies in the map-making business. *What was the name of her company? Did Jerry ever mention it when we were in Cassino? Damn, I should have paid closer attention.*

Mark decided to call a few companies and ask for her. If he couldn't locate her, then the fallback would always be available, calling her at home. He hesitated before dialing the first number, wondering if he was doing the prudent thing. He thought of something his deceased mother often said: "Faint heart never won fair lady." *She'd probably be rolling over in her grave if she knew I was doing this.*

At the first two companies, when he asked for Joan Soric, the response was similar. "Sorry. Nobody here by that name." But at the third company he called, a female voice responded politely, "Just a moment, sir, and I'll connect you."

Mark's heart beat faster, his mouth became cotton-dry, and his mind almost went blank as he fumbled for the words that he had readied but were now absent.

She answered after two rings. "Joan Soric" was her crisply professional greeting. But after several seconds of silence, she asked, "Hello? Anyone there?"

"Hey there, Joan. It's Mark Holloway. How are you doing?"

This time it was Joan's turn to be shocked into silence.

"Joan, it's Mark. Can you hear me?"

"Yes, Mark, I can hear you fine. This is quite a surprise. You're about the last person I expected to hear from."

"That's odd. Didn't Jerry tell you about our meeting in Cassino?"

She took a deep breath and said, "Yes, he did. But I got the idea that you weren't interested in contacting me. That's the impression he gave."

"It's probably true. I didn't pursue it with him."

"Now I'm confused," she said. "How did you get my office number?"

"He said you were a manager at a map making company." Mark then stretched the truth a little. "So I just looked up your company in the Yellow Pages and dialed your number."

She paused for a moment to let it all sink in. "Where are you calling from?"

"I'm here in St. Louis, out by the airport."

"You're in town? I can't believe it. I thought you were a pilot. Jerry said something about you flying to Paris a lot."

"That's right. New York to Paris is my usual route. But I'm working here with a company called SIMFLIGHT. Probably for a few more months."

"You're at SIMFLIGHT? What a coincidence. They're one of our customers."

"How about that?" He wondered. "It's really a small world, isn't it."

They both laughed nervously at Mark's trivial comment and became silent. Joan spoke up first. "So why did you call, Mark?"

"I'd like to see you while I'm here. How about lunch?"

Joan's heart skipped a beat, her face flushed, and her body shivered slightly. "Really? You want to see me again?"

Mark relaxed as he sensed that Joan was also excited about the possibility of a reunion. "Sure," he said. "You do eat lunch, don't you?"

"Some days I just skip it. If I play tennis that day."

"That's right. Jerry said you played tennis several times a week."

"Thursday or Friday would work for me."

"Thursday is fine," said Mark. "I could meet you at your office."

"Tell you what," she said. "Meet me around noon at the Petit Auberge. It's near the corner of Kingshighway and Gravois, close to my office. I'll make reservations. Think you can find it all right?"

Mark remembered that part of the city from their college days, an area not too far from her parent's house. "No problem. You've got a date."

After they hung up, each sat perfectly still and stared at the phone, wondering what was waiting at the end of this new, exciting, and

CHAPTER NINETEEN

dangerous path.

Mark slept poorly Tuesday and Wednesday nights, plagued by bizarre and unsettling dreams. In one particular sequence, which seemed to last for at least an hour, Averil and Joan were standing together on a Park Avenue sidewalk, watching Mark pedal a toy scooter down the street while dodging taxis. The two women were so overcome with laughter at Mark's antics that they had to hug each other strongly and support each other so they wouldn't fall down.

On Thursday morning, Mark dressed for work in his pilot's uniform, just as he'd done every day since arriving at SIMFLIGHT. The last thing he wanted to do was attract undue attention by showing up for work in "civvies."

At 11:15 A.M., he left his office and said to Nancy on his way out, "I'm going into the city for lunch. I'll probably be back a bit late."

Nancy looked up from her desk and smiled. "She must be something pretty special if you're going all the way downtown."

Mark stuttered back, "Just an old friend. Somebody I went to college with."

Just before Mark was out of earshot, Nancy called out to him, "I'm available for lunch, Captain. And you wouldn't have to drive very far."

Traffic was surprisingly heavy but Mark moved steadily along the interstate and then on major surface streets, arriving at the restaurant just before noon. Joan had not arrived so Mark waited in the lobby, near the door, in a spot that allowed him a good view of the parking lot.

He spotted her immediately when she got out of her white compact sedan. She wore large sunglasses and a pale cranberry suit. She walked briskly up to the restaurant's entrance, her head held high and her shining dark brown hair bouncing off her shoulders. *Jerry was right. She dresses better than any fashion model I've ever seen.*

When she entered the restaurant, she saw Mark immediately and pushed her sunglasses on top of her head. Mark smiled but was unsure of just how to greet her. She solved the problem by extending her right hand, smiling back at him. "Hello Mark, so good to see you again. You haven't changed at all."

He took her hand and gave it a soft but firm squeeze. "I don't know about that. There's a few gray hairs up there on top now. But you look fabulous. Not like the college girl I remember, but obviously a successful business woman."

Joan touched the lapels of his jacket and commented. "This outfit of yours—all black and white. Is this your pilot's uniform?"

"Yes, is something wrong?"

"No. It just reminded me of Jerry for a second."

They were seated at a small corner table and given elaborate menus by their waitress. Mark looked over the extensive wine list and first ordered a pricey bottle of Sancerre to accompany their lunch.

Joan laughed softly. "After you phoned, I had second thoughts about suggesting a French restaurant. I mean—since you you've probably eaten at any number of fancy ones in Paris."

"Not to worry. This is a charming place."

"You seem to know what you're doing with the wine. I think I'll just let you order for the both of us."

After the waitress returned with the wine and poured some into their glasses, Mark offered a toast. "Old friends are the best friends." Joan blanched at his use of the word 'old' but managed a weak smile as she clinked her glass against his.

They became quiet, each wondering how to start the conversation that would try to bridge a thirty-five year time gap. Mark picked a topic of recent common interest and spoke first. "So how is Jerry getting along? I assume he's back from Rome."

"Oh yes, he's been back for about two months. He stayed with us for a while and then moved into Jesuit Hall on the St. Louis U. campus. He has a heavy teaching load at the high school but he seems to thrive on all the hard work. He even helps out at Holy Family church on Sundays. I don't know how he does it."

"I was very much impressed when I met him in Italy. He's a fine young man and I have to believe it's because of the outstanding job you did as his mother. You should be very proud of him."

Joan broke eye contact and looked around the room before changing the subject. "Tell me about your job here in St. Louis. How long will you be here?"

Mark relaxed, grateful for a conversation topic that was not as delicate as Joan's relationship with her son. He rambled on about the job and

CHAPTER NINETEEN   113

managed to cover the topic exhaustively, ending his story as their Caesar salads arrived.

As they began eating, Mark reciprocated by asking about her career in the map making business. As she described the job, it was not a particularly exciting part of her life; at least that's the way it appeared to him. But he was attentive and asked relevant questions.

Over the main course of a baked filet of sole, pommes frites, and steamed vegetables, the conversation became more personal. Instead of asking about Mark's Navy career, Joan was curious about the women in his life. "Jerry told me that you've been married twice. Was your first wife from St. Louis?"

"Yes, she was. I knew her from the Cathedral Club. She didn't go to college but she had the one qualification that was a big problem with you and me. She was Catholic, you see."

Joan looked down. "If this is upsetting, you don't have to talk about it."

"No, I want to talk about it. It's something that you should know and understand. Religious compatibility isn't everything in a marriage. We had lots of problems, even though we were both Catholic, and the main one was a lack of communication. I don't know how I stuck it out for twenty years."

"For the sake of the kids?" she offered. "That's often the reason couples stay together in unhappy marriages."

"If only Margie and I could have talked to each other—like you and I used to talk—then maybe we'd still be together."

Joan blushed slightly at his oblique reference to her but disguised it by taking a sip of wine. "This is wonderful," she said. "I'll have to write down the name."

"How about you? Do you and Frank get along well—isn't that his name?"

"He's been a good husband. And I have to give him a lot of credit for the way Jerry turned out. I owe Frank a lot, encouraging me to be independent, have my career, and all the other outside interests that I like to pursue."

"Like tennis?"

"Sure, tennis. But there's lots more than that. I do a lot of volunteer work for our church."

Mark stared intently at her face while she talked and noticed that her eyes had clouded slightly and the edges of her provocative mouth had turned down. He thought she might be dissembling but concluded that this was probably the only way she could handle such a question. She would never admit to her jilted college sweetheart that her long and only marriage had not been a complete success.

Joan changed the subject again. "Jerry told me your present wife is British."

"That's true. We've been married for ten years. When I met Jerry, we were on a two week Italian vacation—an anniversary present."

"How did you meet her?"

"On a business trip to London. She was working at the hotel where I stayed. She had a pretty rough time with her first husband but he's in prison now. Oh yes, she's Protestant, too. But we don't have any children so we don't have any religious education issues to contend with."

Joan ignored this comment and asked about his current lifestyle. "What's it like being an airline pilot?"

"Well, I spend a lot of time away from home, but Averil gets to travel with me, whenever she can get away. It's fun knocking around different places in Europe when I'm not in the cockpit. Paris is such a great city. One of my favorite things to do is walk down the Champs-Elysees, especially in the early summer."

Joan rested her chin in the palm of her right hand. "That sounds so romantic. I'd love to go there someday. Hell, I've never been out of the country."

"You would love it. Paris is definitely a walking city. I remember how much you enjoyed walking and exploring different places." Perhaps it was the wine that prompted Mark to add a postscript. "If we had married, you could have traveled to all these places with me." Joan did not respond verbally, but stared at him intensely, her anger slowly rising inside.

The wine had been drunk but neither Mark nor Joan felt to compelled to end the luncheon experience just yet. Mark ordered profiteroles filled with French vanilla ice cream and two cups of coffee.

"One thing still bothers me," said Mark. "After I left St. Louis for flight training, I wrote you several letters but you never answered. How come?"

"There was no point. I was in Columbia and you were in Florida. We

CHAPTER NINETEEN

had no future together anyway. I thought I made that clear after the Christmas dance."

"Yeah, you made it clear all right. Painfully clear."

She stiffened and scraped her high heels on the floor. "I'm sorry, Mark. I was only doing what I thought was the right thing."

They both sipped their coffee until Mark decided to probe a little further. "When I met Jerry at Cassino, he seemed very troubled about his relationship with you. He said you were very negative about his conversion to Catholicism and becoming a Jesuit."

"What about it?" she asked with a slight edge to her voice.

"Are you two any closer to getting your differences resolved?"

"I can't see that it's any of your business."

"Hey, you don't have to get defensive with me. I just hate to see two people I care about go through all this unnecessary strife."

Joan took a deep breath and waved a hand across the table. "If it will make you feel any better, yes, we're coming closer together."

Mark relaxed and smiled. "That's good news. If I didn't know you as well as I do, I would guess that your rejecting him had something to do with our own breakup in college."

"What do you mean by that?"

Mark leaned forward. "It seems to me that you've been punishing him for a mistake you made before he was even born. You dump me because I'm Catholic and then he converts to the same faith. Only he goes one step further and becomes a priest. That must have been a really bitter pill for you to swallow."

Joan threw her napkin on the table. "Well, Mr. Holloway, you are way off base. You don't know me at all and I resent your thinking that you do. What you just said was the biggest pile of sanctimonious psycho-babble I've ever heard."

Mark was now alarmed. "Take it easy and lower your voice. People are starting to stare at us."

"Let them look. I don't give a damn." After pouting for a few seconds, she got her second wind. "Just why did you call me, Mark? Was it to tell me how crappy I'm treating my son? Or did you just want to rub my nose in it—show me how I made a big mistake by not marrying you when I had the chance?"

Mark was too stunned to answer. An hour later, he would be able to come up with a series of eloquent rebuttals but, for the moment, he remained speechless.

Joan stood up, grabbed her purse, and put on her sunglasses. "Thanks for the lunch, Mark. I'd offer to pay my share, but since you're probably rolling in dough, I'll just let you take care of the bill."

Mark did pay the bill and left the restaurant as quickly as possible. He drove slowly back to his office, grateful for the opportunity to calm down and reflect on Joan's emotional outburst and abrupt departure. He had handled it badly and he was upset with himself. He also had to admit that she was right about one thing. It was an act of petty revenge on his part, suggesting that she had made some poor choices earlier in her life. He was ashamed with the perverse pleasure he took by hurting her, but he diminished it through a convoluted internal process. She had hurt him badly thirty-five years ago—but the score was now settled and he could get on with his life without her image haunting his dreams.

Chapter Twenty

Mark stayed late in his office Thursday afternoon, trying to get through a thick software performance specification, but he found it difficult to concentrate. Finally, about six o'clock, he gave up and went to his hotel. He knew himself well enough to recognize all the symptoms of his discontent. One of his tried and true methods for getting his mind off contentious problems was vigorous physical exercise, so he changed into swim trunks, put on a light weight warm-up suit, and walked to the hotel's pool and weight room.

He was the only person in the weight room and the stale air smelled sweat-heavy. Even though he was aware of its presence, this was the first time he used the facility. He promised himself that, starting next Monday, he would work out every day, either before or after his work day in the office.

He first tried out all parts of the Nautilus exercise system. Then he took a quick rinsing shower before swimming laps for fifteen minutes in a barely adequate, heavily chlorinated pool filled with tepid water. All this exercise did the trick; he not only felt refreshed and mentally restored, he was even hungry for dinner.

He changed into jeans and a white polo shirt and walked to a nearby grill, a place popular with twenty-something professionals, with a cocktail lounge almost as large as the dining area. He took a seat at the bar and had a double Jack Daniel's on the rocks before ordering a steak sandwich.

While he sipped the smooth sour mash whiskey, he reflected on his earlier lunch date with Joan. *You are such a jerk, Holloway. You didn't have to treat her that way. That business about her relationship with Jerry was obviously a sore point. You were rubbing salt in the wound, as she implied. And your fantasy of having some kind of romantic reunion with her? Dream on, you silly fool.*

Mark slept well that night, aided by two glasses of Merlot he drank with his meal. But the whiskey and wine were more than he usually had at one sitting and this was brought home to him in a painful manner the next morning. He had to take three aspirin before he showered and shaved, a remedy along with several cups of black coffee that managed to get him through a busy morning.

In mid-afternoon, after ruminating about his encounter with Joan, he called a downtown florist and ordered a dozen red roses to be delivered to her office on Monday morning. When asked what words he would like to have written on the accompanying card, he chose only two: Sorry, Mark.

Mark arrived at his Huntington home about seven o'clock that evening and found Averil on the patio, sitting on a chaise lounge and browsing through a magazine. Mark bent over and kissed her in a perfunctory manner. "Hi there good looking. What's cooking?"

"I thought I'd grill some chicken tonight and we could eat out here. It's such a lovely evening. Too nice to be cooped up inside."

"Sounds good to me," he said. "Give me time for a quick shower and I'll be right back down."

Twenty minutes later he came down from his office, dressed in a dark red jogging suit that he often wore about the house, clutching a stack of mail that Averil had placed on his desk.

Averil entered the kitchen from the patio and asked, "Care for a toddy, luv?"

Mark grimaced and said, "Oh, I don't know. Maybe a Bloody Mary would do the trick."

Averil gave him a puzzled look. "Don't tell me you've got a hangover?"

"Yep, I guess I do. Had a bit too much to drink at dinner last night. When will I ever learn?"

"All right then. A Bloody Mary it is—a little hair of the dog to make you well again." Averil went to work fixing his drink, adding several dashes of pepper, Tabasco, and Worcestershire sauce to make it spicy hot, the way he liked it. She brought his drink out to the patio on a large tray that also contained a gin and tonic for herself, two large chicken breasts, and a bowl of red, green and yellow peppers and onions, all of which she placed on the preheated grill.

CHAPTER TWENTY

Mark sipped his drink while wading through the mail, pausing occasionally to make a brief comment about some item he had just read.

"How was your week at SIMFLIGHT?" she asked.

"It was pretty quiet this time. Not like the first two weeks."

"That's good. You can't be expected to keep up that intensive tempo all the time. You need some kind of break every now and then."

Mark picked up an annual report from one of their jointly-held mutual funds and began to study it intently. His almost absent-minded comment to Averil's last statement was a casual, "Whatever."

Conversation throughout the meal was minimal. Mark spoke about the current state of the simulator project and Averil talked about a shopping trip that she made with her neighbor, Laura Carnahan. Toward the end of dinner, Averil couldn't stand it any longer and asked in a strained voice, "*What* is bothering you?"

"Who, me?"

"I don't see anyone else out here that I might be talking to."

"Nothing's wrong. Where did you get that idea?"

"You're not your usual self, that's why. In fact, you remind me of something that happened several months ago when we were in Italy. That night we had dinner in Formia—the same day you met that Catholic priest."

Mark stopped eating and stared at her for a few moments before answering. "You amaze me. How the hell do you do it?"

"Do what?"

"Put your finger right on the problem like you do." He took a sip of water, sat up in his chair, and with considerable difficulty looked her in the eyes. "OK, there's something else that happened this week that I didn't mention. I had lunch with Joan Soric yesterday."

Averil stared back and paused before speaking. "Is that so? How did she know you were in St. Louis?"

The spicy Bloody Mary and Averil's icy demeanor caused Mark to start sweating and he unzipped his warm-up slightly before answering. "Well . . . uh . . . I called her. I invited her to lunch and we met at a place near her office."

"And how is your long lost love? Is she keeping well?"

"Look, Av, I was going to tell you about this. At the right time. I guess there is no right time."

"What prompted you to call her?"

"Curiosity, I guess. I've never felt right about the way we broke up in college. I left St. Louis without ever resolving all the issues between us. And I wanted to see how she and Jerry were getting along."

"What a conscientious fellow you are. It's almost overwhelming."

Mark could almost smell the sarcasm dripping from her lips but felt he had to continue, hoping to better justify his actions. "It's just something I had to do. If I'd let this opportunity go by, I'd regret it for the rest of my life."

Averil placed her cloth napkin on the table, leaned back in her chair, and continued looking at him in silence.

"Anyway, we talked a lot and got things settled. Only the meeting ended on a sour note. She got mad and stormed out of the restaurant in a big huff."

"Do I really need to hear this?"

"Yes, I think you do."

"Why was she angry with you?"

"I said some things about her relationship with her son and she took it pretty badly. I guess I went a bit too far."

"That's really not your concern anyway, is it?"

"In a way, it is. I think she's been punishing him for converting to Catholicism and becoming a priest. All because of me and our breakup in college. And I think it's really unfair to Jerry."

"So you're a family counselor in addition to being a pilot?"

"OK, OK. I get your point," he said. "Anyway, I think the whole business is moot. I don't intend to contact her again, and I'm sure she doesn't want anything more to do with me. Case closed."

Averil got up, collected their dishes and silverware, and took them inside to the kitchen sink. After a few minutes, she returned and stood momentarily behind her own chair. "I've been thinking of taking you up on your offer. Perhaps I could come over to St. Louis and keep you company."

"You don't trust me, do you?"

"I didn't say that."

"I said I wouldn't call her again and I keep my promises. You know that."

CHAPTER TWENTY

She smiled faintly. "Didn't a wise man once say that idle hands are the devil's workshop? Or was he talking about some other piece of the male anatomy below the belt? I'm never quite clear about that point."

"Good grief, Av. Give me a break."

She turned and picked up a few more dinner items from the grill and started to go back into the kitchen. She stopped at the sliding glass door and added a postscript before going inside. "Perhaps Mrs. Soric and I could get together for a chat over a cup of tea. Catch each other up and all that sort of thing. Wouldn't that be a jolly time for us?"

Mark continued to sit in his chair and think about the two women he had alienated by his actions. It was now dark outside and the back yard was illuminated by the half dozen solar-powered garden lights. After fifteen minutes had passed without Averil's return, he concluded that she wasn't coming back. He brought in all the mail and the remaining dinnerware and went to his office where he puttered around for an hour until he became sleepy.

When he finally went to bed, he was able to see Averil's reclining form in bed, aided by a pale light coming from the bathroom. She was wearing the most dowdy nightgown in her possession, one she didn't wear very often, and lying far away on her side of the bed with her back turned towards Mark's position. After turning out the bathroom light, he quietly crawled into bed. He heard no noises coming from her so he wasn't sure that she was asleep. He decided that it didn't matter because he was being punished for his behavior. He would have to make it up to her—big time—to get back in her good graces.

Chapter Twenty-One

On the following Monday morning, Joan was seated in her office when her secretary, Penny, came bursting in with a vase holding a dozen dark red roses. Penny set the vase on a front corner of the desk as Joan arose and walked around, wide-eyed and speechless.

"Isn't tomorrow your birthday?" asked Penny.

"Yes, it is," replied Joan.

"What a thoughtful husband you have."

"Yes, he's just full of surprises." *Frank hasn't sent me flowers for years. Why is he doing this now?*

After Penny left her office, Joan took a few moments to examine the roses and enjoy their fragrance. When she found the card and read Mark's brief note of apology, her first reaction was mild irritation. *Damn him. If Penny had seen that card, the whole office would know about it by noon.* She placed the card in her desk drawer, sat down while continuing to stare at the roses, and had second thoughts. *Still, it was very sweet of him to do this. Maybe I was too harsh on him.*

That afternoon, Joan received a telephone call from Stephanie. She had checked with the rectory at Holy Family Church and was told that Father Jerome was scheduled to say the ten o'clock mass the following Sunday. "I'm planning to attend," she said. "Are you still interested in coming with me?"

"Does Jerry know anything about this?" asked Joan.

"Not as far as I know. It should be a complete surprise."

"OK, I'll do it."

"How about me picking you up about 9:30?"

"That's fine with me," said Joan. "I'd like to get there a bit early and find a good place to hide."

When Sunday rolled around, Joan and Stephanie arrived at the church about ten minutes before mass was to begin. Autumn was in the air and

CHAPTER TWENTY-ONE

both women wore wool; Joan in a dark blue suit and Stephanie in a long beige dress. Frank was on the golf course again, trying to improve his game, and Joan was mildly irritated with him for this. She was willing to overlook his absence today, however, sensing that the outcome of this expedition into foreign religious territory would best be handled by her and Stephanie.

Today also marked the first time that either woman had been inside a Catholic church. During a whispered conversation, they agreed the best course of action was to mimic the movements of the faithful around them.

When Father Jerome emerged from the sacristy with a deacon and two servers, Joan was overcome by an avalanche of emotions; pride was not only the most prevalent but surely the most surprising to her. He wore dark green satin vestments trimmed in gold and she watched him in rapt silence as he moved about the altar, leading the congregation in the introductory recitations: the Entrance Antiphon, the Penitential Rite, and the Kyrie. She even marveled at the maturity and wisdom he seemed to radiate as he spoke these traditional prayers.

Deacon Ray Moore, a white haired man of about sixty, read the gospel for that Sunday, a text attributed to St. Mark. Joan flinched when she heard the deacon announce the name "Mark," but willed herself to focus on the gospel reading.

After the gospel was read, the congregation was seated and Father Jerome walked to the lectern. As he adjusted the microphone, Stephanie turned to Joan and smiled warmly, squeezing Joan's hand in joyful anticipation.

"Good morning, brothers and sisters," he began. "It's customary to have the homily deal with a topic in one of today's readings, but today I want to talk to you about something else. First, I'd like to read from the gospel of St. Mark."

My goodness, thought Joan. *That St. Mark was sure a prolific writer. I wonder if Mark Holloway still has that fountain pen I gave him.* An image flashed through her mind: six letters from Mark Holloway, hidden inside a cardboard shoe box, tucked away on a high shelf inside a dark closet.

Father Jerome continued, "This is Jesus talking to his disciples: *Learn a lesson from the fig tree. When the branch becomes tender and sprouts leaves, you know that summer is near. In the same way, when you see these things happening, know that he is near, at the gates. Amen, I say to you, this generation will not pass away until all these things have taken place. Heaven and earth will pass away, but my words will not pass away. But of that day or hour, no one knows, neither the angels in heaven, nor the Son, but only the Father."*

He cleared this throat and raised his voice slightly. "Let me paraphrase that last sentence for you. No one knows when the end of the world is going to happen. Not even Jesus Christ, but only God the Father."

Joan turned to Stephanie and whispered, "Something's wrong here. He sounds troubled."

"Now let me tell you about a man, a fellow priest by the name of Ryan Mahoney. I first met him in Rome, a little over a year ago, when we both entered the Gregorian Pontifical Institute as students. We became close friends almost immediately and did many things together. He was older than I, forty-two at the time, for he had received his calling relatively late in life. He even gave up a very lucrative law practice in Santa Fe, New Mexico, to enter the priesthood. During our time at the Institute, he was a faithful and wise counselor for me when I was troubled and needed to talk with someone. If I could sum up our relationship in a single phrase, I would say he was like an older brother to me, the brother that I never had but always wanted."

On hearing this, Joan flinched again as a large dry lump came into her throat.

"We both left Rome in mid-July and Ryan returned to his home in Santa Fe where he was ordained just two months ago. He was very happy when the Archbishop assigned him to a small parish in the northwestern corner of the state near a city called Farmington. This is what he was striving for. It was here that he found his greatest happiness in the most difficult and unglamorous of situations, ministering to the poor and downtrodden members of his parish."

"Now you may be asking yourselves why I am telling you all this. Just two days ago, Father Mahoney visited a very sick elderly woman out in the country and gave her the last rites. Then coming back home, on a dark and lonely desert road, he was struck head-on by an old beat-up truck. The driver of the truck must have fallen asleep at the wheel. Father Mahoney

CHAPTER TWENTY-ONE

died instantly and I'm sure he experienced no pain."

Many members of the congregation murmured to each other on hearing this. Father Jerome let the noise subside before continuing.

"The man driving the truck was also alone and, by some miracle, survived the terrible collision. When the police arrived on the scene, they discovered that this man was drunk—so drunk that he could barely stand up. The man had prior DWI—driving while intoxicated—convictions and was driving his truck without a valid license. This leads the caring and compassionate Christian in each of us to ask many questions: Why does a just and merciful God allow this to happen? Wouldn't it have been better if Father Mahoney had survived and the drunk had been killed instead? Wouldn't God's work on earth be further blessed if Father Mahoney had been allowed to continue his ministry and live to a ripe old age?"

At this point, Father Jerome's voice cracked and he was overcome with grief. He stepped back from the lectern, retrieved a handkerchief from his trousers, and wiped away his tears. Stephanie turned to Joan and said, "This is terrible. I can't stand to see him suffer like this."

Father Jerome composed himself and came back to the lectern. "I'm sorry for that. Please excuse me." He stuffed his handkerchief back into his pocket and continued. "The point is this: we don't have a clue how God operates or why he allows such things to happen. But we can rejoice in the faith of good and holy men like Father Mahoney, knowing that he is in heaven today with Jesus, while we here on earth must continue to cope with our daily problems."

"Recall the words of Jesus, written by St. Mark, that I read to you at the beginning of the homily. *But of that day or hour, no one knows, neither the angels in heaven, nor the Son, but only the Father.* Each of us can take these same words and use them to guide us in the conduct of our everyday life. None of us knows how long we have. I could live to be ninety-five and die in my sleep. Or I could be taken tomorrow in an accident, just like Ryan Mahoney."

"That's the thought I want to leave with you today. Love each other as Jesus instructed the Jews almost 2000 years ago, loving your neighbor as yourself. And live each day of your life as if it was going to be your last day on earth. Be ready and always watchful for we don't know when that final moment will arrive; when Jesus calls us to join him and share his glory in heaven for all eternity."

Father Jerome turned around, walked to a position between the two servers, and asked the congregation to join him in reciting the Nicene Creed as a profession of faith.

After the mass concluded with the final blessing, Father Jerome led Deacon Moore and the servers down the center aisle to the church entrance while the organist played a stirring recessional anthem. Joan took Stephanie's arm and said, "Let's walk around to the front and try to catch him before he gets away."

Father Jerome stood on the front steps, surrounded by parishioners, when the two women came within view. He spotted Joan out of the corner of his eye, walked over to her with his arms opened wide, and gave her a warm and strong embrace. "This is such a wonderful surprise, Mom. What are you doing here?"

Joan started to cry. "Oh Jerry, I'm so sorry that you lost your good friend."

"You were in the church just now? Hearing my mass?"

"Yes, I was." Joan turned around and waved her hand at Stephanie, inviting her to join them. "Stephanie wanted me to come with her."

Stephanie moved forward and shook his hand warmly. "I told you I'd sneak in here one day and hear your sermon. I had no idea it was going to be such a sad one. I know it's a tragic event for you, but the way you ended your talk—well, it gives us something to hope for, doesn't it?"

Because of the many people moving about him and several simultaneous conversations taking place, Jerry didn't answer her question immediately. Instead, he took advantage of the opportunity to proudly introduce Joan and Stephanie to Deacon Moore and the remaining parishioners standing nearby.

After the crowd had thinned out significantly, Joan extended an invitation to her son. "Why don't you ride over to the house with us and I'll make us a big brunch. You can tell Steph and me about Father Mahoney."

"Sounds great, mom. Just give me a few minutes to change my clothes. I'll meet you in the parking lot."

Deacon Moore interrupted them before they could disperse and spoke to Joan. "It's a great honor to meet you, Mrs. Soric. Will you be joining

CHAPTER TWENTY-ONE

our parish, now that Father Jerome is almost a permanent fixture here?"

Joan made a short, croaking laugh before answering. "Me? I don't think so. I'm not Catholic."

Deacon Moore looked puzzled. "You're not? But your son . . ."

"Don't go there, Ray," Jerry admonished.

Chapter Twenty-Two

The morning after she attended mass, Joan placed a call to a startled Mark at his SIMFLIGHT office. "Why are you so surprised?" she asked. "Did you think that you'd never hear from me again?"

"Frankly, yes. After the way our lunch ended, you'd be completely justified in forgetting I ever existed."

Joan's voice softened. "I want to thank you for the roses. They were beautiful and it was very thoughtful of you to send them."

"I'm glad to hear that. I hope it didn't create a problem."

"It didn't. Now if you had sent them to my house, that would have been a *big* problem. Everyone thought they came from Frank for my birthday."

"Hey, that's right. You just had another birthday, didn't you?"

"It's no big deal anymore, especially at my age. And you have one coming up later this week, as I recall."

"Yep, this Friday, and I'll still be ten days younger than you."

Joan laughed lightly at his needling humor. "I also remember back in college how you bragged to your buddies about dating older women."

Mark chuckled. "I think we should change the subject right now."

"Agreed. There's another reason for my call."

"It's your nickel. I'm all ears."

"I want to apologize for the way I behaved at lunch the other day. Some of the things you said really upset me, but after careful thought, I realized that I've probably been avoiding the truth for a long time."

"Now wait a minute. I have to take part of the blame too. I was pretty rough on you and said some things that were none of my business."

"Mark? Let's stop this finger pointing, OK?"

"Sounds good to me."

"I'd like to make amends and treat you to a birthday dinner. How about Wednesday evening?"

CHAPTER TWENTY-TWO

"Sure. A home cooked meal would be nice."

"No, not that. I want to *buy* you dinner. There must be some decent restaurants near your hotel."

Mark paused for a moment, realizing that somewhere, somehow, and sometime during the last week or so, the winds of their relationship had shifted slightly. "What about your husband? Is he happy with this?"

"Frank's out of town on a business trip, so it will be just you and me."

Mark's mental gears were now spinning rapidly, considering not only the opportunities presented by her invitation, but also the dangers. There was still that tiny element of mistrust in his heart, sensing that another meeting with Joan could end in a bitter quarrel; he didn't want that to happen. Any thoughts he had about Averil at this point were conveniently swept into his conscience's dustbin.

"There's a place close to the hotel called Hooligan's. It's pretty informal but they have good food and the bartender has a generous elbow."

"I love Hooligan's. There's one by our office."

"Wednesday is good for me," he said. "Where shall I meet you?"

"I have a tennis match after work so I'll drive out to your place after I change clothes. Is eight o'clock too late?"

"No, that's fine. I'll be able to have a swim after work."

"Great," she said. "I'll meet you in the lobby."

After Joan hung up, she made an appointment for late that afternoon with her hair stylist for a haircut and coloring. Then she wrote the initials V.S. in her day planner for Tuesday, a cryptic message that would remind her to go shopping for new underwear.

Mark went to the hotel lobby about fifteen minutes early and killed time flipping through a discarded copy of *USA Today*. He had dressed casually in a pair of off-white slacks and a blue and white striped sport shirt.

Joan walked through the lobby's front door about five minutes before eight o'clock and Mark almost didn't recognize her. She wore tight stone-washed jeans, a long sleeve red turtleneck sweater, large hoop gold earrings, and the gold chain with heart that he'd given her many years ago. She smiled when she recognized him, walked up close and gave him a light kiss on the cheek. "Hi, Mark. Hope you haven't been waiting too long."

Mark stepped backwards slightly and said, "What did you do? You look so . . . *different*."

She frowned coyly. "I don't know how to take that. Do you like it?"

"Yes, I do. You look wonderful. Almost like a college girl again."

"It's probably my new hair style. It caused quite a commotion at work yesterday." She turned around so Mark could get a better look. It had been cut short, to the nape of the neck, and was now layered with blonde highlights on top.

"What does Frank think of the new look?"

"Oh, he hasn't seen it yet. It'll be a nice surprise—if he notices, that is."

"Do you mind walking to Hooligan's? It's only a couple of blocks away."

"Not at all. It's very pleasant outside tonight." After they left the hotel, Joan took his hand in hers as they walked. At first, Mark grinned nervously, reflecting some embarrassment, but he overcame the awkwardness and felt comfortable holding her hand all the way to the restaurant.

Hooligan's was unusually crowded for a Wednesday evening. Mark had not made reservations so they went to the bar to wait for a table where they luckily found two empty stools next to each other. Joan ordered a Manhattan and Mark had a vodka martini. When their drinks arrived, Mark toasted her belated birthday and Joan returned it with an early birthday wish for Mark.

Because of the high ambient noise level, they had to lean close in order to hear each other. The scent of her jasmine perfume and the occasional touching of cheeks aroused him, making it difficult to concentrate on what she was saying.

"That chain around your neck," he said. "Looks kind of familiar."

Joan twisted her finger under it and rubbed the small golden heart. "Oh, this? Just something from an old boyfriend. A long time ago. I don't even recall his name anymore." Mark recoiled in mock horror, prompting her to pucker up her lips and offer him an 'air kiss.' Both laughed heartily after this exchange.

"I'm glad you called," he said. "I didn't want us to be mad at each other for the rest of our lives."

"Me either."

"I get a feeling that something's different with you. Am I imagining things?"

CHAPTER TWENTY-TWO

Joan took a sip of her drink and continued, "You're pretty observant. I went to mass yesterday at Jerry's church with Stephanie."

Mark's eyebrows shot up. "If this is going to upset you, I'd rather not hear about it."

"No, not at all. It's something I want to share. His sermon was very personal and quite emotional for all of us. His best friend, a priest he studied with in Rome, was just killed in a head-on traffic accident."

"Oh no, that's terrible."

"It's so tragic, something that Stephanie and I weren't expecting. But it caused me to think and realize what the important things in my life are—my son, my husband, and all the other people that I care about. You, for instance." She put her hand on his but he withdrew it quickly to signal the bartender for another round.

"In Jerry's sermon—did he come to any conclusions? Priests normally like to place such tragedies in some kind of context and draw a moral."

"At the start of his talk, he quoted something written by St. Mark—your namesake. How nobody knows when the world will end. Then he ended on an optimistic note, urging each of us to live our life as if each day might be our last."

"I know that gospel. Sounds like it made an impression on you."

"You might say that."

"Are you getting hungry?" he asked.

"I sure am. Maybe we should have an appetizer before I get so drunk I won't be able to sit up for dinner."

Mark agreed and ordered a combination plate of every appetizer that was on the extensive bar menu. It came quickly, right after the second round of drinks.

"So, Mr. Holloway, you are the first to witness the emergence of the new and improved Joan Soric. The hair is only the beginning."

Mark grinned and said, "I really haven't had a chance to get reacquainted with the old—sorry, the former—Joan Soric. Will I like this new woman better?"

"You bet your sweet bippy," she said, helping herself to a mini-kebob. She wiped her hands on a napkin and continued, "Can I ask you a personal question?"

"Ask me anything you want."

"How come we never had sex in college?" When Mark withdrew in mild shock, she rephrased her question. "I mean, after all the chances you had, why didn't you try to get me into bed?"

Mark nibbled thoughtfully on a buffalo wing. "You like to go for the jugular, don't you? But it's a fair question. Now, don't think I didn't want to—lots of times. But back then, it was continually hammered into me by the priests and brothers that having sex before marriage was a mortal sin."

"I understand that very well. There were similar pressures on me."

"So I guess one of the reasons for wanting to marry you was so that we could do it, legally and morally."

"Did you hear what you just said? That's *not* a foundation for marriage."

"I know that now. I learned it the hard way with my first wife."

"So, that's it?" She asked. "Your religion was holding you back?"

"There was something else. It was this great respect I had for you. Like if I tried to go too far, you'd get mad at me and break it off. Besides, I was a virgin then and I didn't have a clue of how to go about doing it."

Joan smiled sadly and moved her head slowly from side to side as a dreamy gaze came into her eyes. "That's very sweet, Mark." She took his left hand and pulled it hard, bringing it around her waist, and placing it firmly on her butt. "Can you feel that? It's flesh and blood, solid stuff with needs and wants. I don't want to be put on a pedestal."

A silly grin came over Mark's face. "Yeah, I can feel it. You have a very nice ass, lady."

Joan leaned closer, put her hand on his neck, and kissed him hard on the lips. After she pulled back, Mark looked around the bar to see if anyone had noticed their affectionate moment. Nobody was paying them the slightest bit of attention.

He slid his left hand up under her sweater and rubbed her back softly. Joan closed her eyes and whispered in his ear, "I remember how you used to do that when we danced. You haven't lost your touch."

Mark pulled her closer and kissed her softly while she rubbed his neck with her right hand. "Does your hotel have room service?" she asked.

"I think so."

"Let's go back to your room. I need privacy when I give you your birthday present."

Chapter Twenty-Three

Joan moved about the suite's living room, oohing and aahing at the space and creature comforts it provided. "You must be doing pretty good with Trans-Global. My company would never spring for something like this."

"It is better than I'd get for just a one night layover. But this is my home-away-from-home for a few months so they agreed to pay for a suite."

Mark tuned the stereo radio to an FM station that was playing soft orchestral music and Joan floated into his outstretched arms, greeting him with a tender kiss. They danced silently in an almost stationary position, swaying back and forth, while Mark slipped his hands under her sweater and ran them across her back.

"Now, what were you saying about a birthday present?"

"It's standing right in front of you—me."

"You?"

"That's right. I'm yours. Do what you will. You can finally have your way with me."

"Sounds like some lines from a very bad Victorian novel."

She stepped out of his embrace and started to remove her red turtleneck, but Mark gently stopped her. "Oh no you don't. I get to unwrap my present."

"Be careful with the chain," she pleaded. "I don't want it broken."

He tucked the chain inside her collar and carefully removed her sweater. "So lovely," he said, looking at her champagne lace demi-bra, contrasting nicely with her tan body. He took a long time to kiss both sides of her neck, the top half of each breast, and her stomach just above the navel.

"Can you maybe just hurry this up a bit?"

"No, I can't," he scolded. "I've waited years for this, so don't rush me."

After kissing almost every piece of her exposed flesh, he reached around and unhooked her bra. As he removed it, he cried out, "Ouch."

"What's wrong?"

"I cut my finger on something." He held up the end of the bra strap in the light and then laughed. "I nicked it on the price tag."

"Let me see that," she said in shocked embarrassment. "I can't believe I forgot to cut it off." Then she threw it across the room where it landed on the brown leather couch.

"Where was I?" he asked, pulling her closer and unzipping her jeans. After he had removed them and placed his hand inside the back of her matching champagne panties, he made another comment. "Maybe I better check these things out real close—just in case you've planted any more booby traps."

In a few heated minutes, they were totally nude and locked in a feverish embrace, rolling around his queen-size bed. The room was dimly lit by a lamp in the living room, giving the lovers just enough visibility to see each other's face and body while their hands caressed, pressed, and rubbed all the intimate areas that were dreamed about but never reached when they were young.

Joan's voice suddenly acquired a business-like tone. "I hate to go practical at a moment like this, but I have to ask. Do you have a condom?"

"Hell no. I haven't carried them around for a long time. Averil's been the only woman I've slept with in the last ten years."

"Well, I don't have one either. Never thought about it until now."

Mark's hand rested on the inner part of her thigh. "I'm not really worried about you having anything. Should I be?"

"Well thank you very much for that vote of confidence. I guess I'm not going to be elected poster girl for safe sex."

Mark moved his hand upward until he felt her wet warmth. "I don't think we should be too concerned about this. Let's just trust each other."

And so their bodies joined together in an ecstatic and joyful consummation of their hungry desire, a passion deeply satisfied after thirty-six years of secret hoping and dreaming. Afterwards, they both lay on their backs, side by side, her left hand in his right.

"Awesome," he said.

"Fantastic."

"Stupendous."

"Was it worth waiting for?"

CHAPTER TWENTY-THREE

"Hell yes, but if we have to wait another thirty-six years, we'll be too old to enjoy it."

"I can't do the math," she said, "but I have the feeling we'll both be dead."

Mark looked over at his bedside clock. "I'm going to call room service before they shut down for the night."

"Is there a menu anywhere in the room?"

"Let me order for us," he said. "I've got something special in mind."

"Ooh, I just *love* surprises."

Mark got out of bed, put on his jogging suit, and went out to the living room to call in their dinner order. When he returned, he noted that Joan had turned on the lamp at her side of the bed and ducked into the bathroom.

Mark busied himself straightening out the jumbled bed covers and propping up the pillows. Joan finally emerged from the bathroom wearing her panties and Mark's undershirt. "Don't I look glamorous?"

"Good enough to eat," he growled in his best macho bravado, at the same time harboring another and more sobering thought. *Now I'll have to throw that undershirt away. Can't have Averil pulling that one out of the hamper. Her nose would pick up on Joan's perfume real quick.*

"Speaking of things to eat," she went on, "what about our dinner?"

"I caught room service just in time. Should be here any minute now."

Soon thereafter, a young waiter brought their order on a large tray. Joan stayed in the bedroom while Mark signed the order ticket, adding a generous tip. After the waiter left, Mark carried the tray and placed it in the center of the bed.

Joan sat at the foot of the bed, her legs crossed with her feet tucked under her knees. She looked briefly at the juicy cheeseburgers, the crisp French fries, and the chilled bottles of beer before hungrily diving in. "A special meal, huh?"

"Not for most people," he said. "Do you remember our first date? The movie and the dinner afterwards?"

"Of course I do. This is what we ate and drank after the movie. Then we went down and looked at the Arch."

"Hey, we could do that tonight, after we finish eating."

Joan cocked her head, her mouth full of cheeseburger, and gave him a quizzical look. "Are you serious?"

"Oh, I don't know. It was just a thought."

"It has potential, though." She paused and then added, "We could make love under the Arch. *That* would be a birthday present neither of us would forget."

Mark shook his head. "You are a wicked woman."

"Like we would be the first to do that? I hear it's a popular make out spot for the high school kids. We'd probably have to fight them for blanket space."

Mark sighed wistfully. "Do you ever get the feeling we were born thirty years too soon?"

"All the time, my friend. All the time."

Mark took a swig of beer and giggled.

"What's so funny?"

"This is a brand new experience for me. Being seduced by an older woman with fancy new underwear."

Joan's only response was to throw a handful of French fries in his face which prompted more giggling by both of them.

"Maybe I should call Jerry and thank him for the words in his homily."

"What do you mean by that?" she wondered.

"I'm guessing that his sermon had some impact on you. Enough to make you drive out here tonight and hop into my bed."

Joan finished chewing a bite of food before answering. "Listen, Holloway. Don't you go analyzing this thing to death or you'll spoil it for both of us."

"Sorry, that was a joke. I didn't mean to make it sound like that." Mark drained his beer bottle and placed it on the tray.

"You like the beer, huh?"

"I did. It really hit the spot."

"You can thank Frank for that. Some of the grains he bought probably found their way into your bottle."

"Is that what he's doing this week?"

"Yes, he's in Kansas and Iowa. Visiting some really exciting places."

"When he calls, won't he wonder about you not being at home?"

"He never calls me when he goes on the road. Do you call your wife?"

"I do, but not when I'm in Paris."

"Why not?"

CHAPTER TWENTY-THREE

"Overseas phone calls are pretty expensive. Besides, I'm always back home the next day."

Joan loaded up the tray with the remainders of their meal and took it out to the living room. When she came back to the bedroom, she cuddled up next to Mark who was sitting up in bed with three pillows propped up behind his back. As she slid into his waiting arms, he kissed her on top of the head.

They remained silent for a while, content to feel the presence of each other's body and listen to the rhythmic breathing. Joan was first to break the silence. "I guess I should be thinking of getting dressed and going home."

"Why don't you stay and have breakfast in the morning? That would be something else we've never done together."

"Sounds like fun but I have to work tomorrow. I need to get into my closet before I show my face at the office."

"Oh, the trials and tribulations of the female executive," he moaned, followed by Joan's gentle slap of his cheek. Mark lowered his body, turned to face her, and slid his left hand inside his undershirt she wore to cup her right breast. After he kissed her, he licked his lips and said, "You taste like French fries."

"What are you doing?"

He moved his hand back around to her rear, slid it inside her panties, and pulled her closer. "Just playing with your beautiful body."

"You want to do it again? *Can* you do it again?"

"Hell, I don't know. Let's give it a try and see what happens."

They took off their own clothes this time and settled down into a close and comfortable embrace, pleasantly surprised at not only Mark's stamina, but also their ability to again give pleasure to each other. This time, they made love slowly and deliberately, talking and laughing frequently until they reached an almost simultaneous climax. Afterwards, the exhausted lovers fell asleep while entwined in each other's arms.

Several hours later, Mark awoke and sensed that Joan had left his bed. Before he could call out, she came out of the bathroom in her underwear, went into the living room, and returned with the rest of her clothes. Mark watched silently as she pulled on her jeans and then her sweater. "You are such a beautiful woman."

"No, I'm not. I look like the wreck of the Hesperus right now."

She put on her tennis shoes while sitting at the edge of the bed next to Mark, and then turned to face him. "How are you doing there, my friend?"

"You know something? You are even sexier getting dressed than you are getting undressed."

"And you are out of your mind."

"Why don't you come back to bed? We've still got some time left."

She pushed him backward and went into the bathroom while calling out, "You talk a big game, Holloway. Three times in one night would be too much even for Superman."

After applying some lipstick touches and brushing her hair, she came back and sat down again next to Mark, brushing his lips with a light kiss. "I've had a wonderful evening. Will you call me?"

"Of course I'll call you. We need to talk some more. A lot more."

"Yes, we'll talk. What do you want to talk about?"

"I'm not sure. What's going to happen next? About us, I mean."

"I don't know, Mark. There's lots of options open. Maybe we can—no, that's enough excitement for one night. Let's just leave it there for now."

She kissed him once more and quietly left his suite and the hotel.

Chapter Twenty-Four

Mark found it difficult to focus on his office work the next morning; his brain swirled with conflicting scenes and emotions. On the one hand, he felt a warm glow thinking of Joan and their lovemaking the night before. But on the other hand, the guilt weighed heavily on his conscience. He had been faithful to Averil since their wedding and now he had broken that bond of trust.

In spite of his misgivings, he called Joan at her office that afternoon. "Just thought I'd check in and see how you're doing."

"I'm doing OK. A little tired and a little sore, but otherwise, pretty good."

"You're sore? How come?"

"If you must know, I exercised some body parts last night that haven't been used much in the last few years."

"Oh. I see," he said, somewhat embarrassed.

"In fact, I was just thinking about last night when you called. It was very nice and so . . . whoooo!"

"Are you blushing?" he asked.

"Are we having phone sex?"

"Whew—I don't think so—it couldn't be as good as the real thing."

"Hey, Mark. What are you doing tonight?"

"Nothing special. Why?"

"Why don't you come out to my house for dinner? I can demonstrate my talents in another room of the house."

"Will Frank be there?"

"Nope, he gets back tomorrow."

"You know, I don't think it's such a good idea. I'd like to but I wouldn't feel comfortable being there—especially after last night."

"What a chicken. But I think I understand. So, when will I see you again?"

"How about lunch next week?"

"Fine with me. Pick a day."

"Let me get back to you on that. I'll call you Monday when I see how my work schedule shapes up."

"You better not forget," she said.

"No chance of that. There's something else I want to talk about. I'd like to contact Jerry while I'm here."

Joan paused for several seconds before answering. When she finally spoke, Mark sensed a slight change in her mood. "I'm sure he'd be glad to hear from you, but that would complicate the situation a bit."

"How so?" He wondered.

"How would you go about reaching him?"

"I could call his parish or Jesuit Hall. Or maybe I could just drive out to the high school and surprise him."

"Yes, you could do any of those things. But there's a chance that he'd figure out you got this information from me and that wouldn't look good."

"Why do you think he'd connect the two of us?"

"I know how guys think. Jerry doesn't know that I'm seeing you and neither does Frank. So I'd like to keep all this confidential. Do you see my point?"

"I guess so. What a shame."

"But that's the way it is—the way it has to be for now."

"OK, I won't see him. For you."

"You're a sweetie, Mark. I have a meeting now so I have to scoot. Talk to you Monday."

That evening, just before midnight, Mark was awakened by the telephone. He was momentarily confused by the anxious voice of a young woman on the other end of the line. "Hi Daddy, it's Karen. Did I wake you up?"

"Karen, are you all right? Where are you?"

"San Francisco. I'm calling from a pay phone."

"What's going on? Are you in some kind of trouble?"

"Not yet, but that's why I'm calling. Oh shit, things are really screwed up here. I've really made a mess of it."

By this time, Mark was sitting up in bed almost fully awake. "Now calm down, honey, and tell me what the problem is."

"This guy I'm living with—Darrel? I thought he was pretty straight but

CHAPTER TWENTY-FOUR

I found out he's been dealing drugs. And there's some mean looking guys watching our place all the time. They're either cops or suppliers and, either way, I figure he's about to get busted. Or something even worse. I need to get out of here."

"You're asking *me* for help?"

"Pretty strange, huh? Well, after all, you're my dad. Guess I don't have much choice. Darrel has a bad temper and gets mean when you cross him. But if you were here, he wouldn't try any of that macho shit with you."

"Has he been abusing you?"

"Let's not go into that right now. Can you come out here? I need you to help me move away from this place. It's really bad."

Mark leaned back across his bed and sighed. "Sure, I'll come tomorrow. I think there's a Trans-Global flight that gets there in the early evening."

"You're an angel. I'll meet you at the airport and we can talk on the way to my apartment."

"By the way, how did you get my number?"

"I called your home. Averil gave it to me."

"That makes sense. She's probably still awake. I'd better call her and tell her I won't be home this weekend."

"I hope she won't be too disappointed."

"So do I, honey. So do I."

Immediately after hanging up, Mark dialed his home number. Averil answered in a deep sensual voice on the second ring. "Hello there, Mr. Holloway. I had a hunch I might be hearing from you tonight."

"You're right, as usual. I just talked to Karen and she's in a pretty tight spot."

"Yes, I know. We had a long chat when she called. I take it you'll be traveling to San Francisco then?"

"I'll fly out tomorrow after work and spend a couple of days out there, helping her move. This trip is long overdue anyway. You know it's been two years? I haven't seen her since graduation."

"Then it's the proper thing to do. Gives you a chance to get reacquainted with your daughter."

"Then you're not upset?"

"Of course not. Just a little disappointed, that's all. Oh, by the way, happy birthday, luv."

"Oh my god, you're right. I'd almost forgotten all about that. Well, maybe we can celebrate it the weekend after next."

"We may have to postpone it even longer," she said.

"How's that again?"

"I have some family news of my own. A letter came today from Emma and she's very concerned about mum. Seems like her health is much worse and she's reached the point where she can hardly get by on her own. A fortnight ago she fell and broke her wrist and sometimes she has lapses in memory—forgets where she is or where she's going. Emma thinks she should be moved into a home where she can receive assisted health care."

"How does your mother feel about this?"

"Oh, she's fighting it tooth and nail, of course. Doesn't want to leave her home, her garden, all her friends. I knew it would be like this one day."

"So Emma's looking to you for backup?"

"She's asking me to come across and help convince Mum that this is the right thing to do. Return of the older sibling, a united front, that sort of thing."

"Are you going then?"

"I thought I should discuss it with you first. Can you manage without me for several weeks?"

"It won't be that bad," he said. "Most of the time I'll be here or in San Francisco. So go ahead and do what you have to do."

"Good. I thought you'd understand. I'll call Emma in a few hours and let her know I'll be coming. I'm not looking forward to this, you know."

"I know. I feel much the same way about my own trip."

Mark tossed and turned the rest of the night and slept only a few hours. The next morning, he had a short meeting with Tom Campbell and told him that he'd be absent from the office for several days due to a family emergency. He then called Kent Waldorf at Trans-Global, followed by Joan Soric, and gave them essentially the same news. Waldorf was sympathetic and told Mark to take all the time he needed; his absence would be charged against his accumulated vacation time of which he had plenty on the books. Joan was clearly less enthusiastic about his absence, almost whining for him to hurry back so they could be together again. She also implied that he was using this opportunity to avoid seeing her again. Mark didn't feel like arguing the point with her so he let it pass.

CHAPTER TWENTY-FOUR

On the flight to San Francisco, Mark fell into a deep sleep. He dreamed that he was lying nude and spread-eagled on a sunny Southern California beach, with each foot tied to a wooden stake driven into the sand. Ropes were also tied to each wrist; Averil was pulling on one rope and Karen on the other. Both women were wearing khaki police uniforms and each was equipped with a pistol, a nightstick, and a set of hand cuffs. He then watched Joan Soric walk up to him, wearing only her new champagne underwear, and holding a small coil of piano wire in her hand. After she had fastened one end of the wire securely around his testicles, Mark woke abruptly in a cold sweat.

Chapter Twenty-Five

Mark entered the San Francisco terminal and looked tentatively at the people waiting in the gate area. He didn't recognize anyone and concluded that Karen would be late, until he noticed a most unusual young woman heading in his direction. *It has to be her, but what the hell has she done to herself?*

She wore black high heel leather boots whose tops came up to just below the knees, black fishnet stockings, frayed and faded blue jean shorts, and a black leather jacket liberally sprinkled with diamond-shaped silver studs. But her hair was the most striking part of her appearance; it was cut short and the natural dark brown color had been replaced with a shiny bright red hue reminding Mark of candied apples. She had also applied some kind of goop so that her hair stuck up in grotesque spikes. *Margie had mentioned something about a ring in her nose, but I don't see one. Wonder if she got the tattoos?*

She stepped up and gave him a big hug. "Hello, Daddy. Thanks so much for coming." Mark gave her the best hug he could muster under the circumstances with one hand firmly holding his carryon. He also had to blink his eyes several times because her powerful perfume was making them water. *She must have taken a bath in that crap.*

"I'm glad you made the first move," he said. "I'm not sure I would have recognized you." The tone of his voice clearly conveyed his disapproval but she had already anticipated a cool reaction to her appearance. *She sure doesn't look like the girl who graduated from college two years ago.*

As they walked away from the gate area toward the terminal exit, Karen told him her plan. "We can take a bus downtown. The driver will let us out at a spot near my apartment. It's only a block away."

They took a seat near the back of the bus, away from other passengers, so Mark could hear the details of Karen's situation. "Who is this guy, Darrel?"

CHAPTER TWENTY-FIVE

"Boy, he really fooled me. He's a musician, plays the sax in one of those strip joints in North Beach, the ones that have the girls with the big silicone-filled tits. I thought he was on the level, but that job is just a cover up for his real work, selling pot and cocaine to customers in the club and other contacts."

"Are you one of his customers?"

Karen lowered her head. "Shit. Well, I'm not going to lie to you, Daddy. You'll find out everything anyway, sooner or later." She paused before turning to look in his eyes. "Yeah, I get my grass from him. But that's all I do."

"Do I get to meet this wonderful guy?"

She broke out in a grin. "Oh no. That's the good part—we really lucked out. He's down in L.A. trying to promote some new kind of money-making scheme. We should be totally gone by the time he gets back Sunday night." Then she giggled. "Boy, will *he* be pissed."

"Did this jerk ever hit you?"

"Not exactly. But we did get into some pretty physical arguments once in a while. Pushing, shoving, that kind of stuff."

"It's a good thing he won't be around. I'd have to knock him around a bit."

"Don't even think about it. He carries a gun and he wouldn't think twice about using it."

When they got off the bus and started walking, Mark received his second shock of the evening. Karen was now the one dressed like a 'normal' person and he was clearly the outsider. They attracted many curious stares as they passed stumbling drunks, bag ladies, homeless derelicts, and a pair of gussied-up prostitutes plying their trade on a busy street corner. Mark was extremely self-conscious in his pilot's uniform and thought it made an obvious statement: *Mug me. I'm easy.*

As they passed the two hookers, one called out to the other in a mock falsetto voice, "Now looky dere, Monique. Dat little lady done got herself a rich *fly boy.*" Mark grabbed Karen's hand and pulled her along, trying to walk faster, but she only laughed at his discomfort.

Karen's apartment building was a run-down structure on Turk Street near Leavenworth, right in the heart of the Tenderloin District. They had to step over a passed-out drunk just to enter the building's front door.

As they climbed the rickety stairs to the third floor, Mark was almost asphyxiated by the stench of decay: urine, excrement, cheap wine, and rotting food. Once inside her apartment, he noticed another aroma; the sweetly pungent smell of smoked pot or burned incense. He couldn't tell which.

Karen turned on a floor lamp and Mark took a quick survey. The dark windowless living room had a sofa, an overstuffed chair, a large stereo system, and a small TV. A chrome and formica dinette table with two chairs were in one corner, and the adjacent kitchen was equipped with a tiny refrigerator, a two burner gas stove, and a portable microwave. A door on the far side of the living room led to the single bedroom containing a queen-size water bed and the adjoining bathroom.

Dark paint was peeling off the walls and ceiling in random blotches; this place had clearly seen better days.

"You sleep in the bed tonight, Daddy. I'll bunk out here on the couch." Mark was so tired that he didn't raise any objection to this arrangement.

"I didn't have any dinner tonight," he said. "Do you have anything to eat in this place?"

"There's some leftover pizza in the fridge. Just zap it in the microwave."

He retrieved the foil-wrapped pizza and helped himself to a can of beer, but first changed into jeans and a sweat shirt before heating his food. Mark sat on the couch eating while Karen lounged in the overstuffed chair, smoking a cigarette.

"By the way," he said, "I thought you had a car. What happened to it?"

"I still have it. It's in a garage around the corner loaded up with clothes, books, and other small stuff. There's only room for the driver—that's why I didn't drive it out to the airport."

"So what's the plan for tomorrow?" he wondered.

"I made a reservation for a small U-Haul truck—we can pick it up in the morning. Then we load up all my stuff in the truck and blow this popsicle stand. Oh yeah, remind me to drain the water bed first thing in the morning."

"Which stuff is yours?" He asked, looking around the room.

"Almost all of it. But I'll probably leave some of the big furniture for Darrel. I won't have room for it."

"Where are you going? You haven't even told me about that yet."

CHAPTER TWENTY-FIVE

"A house in Walnut Creek. I'm renting a spare bedroom from a very nice couple. It's a much nicer neighborhood than this one. And cheaper, too."

Mark smiled at her. "This is quite a pleasant surprise—seeing how well organized you are for this move."

"Nothing at all, Daddy. I learned it all from you. All those cross-country moves when you were in the Navy."

"The worst move I ever had was when your mother and I separated. Do you remember that one?"

"How could I forget?"

"You were only thirteen then. Spent the entire weekend with me in that crummy studio apartment. Organizing my kitchen, washing my plates and silverware, lining my shelves."

"Yep, I was a real Suzy Homemaker."

She got up, stubbed out her cigarette, went over to the couch, and sat down next to him. Mark put his arm around her shoulders and hugged her tightly. "I don't know if I ever thanked you properly for helping me that weekend."

"You're being here now is all the thanks I'll ever need."

Mark kissed her on the cheek. "We'll talk some more tomorrow, but now I have to hit the sack. My body's still on St. Louis time and I'm fading fast."

Mark had never slept on a water bed before so he was unsure of it when he first settled in. But he quickly found out that if he lay perfectly still, it didn't make him feel like he was on the ocean in a rubber raft. Just before he fell asleep, he compared the stark differences between this place and his suite back in St. Louis.

I wonder how Joan would be on a water bed? We'd probably enjoy ourselves, as long as the bed was in a nice hotel.

Chapter Twenty-Six

The next morning, they managed to load Karen's things into the back of the U-Haul truck in less than two hours. She walked to the garage and drove her car back to the front of her apartment building and parked in front of the truck. The garish orange VW beetle badly needed a paint job and had numerous dents in the fenders and both bumpers. "We'll be heading east on I-80 over the Bay Bridge," she said. "I'll drive slow, so just follow me."

"How could I miss you?"

"Then we'll take I-680 to Walnut Creek after we cross the bridge. It can't be more than thirty-five miles from here."

Since it was Saturday morning, traffic was relatively light. An hour later, they pulled into the driveway of an attractive single story house in a quiet upscale neighborhood. Karen jumped out of her VW beetle and called out, "C'mon, Daddy. I'll introduce you to my new landlords."

She rang the doorbell and was greeted by a tall, thin, and bespectacled woman with short blond hair in her mid-thirties, wearing blue jeans and a maroon sweat shirt. "Hey Karen. You made it."

"Hi, Jessica. This is my father, Mark."

She gave Mark a firm hand shake. "A pleasure to meet you, Mark."

They entered a large living room populated with modern but clearly expensive furniture. Thick beige wall-to-wall carpeting and wide picture windows gave the room a cheerful and inviting look. Shortly after sitting down, they were joined by another woman in her mid-thirties wearing a white jogging suit, shorter and heavier than Jessica with long brown hair. Mark stood as she entered the room and she offered her hand. "Hi, I'm Julia. You must be Karen's dad."

Mark's face fell slightly, something that all three women noticed. Karen explained, "Julia and Jessica are the owners—my new landlords." Sensing his unease, she giggled and added, "Or maybe I should

CHAPTER TWENTY-SIX

call them landladies."

"Let's have a tour of the house," said Jessica. "We'll start with Karen's bedroom." This room was empty except for a floor lamp and a bedside table holding a small reading lamp. The tour continued to another bedroom that had been converted to an office; it contained two bookcases, two desks and two computers. As the group came to the master bedroom, Julia commented that the bed hadn't been made this morning so that room was bypassed. They continued through a small dining room and stopped in the kitchen, a bright room with white cabinets and wood flooring of light pine strips.

"You have a very nice home," said Mark. Then turning to Karen, he said, "You did good, honey."

"Let's start unloading, Daddy. We've got lots of work to do."

"I'll make some sandwiches for you guys," said Jessica. "When you get hungry, just take a break and help yourself."

When Mark and Karen came around to the rear of the truck, he muttered, "You said you were renting from a couple."

"I am. They *are* a couple."

"I thought you meant a *couple* couple. Like a man and woman couple."

"Now don't you go spastic on me, Daddy. These are nice women—professionals in the financial district. They've been very understanding about my situation."

Mark didn't answer but instead opened the truck's rear door and started lifting boxes onto the driveway. The truck was soon unloaded and Karen began setting up the water bed in her bedroom. Mark found a local U-Haul dealer in the telephone book's Yellow Pages and Karen followed him in her VW beetle. After dropping off the truck, Karen suggested that stopping at a supermarket would be the prudent thing to do. "J. and J. are going to a concert in the city tonight, so you and I are on our own for dinner."

They loaded up a shopping cart and the bill was almost $150 which Mark paid with his credit card. "My housewarming gift," he said. When they got back to the house, Karen insisted that Mark be first in the shower. She put the groceries away and started preparing their dinner of garden salad, baked potato, and New York strip steak.

Mark donned his maroon jogging suit after showering and went out to the rear patio with a *Time* magazine, intending to relax before dinner. He thought of Averil in England and wanted to call her, but the difference in time zones was a problem. She would be sleeping soundly and wouldn't appreciate being awakened by an ordinary "checking-in" call. Instead, he went to the kitchen and mixed himself a vodka and tonic using the ingredients they had purchased earlier.

A barefoot Karen came out to the patio after her shower, dressed modestly in blue jeans and mauve polo shirt. Mark looked up at her, momentarily surprised at her appearance. "I don't believe this. Your hair looks almost normal again."

"Yeah, I washed the color out of it. It was just temporary anyway. Have to ditch that punk look if I'm going to make it in the corporate world."

"Want some help with dinner?" he asked.

"There's not that much to do, but you can set the table. Let's eat out here."

Mark brought out the plates, silverware, napkins, and condiments and placed them on the glass-topped patio table; then he lit the gas grill. The back yard was small and the profusion of red and purple bougainvillea growing up the rear and side fences gave a heightened sense of quiet security, as if they were in their own private garden. He opened a bottle of Napa Valley Cabernet Sauvignon and brought it out to the patio while Karen carried their steaks on a carving board. Mark cooked while Karen tossed the salad; it all came together in fifteen minutes.

After they had satisfied their huge appetites, they sipped their wine in the fading twilight. "I'm curious about something," she began. "How come you and Mom split up? I never did hear the complete story."

Mark hesitated before answering, searching for some words that might possibly justify his divorce. "I don't think there's any single reason I can give you. It was just a whole bunch of small things that added up to a bigger thing. I woke up one morning and realized that I didn't love her anymore."

"But you guys stuck it out for a long time, didn't you?"

"Sure, twenty years. That is a long time."

"Was it for us girls?"

"That was a major part of it."

"How come you two got married in the first place?"

He cocked his head and said, "That's an odd question."

"What I mean is that all the time I was growing up, I never saw much

CHAPTER TWENTY-SIX

love *between* the two of you. It was like you guys were just friends, going through the motions, putting on this act for us. Where was the passion?"

Mark gave her a mock scowl. "How did you get to be so smart?"

She grinned. "You never answered my question."

Mark relaxed and continued, "To be honest, it was probably because of loneliness more than anything. I wanted a wife, a lover, a housemate, and some emotional stability."

"And that's it?"

"Not quite. I think I married on the rebound. The girl I really wanted turned me down. A girl I dated in college." Mark continued with the whole story about a young Joan Krenowicz and their different religious backgrounds, conveniently omitting details about their recent reunion. After telling her all this, he felt that a large burden had been lifted and he'd grown closer to Karen in the process.

"That's so sad," she remarked.

Mark shifted the focus of their conversation so that he didn't have to talk anymore about Joan. "Have you talked with your mother about this stuff?"

"I've tried, but she's so uptight that I don't get very much out of her. She drives me up the wall, waving those freaking rosary beads in my face. I think all she needs is a good fuck."

Mark barked a short laugh but quickly turned serious again. "Don't talk about your mother like that."

"Sorry, Daddy, but it's true." She paused and poured some more wine into her glass. Then she smiled and added, "There's hope on the horizon. She's dating a retired Marine colonel who lives in Oceanside and I think it's serious."

"I hadn't heard about that."

"Hey—if they get married, you wouldn't have to pay any more alimony."

"It's not alimony. It's half my Navy retired pay. They just take it out of my check every month and send it to her. She gets it even if she remarries."

"She does? That hardly seems fair."

"It's not, but it's the law."

Karen lowered her head in thought. "But you're still way ahead of the game. You've got Averil."

"Averil? You really think so?"

"Of course I do. I really like her. She's so cool and you're a very lucky man to have her."

"How so?"

"Because you're very good for each other and I can tell you are both very much in love. Look what she gives up for you. Being alone while you fly all over the world. And now with this St. Louis job for—how many months?"

"Oh, probably just a couple more. Then I go back to my usual schedule."

"While she stays at home, waiting patiently for you."

Mark sat silently, absorbing this latest bit of wisdom from his youngest child. He had to admit that he was indeed a fortunate man and should probably show his appreciation and gratitude more for all the sacrifices that Averil had made during their married life. He also thought about his latest trysts with Joan and felt several sharp and unsettling pangs of guilt.

While they cleaned up the dinner dishes, Karen asked, "When do you have to go back?"

"I left it open-ended with my bosses. I didn't know how long it would take to get you moved."

"Why don't you stay over a couple of days? You've never really seen San Francisco, have you?"

"Not really."

"Then stay. We can see the Golden Gate Bridge, Fisherman's Wharf, Napa Valley—all the tourist attractions. It'll be loads of fun."

"Where will I sleep?"

"I believe J. and J. have a futon in the garage that we can borrow."

"What about your new job?"

"I don't have one yet but I'll start looking after you leave. It won't be hard to find something right here in Walnut Creek."

Mark put his arms around her shoulders and gave her a strong squeeze. "OK, I'll hang out with you for a couple of days. But when I start sounding like a *father,* put me on the first plane to St. Louis."

"But you are my father."

"Yeah, well, there are dads and then there are *fathers.* You know what I mean?"

"Sure, Daddy."

Chapter Twenty-Seven

On a cold and wet Tuesday, three days after Karen Holloway had moved to Walnut Creek, Sean Flannery was working his usual daytime shift in Full Sutton Prison's machine shop. Outwardly, he appeared to be his usual sullen self, but inwardly, he was seething with joyous anticipation.

He had been closely observing the daily work routine and had noticed several recent changes that offered a hint of opportunity. The first was the arrival of a new prison guard, a young man who came on duty in the shop at four o'clock each afternoon. The guard was new to prisoner surveillance and was given the evening watch only because the prison staff thought it was a low risk assignment. Flannery made friends with the guard, not because he liked him or respected him, but because he thought the neophyte might be used to his advantage.

The other change of interest involved the weekly trash pickup. For as many months as Flannery could remember, a large and highly mechanized garbage truck would come to the machine shop every Friday afternoon about 4:30. Flannery, or one of the other prisoners, would help the two men operating the truck load all the shop's scrap into its rear compartment while being supervised by the duty guard. But just two weeks ago, the trash pickup schedule had been changed to Tuesday afternoon at the same time. Even more fascinating to Flannery was the fact that the two men usually operating the truck had been replaced by two much younger men, well acquainted with trash hauling but totally new to the prison environment.

Considering both the new guard and the new waste disposal workers, Flannery concluded that this was the moment for his escape.

He began his detailed planning in earnest, ten days before this particular Tuesday, by starting the growth of a mustache. Since mustaches were not authorized for inmates, Flannery placed a bandage on his upper lip, feigning a cut that he falsely reported as an accident while performing a machining job. The second thing he did was to get some pills from an accomplice in the prison pharmacy, a drug called hyoscine that induces a light sleep. His third action was to inform his IRA contact about the plan and request that certain items be made available to him outside the prison, assuming that his escape was successful.

That Tuesday afternoon, the young guard came on duty at the usual time but the trash haulers were delayed by a fine drizzle and a light fog. The guard took a chair at a desk in the corner of the shop, unscrewed the top of his thermos jug, and poured himself a hot cup of black coffee. When the garbage truck finally arrived, the guard got up and went out to the loading dock. He scolded the driver for being late, citing the need to load the trash and get Flannery, the only inmate left in the shop, back in his cell for the afternoon prisoner count.

The truck driver was not sympathetic to the guard's problem, but he and his helper began emptying the trash barrels on the loading dock into the compartment at the rear of the truck. While the guard was on the dock, Flannery slipped one of the hyoscine pills into the guard's cup and gave it a stir with his forefinger.

Flannery moved more barrels of trash out to the dock, one barrel at a time, using a two-wheel "dolly" or hand truck. The guard came back into the shop, grabbed his cup, and walked back and forth between the shop and loading dock, closely watching the loading activity. He took frequent sips of coffee and seemed pleased that the work was proceeding smoothly and Flannery would be returned to his cell in time for the count.

The guard emptied his cup and went back to his desk for more. By now, he was starting to feel drowsy and thought that he needed still another shot of caffeine to stay alert. When he reached the desk, he became so dizzy that he had to sit down. *I should call for help,* he thought. But before he could lift the telephone's handset, he slumped over and his head hit the desk with a thud.

Flannery came back into the shop right after this and howled in glee; the plan was working. He picked the guard up by the shoulders and dragged him into a nearby storage room. Then he began working faster, hauling the last barrel out to the dock and, with the driver's help, unloading its contents into the truck. After all the work had been done, the driver asked Flannery, "Now where did that bloody guard get off to?"

"I got no idea, mate. Last time I saw him he was back in the shop."

CHAPTER TWENTY-SEVEN

The driver turned to his helper and said, "Ian, go back in the shop. Find that guard and tell him we've got to check out."

"Right you are," said the helper as he walked away. After five minutes, Ian returned and shook his head. "I looked all over and couldn't find the bloke. He must have gone to the loo and the pigs ate him." This caused both the driver and Ian to laugh heartily while Flannery joined in with a nervous chuckle.

"Well, we're shoving off," said the driver. "We're already running late and my old lady will give me bloody hell if I'm not on time for supper."

The driver and helper climbed into the truck's cab, but as the driver started up the engine, Flannery ran to the truck's rear, climbed on top, and dove into the trash-filled compartment. When he landed on the scrap metal pile inside, he cut his left hand on something sharp, causing him to press his bleeding palm against his trouser leg. The stench of garbage and other rotting refuse almost made him sick but his adrenalin was pumping so hard that he willed himself to concentrate on the work ahead. *I've got to find a hiding place in here before we get to the gate.*

The truck lumbered slowly through the prison grounds and periodically the glow from passed overhead lights gave Flannery enough visibility. However, about a quarter mile before reaching the prison's main gate, the driver turned on the rotating compactor machinery. Flannery was powerless to stop the rolling as his body was tossed like some salad ingredient amongst all the trash inside the compartment. The last thing he remembered before blacking out was being struck on the head by a heavy metal object.

When the truck reached the main gate, it was halted by the guards on duty. One of the guards climbed on top of the truck, shone his flashlight inside the compartment, and closely examined its contents. He saw nothing unusual during his search and climbed down, telling another guard that everything looked all right. The truck was waved through and proceeded to pick up speed.

Thirty minutes later, the truck arrived at the county dump and backed into an area used for emptying garbage trucks. It was such a common practice to the driver and helper that neither got out of the cab; they let the truck's machinery do all the work, much like a wildebeest giving birth to her offspring. After five minutes of disgorging its litter, the truck pulled away and headed for home.

An hour after the truck departed, Flannery regained consciousness but couldn't figure out where he was. As he became fully awake, he had to push his way out of the hole he'd been lying in, shaking off the garbage that covered him. His head throbbed in pain but he had no broken bones and his palm had stopped bleeding. He became aware of the wetness and cold, shivering as he looked around the darkness of the fog-shrouded dump. He took deep breaths of the moist night air, but instead of being repulsed by the surrounding garbage, he whooped loudly because there was another, more pleasant aroma to be savored, something he had not know in thirteen years. *Freedom. It's me blessed bloody freedom!*

He stood and waved his arms about, trying to generate some body heat, and looked around on all sides. When he spotted a faint light through the fog, he laughed in glee and stomped through trash in that direction.

Presently, he came to the source of the light and discovered it was a small building, an office that was used by workers for recording the identity of trucks using the dump so that their companies could be billed accordingly. He went around to the rear of the building and found a canvas tarp that covered boxes of supplies. When he removed the tarp, he spotted a black canvas bag, the type used by passengers on almost every airline flight. "There it is," he cried out. "The boys came through for me again. God bless 'em."

The bag contained a complete change of clothes, all chosen to make him resemble the average factory worker from that area of England. He also found money, papers giving him a new identity, and a small cosmetic kit which contained, among other things, a dye that would change the color of his red hair. He changed into his new clothes quickly and buried his prison uniform under a pile of trash.

As he picked up the black canvas bag and began walking away from the dump, he thought about his next move. *I would dearly love to have a drink right now, but that can wait. The most important thing is to find a safe hiding place and lie low. All this has to blow over before I can show me face in public again. There's absolutely no hurry now. I've got all the time in the world to do what I have to do.*

Chapter Twenty-Eight

By the following Tuesday, Mark had decided it was time to get back to work, so he booked a seat on the afternoon Trans-Global flight to St. Louis. Karen drove him to the airport and dropped him at the terminal.

Before he got out of her orange beetle, she kissed him on the cheek. "Thanks again, Daddy, for coming. I couldn't have done all this without you."

"You take good care of yourself now. And keep in touch."

"I will." After he got out and looked through the passenger-side window, she added, "I love you."

"Love you too, honey," he said and quickly disappeared into the terminal.

During the flight, he fondly recalled the last few days spent with Karen. It had been enjoyable in various degrees, but the most satisfying part happened earlier that day. They had borrowed Julia's computer for several hours and crafted a resume that highlighted her bachelor's degree in business administration from Cal State San Diego, followed by a one year job with a large graphic arts design company in Long Beach. She had announced her relocation to San Francisco as a career-enhancing move, but it was really to be with a man who had since left for Oregon. She never did find a permanent job. Instead, she worked as a temp in the financial district where she met Julia and Jessica. Jessica promised Karen that she would float her resume, confident that this would generate several promising interviews.

He also recalled their dinner conversation on the patio last Saturday evening. He marveled at how perceptive this young woman was about his relationships with the women in his life; first her mother and then his wife. *How can she be so right about Averil when I can't even see it for myself, even though it's as plain as the nose on my face? I should spend more time with Karen. This trip has been a good start for both of us but I want to get closer.*

Mark's flight arrived at Lambert Field that evening, just after a thunderstorm had passed through and dumped a half inch of rain. He took a courtesy van to his hotel where he received two telephone messages; both were from Joan Soric, asking him to call as soon as he returned. He crumpled them into his trouser pocket.

He ordered a club sandwich, French fries, and a beer from room service and took a quick shower. He was very hungry by the time the food arrived and ate quickly, thinking about returning Joan's calls.

Joan's messages didn't give a phone number so he wasn't sure whether he should call her at home or at the office. *Best I call her at the office tomorrow. No sense in taking stupid risks at this point.* He wanted to talk with Averil, but because of the six hour time zone difference, she would be asleep. *I'll call her in the morning before I go to work.* Before going to bed, he read that day's *Post-Dispatch* and watched thirty minutes of Jay Leno's *Tonight Show*.

Mark slept soundly until a barely audible telephone made him realize it was the real thing and not part of a dream. The bedside alarm clock read 2:30 A.M. as he picked up the handset and mumbled a groggy hello.

"Oh, thank God you're there."

"Av, is something wrong? You sound upset."

"It's the worst possible thing I could imagine. He's escaped from prison."

Mark sat up and almost shouted into the phone, "When did this happen? How did you find out?"

"I saw it on the BBC news. The authorities just released a bulletin—he's been missing since last night sometime and they can't account for his whereabouts anywhere in the prison."

"What else did they say?"

"Hardly anything else. Except they've launched a full-scale investigation."

"Yeah, right. Sounds like locking the barn doors after the horse is gone."

"Mark, I'm terribly frightened. With him on the loose, I don't feel safe."

"Where are you calling from?"

"I'm at mum's, looking after her."

"Any progress getting her moved into a nursing home?"

CHAPTER TWENTY-EIGHT

"Precious little," she said. "Emma's supposed to come over from Portsmouth today and help me inspect two possible places. We haven't found one yet that quite measures up. I'm afraid it's going to take some time."

"I don't like this, Av. You're like a sitting duck there with Flannery on the lam. Do you want me to come over?"

"That would be lovely, but there's really nothing that you can do here. And you must be behind in your work because of your trip to San Francisco. Oh dear, I forgot to ask you about that."

"It was a good trip, but we can talk about that later. Look, I want you to go to the police."

"The police? Do you really think that's necessary?"

"Yes, it's the right thing to do. Tell them who you are and why you're concerned. I'm sure Flannery doesn't know you're in England but he might try to reach your mom or Emma, just to find out where you are. God forbid, he might even hurt one or both of them. Or you!"

"It would be just like him to do something like that."

"Then you'd be helping the police track him down. There's probably nobody in England right now that knows him like you do."

"All right. I'll ring them up straight away."

He couldn't get back to sleep after Averil's frantic call. He was angry because it was one of the few times in his life when he was faced with a life or death situation and had absolutely no control over the outcome. He was also worried about Averil's safety, imagining all types of horrible scenarios involving Flannery. Last, but certainly not least, was the pressing guilt—screwing around with another man's wife while his own wife was being stalked by a maniac.

He tossed and turned until the alarm went off at 6:30 A.M. He was relieved to be fully awake and going back to work where he could engage his mind in something less aggravating.

Nancy was the first person to greet Mark when he arrived at his office. "Oh Captain, I'm so glad to see you. Did you have a successful trip?"

Mark winced at her overly effusive greeting. "Yes, I did. Moved my daughter to a much nicer neighborhood. I think she'll be OK now."

"I'll tell Mr. Campbell you're in. He wants to see you."

Mark hung his hat and coat in his office, dropped his briefcase on his desk, and walked the short distance to Tom Campbell's office. After a few pleasantries about Mark's trip to San Francisco, Tom gave him some exciting news about the project. "Looks like we'll have a few software modules working by the end of the week. Enough so you can try your hand at flying it next week. It won't be the landing part, but some of the routine en route stuff. Are you up for it?"

"I sure am," said Mark. "That sounds great."

"Check in with Dick Hightower. He'll give you a rundown on which parts will be operational."

Mark spent the next two hours with Hightower discussing the software modules. He returned to his office and read engineering notebook entries about the same modules that would be controlling the simulator's operations.

An hour after lunch, he poured himself a cup of coffee from the carafe in Nancy's office and took it back to his desk. Before dialing Joan's office number, he closed his office door so Nancy wouldn't be tempted to eavesdrop.

"You're back," Joan almost screamed. "I was starting to get worried."

"Yeah, I got back late last night. I got your messages, but I didn't want to bother you at home."

"Good thinking. It's better to call me at the office when Frank's in town. So—how about lunch? We don't have much left of this week."

"Aw, it's not looking so good. I've got a lot of work to do. It sort of piled up while I was in San Francisco."

"How did it go?"

Mark spent nearly five minutes giving her the chronology of his and Karen's activities in San Francisco and Walnut Creek.

"My goodness," she said. "You certainly were a busy bee. What a way to spend your birthday. I'll bet your wife wasn't too pleased about your not coming home for the weekend."

"You don't know the half of it. She's off in England right now, trying to get her mother moved into a nursing home."

"Really? I sure don't envy her. One of my close friends at church had to do the same thing for her mother several months ago. It's no picnic."

"I talked to her this morning—real early. Something else happened that really complicates the situation. Her ex-husband just escaped from prison

CHAPTER TWENTY-EIGHT

and that presents a whole new set of problems that she has to deal with."

"Mark, I had no idea. What's this all about?"

"It's a very long story—some other time. I'll give you the whole chapter and verse if you're really interested."

Joan paused for a few seconds before continuing. "So if she's in England, what are you going to do?"

"What do you mean?"

"Are you going to England to be with her? Where will you be this weekend?"

"I'll probably stay here in St. Louis," he said. "No sense in going back to an empty house in New York."

"Then let's have lunch on Saturday. You don't have anything planned, do you?"

Mark instantly realized he'd made a tactical error; he'd given her too much information. "No, I guess not. But how are you going to manage that?"

"Oh, I'll figure out something. Shall I come out to your hotel around noon?"

"Uh, no. Let's meet downtown somewhere. Why don't you meet me under the Arch?"

"Under the Arch?" Mark could sense the peevishness in her voice. "Oh, I get it. Just like we did on our first date. How romantic of you, kind sir. Then we can walk to a restaurant from there."

After hanging up, Mark paced back and forth, stopping occasionally to look out his large office windows. His conversation with Joan had not gone the way he had planned. He felt a loss of control, being manipulated into a luncheon engagement about which he had mixed feelings. At one point in his pacing, he stopped to pick up Averil's photo on his desk. He put the picture back on the desk, face down, and continued pacing.

Eventually he sat down and drained his coffee cup. *Since I have to spend the entire weekend here, I might as well do something that I want to do. Something I need to do.* He riffled through the telephone directory, found the number for Holy Family Church, and called for Father Soric's Sunday mass schedule.

Chapter Twenty-Nine

Averil looked through the Southampton telephone directory, found the number for the local police station, and dialed it.

"Sergeant Fincher at your service. How may I help you?"

"Good morning, sergeant. My name is Averil Holloway and I'm calling about that escaped convict—Sean Flannery."

"Sorry, miss. I don't know anything about an escaped con."

"You don't? Why I should think that the police all over England would know about it by now. I just saw a news report on the BBC."

"Then we should be getting a report about him shortly. Do you have some information for us about this man?"

"You could say that. I was married to him at one point."

"Let me get a pencil and note pad. Would you state your name again please and where you are calling from?"

"It's Mrs. Averil Holloway and I'm calling from my mother's home here in Southampton. Her name is Charlotte Langford."

"And the escaped convict's name?"

"Sean Flannery. He escaped from Full Sutton Prison last evening."

"Oh, that's a nasty place, Mrs. Holloway. Only the worst of the lot are kept there."

"I'm very concerned for my personal safety as well as my mother's. She is not a well woman and that's why I'm here in England at the moment." Averil went on for several minutes, giving him a summary of their marriage, their divorce, and his threats against her.

"I fully appreciate your position, Mrs. Holloway, but we're a bit short-handed about the station at the moment. What I can do is have one of our roving patrols stop by and have a look around the premises. Will you and your mother be home this evening?"

"If that's the best you can do, then so be it. Yes, we'll be home this evening."

Averil gave Sergeant Fincher her mother's address, hung up the phone,

CHAPTER TWENTY-NINE

and returned to watching the TV news with her mother.

When the prisoner count on Tuesday evening didn't tally up correctly, the prison warden ordered an immediate lockdown and a complete search of the premises. A groggy and shaken machine shop guard was found in the cleaning gear storeroom and quickly questioned. "The last thing I remember was Flannery moving barrels out to the loading dock, helping the trash men load the truck. Then I got to feeling dizzy and sat down at the desk. I guess that's when I fell asleep."

The guards at the prison's main gate were also interviewed. Their log book showed the trash truck's departure about the usual time and the guards verbally confirmed that one of them had looked carefully inside the trash compartment before allowing the truck to leave.

Inside the prison, the mood among the inmates was joyful in spite of the lockdown; one of their own had escaped and was enjoying his freedom roaming the English countryside. Those few friends of Flannery marveled at his uncharacteristic restraint in his treatment of the young guard. In their collective opinion, the least he could have done was to beat the screw into a bloody pulp. One con even thought that Flannery should have killed him outright in order to buy a few more minutes for making good his escape.

Late Tuesday evening, the prison authorities acknowledged that they had done as much as they could within their own authority and called the York police for assistance. Early Wednesday morning, the police contacted the trash company's management and arranged for the driver and his assistant, the ones who carried trash away from the prison the night before, to be detained at the central garage for questioning. Sergeant Johnson and Officer Buskirk of the York police drove to the garage and began their interview thirty minutes later.

The trash men told their stories and agreed that it would have been dangerous for Flannery to hitch a ride while riding in the trash compartment. "We ran the bloody compactor while we was moving," said the driver. "If he was back there, he would have been smashed flatter than a pancake."

"If I understand correctly," said Johnson, "you drove straight from the prison's main gate directly to the dump, not stopping anywhere along your route. Is that correct?"

"That's correct, sergeant."

"Then I think we should have a look about the dump. Can you show us the place where you unloaded your trash last night?"

"No problem at all, sergeant."

The men got into their respective vehicles and the policemen followed the trash truck in their squad car to the location where it had stopped nearly sixteen hours ago. The gray sky cast a depressing gloom over the gigantic garbage heap and everything was still wet from last night's drizzle. Both police officers were surprised to see dozens of sea gulls hovering over the site, occasionally landing and picking at food scraps, even though the dump was a good forty miles west of the North Sea.

"Let's have a look around," said Sergeant Johnson, "and see if we can find anything that might give us a clue about Mr. Flannery." Johnson then spoke directly to the two trash men, implicitly deputizing them for the search. "If you spot anything suspicious, call me or Buskirk and let us handle the evidence."

The trash men took to the job with gusto. The two officers, however, moved carefully about the dump, trying to minimize any damage to their uniforms. They poked around the area for almost three hours, and were about to break for lunch, when Buskirk yelled out, "Over here, sergeant. I think I found something."

The three other men converged on Buskirk. Sergeant Johnson put on a pair of latex gloves and held up both parts of Flannery's prison uniform. "Well now, at least we know our boy got this far. But he can't be moving about the country buck naked, can he? I suspect he got his hands on some other clothing. Which leads me to believe that he had some help making good his escape. So where do you suppose he might be headed?"

Hours earlier, Flannery had walked briskly away from the dump, well off to the side of a lightly traveled two lane road. Among the treasures in his black canvas bag was a crudely drawn map that gave him several clues regarding his location. If he'd read the map correctly, and he wasn't sure that he did, he would soon be approaching the intersection of this road with a four lane highway, the A64, which was also a bypass ring around York's walled city.

CHAPTER TWENTY-NINE

After walking another thirty minutes, Flannery spotted part of an interchange ahead, a giant truck stop for long distance rigs. He cautiously approached the brightly lit area, trying to remain hidden in the shadows as long as possible. He carefully looked over the area from several different positions and walked to a large parking area at the rear of the truck stop's restaurant. Five tractor-trailer rigs were parked side-by-side, their diesel engines idling noisily, while the drivers were inside having a meal.

He quickly moved around to a dark spot between a pair of trucks, crouched under one of the trailers, and began his wait. Twenty minutes later, the driver of the truck next to Flannery came out of the restaurant and climbed into the tractor's cab. Flannery darted from his position, climbed up on the truck into the narrow space between the tractor and trailer, and wedged himself into the lowest possible profile. He was not happy in this relatively exposed position and worried that he might be seen. But he also hoped that the combination of a dark and foggy night, along with his dark clothing, would help him remain undetected.

As the truck pulled onto the A64 and gathered speed, a shivering Flannery tightly gripped a metal handle with his right hand and a rubber hose with his left. He had no idea where the truck was going but he really didn't care. The important thing was that he was heading *away* from York; the further and faster the better.

On Wednesday morning, the day after Flannery's escape, Chief Inspector Peter Hungerford arrived at his New Scotland Yard office in Westminster a little earlier than usual. He too had seen the BBC news report on Flannery's escape and was bristling with excitement during his train commute into downtown London.

Peter Hungerford was a small and slight man with a long craggy face and snowy white hair, cut in a manner resembling a Roman Caesar. He had been promoted to Chief Inspector eight years ago and was currently serving as head of a special unit within New Scotland Yard that dealt with anti-terrorist activities.

Hungerford politely refused a cup of coffee from his secretary and went directly to his desk, calling up the latest news on his computer monitor about Flannery's escape. He quickly digested the information available and asked his secretary to bring him the Yard's complete file on Flannery. He was delighted when the bulging folder of faded papers arrived. "I believe that I'll have that coffee now, Miss Harris."

Hungerford went back to the start of the Flannery file and read a memo dated September, 1982, that postulated his membership in a small band of rabble rousers possibly related to the IRA. While sipping his coffee, he found copies of his own reports dated March, 1985, dealing with Flannery's knife attack on Averil, his subsequent interview with her, and other papers dealing with the Brighton bombing aftermath. When he read Charlotte Langford's name and telephone number, he decided to call her.

"Mrs. Langford? Good morning, this is Chief Inspector Hungerford calling."

"Oh, inspector. So good of you to call. Do you have some news for us?"

"Some news? I'm afraid not, Mrs. Langford. But I am calling about this Flannery chap. I suppose you already know that he's escaped from prison."

"Yes, we do, inspector. My daughter just had a chat with your Sergeant Fincher about him."

"Your daughter? Sergeant Fincher? I'm a bit confused. I'm with Scotland Yard here in London and I don't know a Sergeant Fincher."

"Oh goodness. The sergeant is here in Southampton and Averil just talked with him only a few minutes ago. She's quite concerned about all of this."

"Your daughter Averil is there with you? Could you put her on, please?" Hungerford drummed his fingers on his desk while anxiously awaiting Averil to come on the line.

"Good morning, inspector. This is Averil Holloway speaking."

"Did you say your last name is Holloway?"

"Yes, it is. I'm married to an American, Mark Holloway."

"You may not remember me, Mrs. Holloway, but I interviewed you in 1985, several days after you were attacked by Flannery."

"Oh, but I do recall it, inspector. You were very kind to me."

"Your mother just told me that you are aware of Flannery's escape and you reported it to a police sergeant. Is that true?"

"That's correct. I'm very worried about all this. He's a dangerous man, inspector, and he would probably kill me given the slightest opportunity."

CHAPTER TWENTY-NINE

"But he wouldn't know you are here in England, would he?"

"No, he wouldn't. But he knows where my mother lives and also my sister, Emma, in Portsmouth. I'm more afraid for them right now than for myself."

"Mrs. Holloway—I'd like to come down and talk with you and your mother. I can take the train and be there early this afternoon. Would that be suitable?"

"Yes indeed, inspector. We would be most grateful for your visit—I shall look forward to meeting you again."

Chapter Thirty

Mark was already awake when Averil called early Friday morning. "Any more news about Flannery?"

"Afraid not, luv. But I did ring up the police. They promised to have a roving patrol check mum's house. And Chief Inspector Hungerford of Scotland Yard came down from London to talk with us."

"I'm impressed—having Scotland Yard taking an interest in this."

"The local police also intend to phone the house periodically, just to be sure Mum and I are safe."

Mark, who was still in bed, propped himself up on several pillows. "I'm glad to hear all this but I won't rest easy until that guy is back in prison."

"What are your plans for the weekend, luv? Are you going back home?"

Mark paused before answering. "Hell no, I couldn't stand being alone in that house without you."

"That's very sweet."

"I've got loads of office work to catch up on. Stuff piled up while I was in San Francisco. Hey—I forgot to tell you about my visit with Karen." He then launched into a play-by-play description of the time spent with his daughter.

"So you plan to spend Saturday and Sunday working?"

"Oh no, I wouldn't do that. Matt and I may take in a baseball game. I think the Cardinals are in town. Then on Sunday, I'm planning on going to mass." Pausing briefly, he decided to change the subject. "How's your mother doing? Have you and Emma found a nursing home yet?"

"We've made precious little progress, I'm sorry to report. And that sister of mine . . . sometimes she's just one giant aggravation."

"What did she do now?"

"She didn't do anything and that's the problem. She canceled her trip. I think she's actually afraid that Sean might show his face around here."

"I can't believe she'd be so inconsiderate, leaving you holding the bag."

"Believe it. She's very capable of side-stepping issues. I'm afraid I'll

CHAPTER THIRTY

have to make all the arrangements myself."

Before hanging up, Mark promised to call her again on Monday.

Mark awoke Saturday morning with feelings of nausea, mild gloom, and depression, an overall condition that reminded him of an incident that occurred early in his Navy career. He had been given a temporary assignment that required him to be a passenger on an LST, a long slim ship with a flat bottom. While the ship was anchored near a small Pacific island, the captain ordered a reverse movement before pulling up the anchor, causing the ship's propeller to cut the anchor chain. The ship drifted for a short period and Mark became seasick, the first and only time it happened to him—except for now.

Last weekend he was in San Francisco. This weekend he was alone in St. Louis instead of being home on Long Island with Averil; she was off to England and in danger because of Flannery's escape. Averil was his anchor but he was drifting aimlessly, weak and irresolute, responding slavishly to base carnal instincts and the availability of pleasant sex with Joan Soric.

After a light breakfast in the hotel coffee shop, he dallied at his table reading the *Post-Dispatch*. Since he had plenty of time to kill before meeting Joan, he decided to kick his physical exercise routine up a notch. First, he went on a vigorous three mile walk and returned to the hotel in less than an hour. Next, he spent thirty minutes in the Nautilus machine room, followed by another thirty minutes swimming hard laps in the hotel's pool. As he toweled off, he felt physically drained but emotionally strengthened, although still not one hundred percent happy about his current romantic entanglements.

He went back to his room, showered and shaved, and dressed for his lunch date with Joan. He wore cordovan loafers, tan slacks, a maroon sport shirt, and a dark brown leather Navy flight jacket with gold aviator wings and CAPTAIN M. HOLLOWAY USN embossed in gold block letters over his heart.

He made the drive downtown in thirty minutes and parked his rental car in a lot near the northern base of the Arch. The sun shone brightly in an almost clear blue autumn sky; the temperature was in the mid-sixties and there was a slight breeze riffling the dozens of American flags flying about the open areas around each of the Arch's two bases. As he walked to the nearest base, he spotted Joan looking about the promenade, wearing large sunglasses, tan gabardine slacks and a black cashmere sweater. They both smiled simultaneously on recognition and waved at each other as Mark continued closer. *Damn, why does she have to look so gorgeous today? And why is she wearing the gold heart and chain again?*

Joan opened her arms wide and Mark hugged her so strongly that he could feel the pressure of her breasts through his leather jacket. She kissed him lightly and stepped backward. "I'm so glad to see you."

"Hope you haven't been waiting too long."

"Just a few minutes." She ran her hands over his jacket and fingered several cracks in the sleeve's cuff. "I think this jacket has seen better days."

"Hey, it's got lots of years left. It's one of my favorites."

Joan made a quarter turn and took his hand, looking across the Mississippi to the Illinois bank. "Isn't this a beautiful day? I've been thinking about our first date—the night we came down here after the movie. Do you remember?"

"How could I forget?"

"You wanted to be part of a big engineering project like this someday. That wish has come true for you, wouldn't you say?"

"That's a fair statement." He turned to face her and, still holding her hand, asked, "How about you? I don't recall you wishing for anything special."

"To be quite honest, I was hoping that our date was the start of something special, a relationship that would last a very long time."

"Sorry to disappoint."

"I'm not disappointed. It took a long time, but we're finally together again."

Mark cleared his throat and looked away from her shining dark brown eyes. "So, where are we lunching today?"

As they walked hand-in-hand away from the river, she replied, "There's a nice restaurant just a couple of blocks from here."

"I hope it's not too far. I've already had a big workout this morning."

Joan stopped abruptly, raised her sunglasses, and said in a mock serious tone, "You'd better not let me down, Holloway. I'm counting on you having plenty of energy after lunch."

CHAPTER THIRTY

The restaurant was a small but elegantly decorated room next to the Drury Inn. At Joan's request, they were seated in a rear corner that gave them an element of privacy. Since it was Saturday, the restaurant was absent the usual crowd of office workers and only half full with serious downtown shoppers.

After the young waitress took their orders, Mark was first to speak. "How did you manage to get away today?"

"Oh, that was easy. I told him I had to help a friend shop for a dress to wear at her son's wedding. Frank hates to shop. He'd do anything to avoid it."

"What did he think of your hair? Did he notice the new style?"

"Yes, he noticed and was quite surprised. And I was surprised that he even noticed. But he likes it—well, he said he did. I think he's still trying to figure out just why I did it."

After the waitress brought them a chilled bottle of California Chardonnay, Mark told her about his trip to San Francisco. Joan listened attentively and laughed at the part where he and Karen were taunted by two hookers on the street corner. When Mark described his sightseeing activities, Joan remarked wistfully, "I've always wanted to see that city. Next time you go, why don't you take me along? It would be so romantic."

Mark could only make a soft grunt which he hoped would not be considered a commitment.

Both were quite hungry when their meals arrived; a chicken salad for Joan and catfish with rice for Mark. "Tell me about your wife," said Joan. "What is she doing in England now?"

Mark summarized the situation in a few sentences, hoping to satisfy Joan's curiosity, but she wanted to know more. "Why is she so afraid of her ex-husband?"

"The man is an *animal*," said Mark. "They were married for only a short time in the mid-eighties. After he and his cohorts botched up the Brighton bombing, he ran away. But he came back one night and attacked her with a knife. They finally caught him and threw him in prison; that's when she decided to divorce him. He's never accepted it and seems to have this demented idea that they can someday be husband and wife again."

"When did you meet her?"

"In 1988. I was still in the Navy and went to London on a business trip.

She worked at the hotel where I stayed."

"So she was still married then. Is that right?"

"Legally, yes. But she'd been alone for some time."

"And you? Weren't you still married to that Margie-person?"

Mark smiled weakly. "You've got it all figured out, don't you?"

"Well, duh. I can do the math. So you were both having an affair. That's very interesting. Do I see a familiar behavior pattern here?"

Mark quietly and deliberately placed his knife and fork on his mostly empty plate and pushed it a few inches further away, followed by a healthy sip of wine. Joan placed her hand on his and said, "Sorry if I upset you."

"No, you're right. I'm a guy who cheats on his wife. Probably has something to do with my genes. My dad thought he was irresistible to every skirt in town."

Joan patted his hand. "Anyway, your wife's absence is my gain because it gives us more chances to see each other."

As they were having coffee, Mark grew restless. "Where do you see this thing going? Our relationship, that is."

"I can't tell you, Mark, because I'm not looking that far ahead. I'm just living in the moment, taking it one day at a time."

"You're amazing," he said. "I wish I could do that but I can't. I'm always looking into the future. A plan-ahead guy, I'm afraid."

"Yes, I know. You think too much. Why don't we just enjoy each other as much as possible during the time we have? It'll work itself out."

Mark frowned slightly. "I wish I had your confidence."

Joan laughed softly. "You just need some good old-fashioned TLC." She reached into her purse and dangled a Drury Inn hotel key in front of Mark. "A little surprise for you."

"What have you got there, lady?"

"I booked a room this morning before I came down to the Arch. Are you ready for some heavy breathing?"

Mark wavered a few moments before answering her. "Sure. Why not?"

Their room was on the fourth floor and, even though it was not as large as his suite, Mark immediately noticed that the furniture and wall decorations were identical. *They must have bought all their furnishings at one time from the lowest bidder, just like the government.*

CHAPTER THIRTY

Mark hung his flight jacket in the closet while Joan excused herself to use the bathroom. He busied himself adjusting the drapes and sheer white curtains at the large single window so that the sunlight filtering into the room gave a softly diffused glow.

After Joan came out, she pulled the bedspread down and fluffed the pillows while Mark took her place in the bathroom. When he came out several minutes later, Joan was in bed looking up at him coyly, the sheet pulled up and tucked under her chin, with all of her clothing piled on a chair next to the window. "What the heck are you standing there for? Get into bed—I'm hot."

Mark undressed slowly, got in next to her, and slipped into her warm and soft embrace. They kissed, touched, and rolled around for several minutes with arms and legs tightly wrapped around each other. When they paused briefly for a mutual quick breath, Joan reached down between his legs and grasped him firmly in her hand. "Uh, oh. Looks like you're not getting into the spirit of this."

"It has to be that workout this morning."

She stroked him several times and said, "Maybe I can help." When he grew hard, she rolled him over onto his back, straddled him, and placed him inside her while she rocked up and down, forward and back. In a short while, he tried to get up but she placed both hands on his shoulders, bent over, and kissed him. "Just relax and let me do this for you."

As he felt himself reaching a climax, he placed a hand on each breast and clenched hard. While Mark moaned loudly in pleasant release, Joan squealed in pain. It was all over.

Laying side by side, Joan cautioned, "Breasts are meant for soft touching. You don't squeeze them like grapefruits."

"Sorry, guess I got carried away. Did you get any pleasure out of this?"

"It was OK. Don't worry about it." They were silent for a few minutes and she continued, "I'm curious about something. This is the third time we've done it and you have yet to say the L-word. How about it? Do you love me?"

Mark gently rubbed her back and thought about her question a few seconds before answering. *This conversation is about to get serious. Be careful.* "Do I love you? That's a funny thing to ask right now."

"Quit stalling and answer."

"Sure, I love you, but it's not a black and white situation here. We're both married and we also have families to consider. This whole relationship could blow up in our faces if we're not careful. A lot of innocent people could get hurt."

"I can't argue with any of that."

"So what about you? Are you in love with me?"

"Would I be doing this with you if I wasn't?"

Mark laughed and pinched her butt. "Now who's the one that's stalling?"

Joan sighed, apparently taking time to consider her answer. "When we were in college and you went off to Pensacola, I thought I'd die. I didn't think I could ever love anyone again, not the way I loved you. But I'm a survivor and life goes on. And even though we didn't have any contact for thirty-five years, I didn't stop caring about you. I sure as hell never forgot you."

"Is that it then?"

Joan snuggled up closer, her right hand resting on his chest while he hugged her shoulder. "You came back into my life at probably the worst possible time. Or maybe the best time, depending on how you look at it. I'd been feeling very lonely and unloved for a long time, going to bed each night with a faithful but indifferent husband. When you called me, the whole damn thing started up all over again. You gave me a second chance to finally do all the things we never did in college. The deeper affection, the mature love, the caring relationship, the bonding of two souls—and the great sex, of course. But now that our respective religions are no longer an obstacle, neither of us is free to make the relationship something more permanent. An ironic situation, eh Mark?"

He gave her a hug and drew a circle around her navel with his forefinger. He thought of saying something like *you should have married me when you had the chance,* but instead gave her the mundane, "You're right about that."

After cuddling quietly for a short while, both grew colder and pulled up the bedspread for warmth. Mark fell asleep and awoke nearly an hour later to see a fully dressed Joan, standing by the window with her arms crossed, looking absently at the street below. He felt depressed again, a combination of the wine and angst over his latest act of unfaithfulness.

CHAPTER THIRTY

When she noticed that he was awake, she came over and sat on the bed. "Hey there, sleepy head. Are you going to be all right?"

"Oh sure. I bounce back quickly."

"I have to go. Frank will wonder what happened and I don't want to push my luck." She bent over and kissed him softly. "Call me Monday?"

Instead of answering directly, he only looked away from her glistening chocolate eyes and stared at the window.

"What's wrong? Are you thinking about your wife?"

A loopy grin came over Mark's face. "No, I was thinking about a big black dog and the first of May."

"Huh?"

"Never mind. I'll call you Monday."

Chapter Thirty-One

In the morning's cold damp dark, Flannery continued his bouncing ride on the large truck heading southwest. He shivered and trembled almost continuously but his self-discipline, steeled by years of prison confinement, overcame his discomfort as he reminded himself that it was all worth it. He was again a free man and the longer he held on, the farther he would be from Full Sutton.

About 1:00 A.M., after riding wedged between the trailer and tractor cab for nearly three hours, the truck pulled off the M42 motorway near the industrial city of Birmingham and into a large truck stop. The driver parked his rig off to the side, away from the gasoline and diesel pumps, and left the engine running while he went inside to urinate and refill his thermos with coffee.

Flannery decided he'd had enough of this wild overland express and jumped off the truck. He sprinted to a dark area at the rear of the repair shop, dropped his bag, and went through a short routine of vigorous exercises to get the blood moving again and work out some of the kinks in his joints.

At this point, he recognized the onset of another problem, acute hunger and thirst. He hadn't had anything to eat or drink since lunch the day before. If he was going to make good his escape, he would soon need some nourishment.

He had noticed a convenience store next to the truck stop that was open, one that sold food and drink for takeout. He judged it would be safer to buy something there and take it away rather than have a sit-down meal at the truck stop's cafe.

Before he went into the convenience store, he decided that his appearance needed some camouflage. He found a small pile of dirty rags next to an open barrel of discarded motor oil and went to work. He dipped one of the rags in the oil and then wiped his head, face, and hands, covering his exposed body parts with grime. He laughed quietly as he finished. *Me*

CHAPTER THIRTY-ONE

own sainted mother, God rest her soul, wouldn't recognize me now.

He entered the store, walked to the area containing refrigerated foods, and picked up a jug of milk and two plastic-wrapped Cornish pasties; minced meat and potatoes wrapped in pastry dough. When he took them up to the check-out counter, a young woman clerk with glasses and long stringy hair asked him, "Can I heat those up for you?" A befuddled Flannery didn't know what she was talking about. "Your pasties. Would you like them heated?"

Flannery mumbled an approval with a hand over his mouth, hoping to disguise his Irish brogue. The woman took the pasties, put them in a microwave oven behind her, and rang up the items on her register while Flannery looked on in wonderment. He had not seen microwave ovens in prison and couldn't remember just when they'd been invented.

He left the truck stop with his food tucked in a brown paper bag. He walked along a secondary road toward the city of Birmingham, its lights reflecting off the low cloud cover above, and soon came to a large culvert under the road through which a single railroad track passed.

He left the embankment and crawled around the edge of the culvert, cautiously entering it in case there were rats or other humans inside. He was alone. He sat down and greedily ate the pasties and gulped the milk. He looked around his immediate area and found several large cardboard boxes, easily constructing a temporary shelter that provided enough warmth. He then dozed off and slept rather well under the circumstances until the morning sunrise woke him.

Flannery walked for nearly five hours, continuing on a course toward the center of Birmingham. He moved in a deliberate manner at a strong pace, giving the impression to passersby that he knew where he was going and wasn't interested in hitching a ride. Besides being hungry and thirsty again, his feet were hurting; prison boots were made only for doing manual labor and not for hiking.

A half hour before noon, he came to a densely populated residential area of three story tenement houses, one after another on both sides of the street, for as far as he could see. The neighborhood appeared promising so he looked carefully at each house he passed. When he saw one with a sign in the window advertising ROOMS TO LET, he went up and rang the door bell.

A small elderly woman answered the door, thin with gray hair and wearing a soiled white apron over a frayed blue house dress. When she got her first look at Flannery, her jaw dropped and she was speechless.

"Begging your pardon, missus," he said, "but I saw your sign and I'd like to rent one of your rooms."

"Good heavens. You look like you've been in the mines for months."

Flannery smiled. "Oh no, missus, I'm a mechanic and I had to work some extra shifts to get our lorries back on the road again."

"Well come inside then." After he passed through the door, she added, "But don't touch anything."

Her entry parlor was warm and the smell of food cooking in the kitchen almost caused him to double up in pain.

"I've several rooms available," she said. "It's forty-nine quid a week with a private bath and thirty-five without. You pay each week in advance and I don't allow any food in the rooms because the insects would be taking over the place. Any meal you have in my kitchen is extra. Would you fancy a look around before you decide?"

"No need for that, missus. I'll take the room with a bath. And a bit of lunch for now if it's not too much trouble." He pulled out a wad of crumpled bills from his pocket and gave her fifty pounds.

"Thank you very much, mister—you haven't told me your name."

"It's Sullivan. Paul Sullivan."

"Then come with me, Mr. Sullivan, and I'll show you to your room."

They climbed the stairway to the second floor and walked down the hallway to a room on the right. It was open and when they entered, a slight breeze came through the open window, billowing the sheer white curtain.

"It's a lovely room indeed," murmured Flannery.

She picked up a room key from the top of a chest of drawers and handed it to him. "I should think you'd wish to clean up a bit before you have your meal." Then she sniffed the air several times and said as she left, "Yes, please do have a good scrubbing."

He dumped the contents of his black bag on the double bed and separated the cosmetics from the rest of the items. He took the bottles into the bathroom, stripped off his clothes, and took a hot bath.

After he toweled off, he pulled the soggy band-aid from his upper lip and inspected his mustache. It was not as full as he wished but given

CHAPTER THIRTY-ONE

another week it would be to his liking. He went to work with the bottles of dye and changed his red hair to black. He gave himself a close shave and, after thirty minutes had elapsed, rinsed the dye from his hair. As he dressed, he made a mental note to find a Marks & Spencer and buy some more underwear and a new set of outer clothes to replace his factory worker coveralls.

The landlady was pleasantly surprised when a freshly scrubbed Flannery appeared in her kitchen. Since he was the only boarder present at this hour, she invited him to sit at the small table near the rear window instead of the long trestle table in the dining room. She served fried plaice, a popular whitefish from the south coast of England, along with boiled potatoes, wheat bread and butter, and a hot cup of tea. He ate in silence and devoured everything he was given, content to look out and admire her abundant pink and yellow roses.

After his filling lunch, he went back to his room, took off his boots and coveralls, and lay down on the ultra soft bed. He immediately fell into a deep sleep.

Hours later, Flannery awoke with a start, cold and confused. He momentarily forgot where he was and looked about the darkened room for clues. He relaxed upon remembering he had rented this private room and, after several minutes of quiet contemplation, decided that his life's quality had improved one hundredfold in the last twenty-four hours. *This calls for a tiny celebration. There must be a pub nearby where I can have a pint or two while enjoying me freedom.*

There was indeed such a place, the landlady informed him, and gave him directions to the Globe & Anchor only two short blocks away. He found the pub within ten minutes, but before entering, he looked cautiously through several plate glass windows to gauge the relative safety of the premises. Like most English pubs, this one was divided into two parts: the 'public bar' which was dominated by a dozen or so men, and a 'saloon bar' that was less crowded and had more comfortable places to sit. Both bars were smoke-filled and rather dimly lit so he chose the saloon bar where he could have a few pints and a meal in quiet mixed company.

He found an empty booth in the corner where he could watch the other clientele as well as the main entrance. He also took note of a door to the alleyway at the rear of the bar, a possible escape route if he felt in danger of being caught. Halfway through his second pint of bitter, he relaxed again, feeling the glow of the beer's alcohol, opening his senses to the loud rock music coming out of the pub's sound system, and savoring several cigarettes. He was enjoying the experience immensely when a forty-something woman walked into the pub and took a seat in the booth next to his. *Here now, 'tis the icing on the cake.*

The woman was only a few inches over five feet, but seemed taller because of her stiletto heels and tight black leather pants. She wore a tan leopard skin top that was tight and cut low in front, exposing a large quivering pair of breasts. Her hair was a beehive of dirty blond curls and her pudgy round face was overly made up to accentuate thick ruby lips and saucer-like blue eyes. Flannery concluded that she would be his before midnight and flashed her a wide smile. She returned his smile in what appeared to be a friendly invitation.

He picked up his beer and ambled over. "You look like a girl that would enjoy some company. Mind if I sit down?"

"It's a free country," she replied with casual indifference, "but I'm expecting a friend to join me soon."

"Would you fancy a drink?"

She gave him a faint smile and said, "A gin and orange squash would be lovely, thank you very much."

Flannery ordered her drink and another pint for himself. Their initial conversation was guarded at first and limited to generalities. The woman gave her name as Sophie and said she was employed as a spot welder. Flannery gave her his phony name and concocted a story about recently moving from London to Birmingham in search of a truck mechanic's job. As their talks progressed, he took in several deep whiffs of her perfume and his eyes darted between her eyes, mouth, and heaving bosom. He was not only nervous in this first close encounter with a woman in many years, but had become fully aroused. If he had to stand up right now, he and Sophie would probably be embarrassed by the large bulge in his trousers. He decided that the pace of courtship should be speeded up.

"Looks like your friend may not show," he said.

"Not to worry," she replied. "He often runs a bit late."

"Look, why don't we go back to me own place? We can have a lot more

CHAPTER THIRTY-ONE

privacy and get to know each other much better."

She grunted a short laugh and gave him a startled look. "You want me to go off with you? Now why should I do that?"

Flannery eagerly reached into his pocket and pulled out a wad of bills. "See, I've got money. I can make it worth your while. What's your usual? A hundred? A hundred and fifty quid?"

Sophie answered in a loud angry voice, "Put your bloody money away. What do you take me for?"

Before Flannery could answer, a large presence loomed next to their booth in the form of a huge man who was a head taller than Flannery and outweighed him by at least fifty pounds. When Flannery looked up and noted his shaved head, black mustache and goatee, and the absence of any neck, his erection shriveled.

"Here now," the man barked. "What's the problem, Sophie?"

"Oh hullo, Bruno. This *gentleman* here just offered me money to go with him to his room. He thinks I'm a whore."

Bruno leaned over, grabbed the front of Flannery's coveralls with his right hand and stood him up, his left hand cocked for a punch. "You've insulted my lady, you bloody fool. You apologize right here and now."

Flannery had mixed emotions at this point: half anger at Sophie for sandbagging him and half fear of being found out and arrested by the police should they be called. *If this encounter had taken place in prison, Bruno would have a knife sticking out of his gigantic belly by now.* Prudence and caution were the watchwords so Flannery backed down meekly. "Very sorry, I am. I meant no harm. I was truly in the wrong and I offer me sincerest apologies."

Bruno loosened his grip and pushed Flannery back down in his chair. For good measure, Flannery turned to Sophie and offered some more words of contrition. "I don't know what came over me. Talking that way to a fine lady such as yourself. Me sainted mother would truly be ashamed, God rest her soul."

Bruno crossed his bulky arms across his large chest and boomed, "Another drunken Mick. I should have known."

Sophie got up and took Bruno's hand. "Let's go somewhere else," she said. "This place wouldn't be the same with *him* about."

As Sophie and Bruno left, Flannery picked up his glass and returned to his former booth. The rest of the pub's clientele returned to their own drinking, eating and conversation.

Flannery quietly and slowly sipped his beer, ruminating on the disturbance he had just experienced. In less than two days after his successful escape, it had almost gone down the sewer in an ironic disaster. He would have to curb his lustful appetite and be much more careful if he was going to accomplish his all-important mission of finding and dealing with Averil.

Chapter Thirty-Two

A light thunderstorm passed through St. Louis late Saturday evening and the streets were still wet when Mark left his hotel the next morning for the drive to Holy Family Church. He knelt in a pew at the rear, folded his hands, and looked straight ahead to the rear wall. As he stared at the figure of Christ hanging on the cross, his mind articulated a rambling prayer:

Here I am again, God, your unworthy and miserable servant. I probably shouldn't even be here today, given the sins I've committed lately. But it gives me something I really need, a place where I'm at peace with you and the world.

So what is it with you, anyway? You give me a healthy sex drive so that I can't resist this married woman who comes back into my life and wants to jump into bed with me. But it's a sin, a mortal sin. You know it. I know it. I suppose it's a worse sin against Averil than it is against you, although I wouldn't find out about that unless I died right now and you decided to ship me off to hell instead of being with you in heaven. Sounds to me like a classic case of double jeopardy, but I'd be the last person to haggle over the legalities of the situation with you.

OK, I know I've done some heavy duty sinning and I'm asking for your forgiveness. Yes, I should go to confession, but you know how busy I've been. I just haven't had the time. I could have probably gone to confession instead of rolling around in bed with Joan Soric those couple of times. But it's been so long since my last confession, I wouldn't know where to start. Heck, I've never even told a priest about having an affair with Averil and, of course, getting married to her in a civil ceremony instead of a mass means that I'm excommunicated, doesn't it? So it comes back to maybe I haven't the right to be here at all.

But you're a merciful God, right? I mean, everything I've read in the missal says you are and you know my heart's in the right place even though this plumbing below my belt is often not in the right place. You probably don't want me to see Joan again and you'd surely advise me to avoid the temptation. Well, I can probably do that, but I need some help. Your help. Please give me the strength to handle this situation if and when it comes up again. What was it that St. Augustine said before he cleaned up his act? 'Oh Lord, make me chaste—but not just yet.'

It's pretty clear to me now that nothing but trouble can come from continuing to fool around with her. I don't believe we have a future together so what's the point of taking all these risks? For a few moments in some hotel room? Her marriage could be threatened and so could mine and neither one of us would be very happy if we were found out. And Joan's relationship with her son? That could turn into a real nightmare. Hey, I've been through this sorry routine before, but Joan hasn't, so she has no idea of the grief she's courting by trying to make up for lost time.

And please watch over Averil while she's in England and get her back home to Long Island as soon as possible. This guy Flannery—what are you going to do about him? How long is he going to remain on the loose while terrorizing the English countryside? Couldn't you arrange for him to be killed in some kind of accident? Maybe the police could find him and pump a couple of hundred rounds of thirty caliber armor piercing into his worthless scumbag body.

If Averil ever found out I was cheating on her, she'd be devastated. I've only seen her crying a few times and if I were to cause her any pain, I'd never forgive myself. Somehow, I've got to take control and be a more responsible husband to this woman. I can't take any more chances and lose the dearest thing I have.

His prayer was interrupted by an elderly couple who entered his pew and knelt down next to him. Mark sat down and shortly thereafter, the organist began playing an anthem he recognized from another time and place many years ago. A few minutes later, Father Jerome and Deacon Ray came out of the sacristy in their green vestments and the mass started.

CHAPTER THIRTY-TWO

Mark wallowed in the graceful pomp and comfortable ritual of the service and even welcomed the acrid suffocation of burning incense. He responded to all the prayers without having to refer to the missal tucked into a wooden pocket on the pew back in front of him. It was almost a mechanical process, the words having been engraved into his subconscious in grade school.

All was going well until Deacon Ray began reading the assigned gospel, a text by Saint Mark. Mark Holloway tried to swallow but something rose suddenly in his throat that produced a mild coughing fit. The spasm quieted long enough for Mark to hear the deacon reading this portion of the gospel:

> *"Good teacher, what must I do to inherit eternal life?" Jesus answered him, "Why do you call me good? No one is good but God alone. You know the commandments: You shall not kill; you shall not commit adultery; you shall not steal; . . ."*

Mark looked heavenward with his eyes closed and said another silent prayer. *Good timing there, Lord. Right on, the old sixth commandment trick again. OK, I get the message. You made your point.*

When the deacon finished, Mark awaited Father Jerome's homily with mixed emotions. *I'm really anxious to hear him speak, but I hope he doesn't harp on this adultery business. I couldn't bring myself to look at him, thinking all the time about screwing his mother.*

But instead of Father Jerome talking to the congregation, the podium was turned over to a pair of tiny Franciscan nuns from Mexico. They were touring the Mid-West and asking for donations to help the poor members of their missions. Mark was so taken by their heartfelt appeal that he plopped a twenty dollar bill into the collection basket when it came around, hoping to ease his restless guilt over his extra-marital dalliances with Joan.

As the mass progressed, Mark wrestled with another problem; what should he do about communion? He went through a long and convoluted process of rationalization and finally decided that he would receive, but not from Father Jerome. His conscience could only be stretched so far.

He entered the line on the right side of the main aisle, a queue served by Deacon Ray. But just before Mark got to him, the deacon ran out of hosts and had to retreat to the altar for a new supply. To Mark's surprise and mounting panic, Father Jerome beckoned to all those in the deacon's line. Father Jerome was out of customers so those in the deacon's line wouldn't have to wait for his return.

Mark was trapped. He couldn't turn around and go back without causing a scene, so he meekly and obediently took the wafer in his hands from Father Jerome and then returned to his pew.

Instead of ministering to the next person in line, Father Jerome paused while watching Mark retreat. The next person in line was an elderly woman who, tired of waiting for Father Jerome to snap out of his daze, made an impatient grumble.

The mass concluded without any more unusual incidents. Immediately after Father Jerome gave the final blessing, Mark was out of his pew, exiting the church smartly, and driving his rental car out of the parking lot. This was enough excitement for him in one morning.

As Father Jerome came down the main aisle with Deacon Ray and the servers, he strained his neck right and left, looking out among the departing parishioners to get a glimpse of his mystery guest. But the man was nowhere in sight. While he was standing in front of the main entrance talking to congregation members, Father Jerome received another surprise. Stephanie, wearing a long dark blue wool dress, walked up and greeted him in a formal but cheerful manner.

"Well, this is a pleasant surprise," he said. "Have you been inside the church all this time?"

"I sure was, but I was on the side of the altar today so that's why you didn't see me." She looked keenly at his face and asked, "You look a little funny. Is something wrong?"

Suddenly his face lit up. "That's it. It was him—Mark Holloway."

"Jerry, what are you talking about?"

"There was a man at mass today and I gave him communion. I knew I'd seen him before, but I couldn't put a name with his face. I just now figured it out. It had to be Mark Holloway, the airline pilot I met this summer at the Abbey."

"The same man your mom dated in college?"

CHAPTER THIRTY-TWO

"Yep, the very same gent. But if it was, why didn't he stick around and say hello? I would have loved catching up with him over a cup of coffee."

"That is strange. But they say that everybody has a twin somewhere on earth, someone that looks exactly like them." Father Jerome didn't answer but bowed his head slightly and rubbed his hands together. "If it was Mark Holloway, wouldn't your mom know about him being here in St. Louis? Surely she'd tell you about that, wouldn't she?"

"You're right, Steph. Guess this was just another one of those amazing coincidences. Which prompts another question. What good fortune brought you to my mass today?"

"I need to talk with you. Do you have a couple of minutes?"

"For you, always. If you don't mind braving a small crowd, we can get some coffee in the parish fellowship hall. Give me a few minutes to change."

He joined her ten minutes later in the fellowship hall, dressed in his black secular clothes, and they sat opposite each other at a rectangular dining table. They didn't attract the kind of stares experienced on their dinner date several months ago because, by now, the parishioners were quite accustomed to seeing Father Jerome counsel attractive young women during his after-mass coffee klatches.

"All right then," he said, "what's on your mind?"

Stephanie tilted her head slightly and, with a casual flip of her hand, brushed her loose blond hair back over her ear. This unconscious feminine movement did not go unnoticed and he smiled in affectionate appreciation. "It's several things," she began. "First of all, I'm going back to college, just after the first of the year."

Jerry arched his eyebrows slightly. "You're not wasting time, are you?"

"Justin came through with the first payment on our property settlement agreement, so I thought I'd make a move while I'm still in the mood."

"Are you going back to Washington U?"

"Oh no, the University of Illinois. At Urbana-Champaign."

"That's a surprise. Why did you pick that one?"

"A couple of reasons. Their law school is one of the top ten in the country and it's only a hundred and seventy miles from St. Louis. I can get back here often—it's only about three hours on the interstate."

"You mean you're going right into law school?"

"No, not really. I'm taking a semester of pre-law courses first. I want to get those good study habits back under my belt before I tackle the heavy stuff."

"I'm very pleased for you, Steph. Sounds like you're making that dream come true. I know you'll do well in law school."

"There's something else. Something a bit more personal. I'm dating a man and it's starting to get serious."

"Uh oh, do I really want to hear this?"

"C'mon now, Jerry. You're still my friend. No need to get defensive."

"OK, so what's he like?"

"Well, he's a few years older than I. I wouldn't use the old tall, dark and handsome cliché, but he's attractive to me. He's an attorney but not with our firm. I met him when I had to take some papers to his office. He was on the opposite side of a case we were litigating."

"Does he have a name?"

"Timothy, but I call him Tim-the-Timid. That's a joke—he's anything but timid. We have some really lively discussions. Not quite arguments."

"Opposites attract, so they say."

Stephanie rambled on excitedly for a while and Jerry's mind started to wander. A slightly conflicting situation presented itself because the only woman he'd ever loved was now seriously attracted to another man. He even felt the tiniest pangs of jealousy, envy, and God knows what else. But the analytical part of his brain was telling him he had made *his* choice and could never be with her again; he should rejoice in *her* happiness, *her* good fortune, and wish her well.

She got his attention again when she concluded her spiel. "The only fly in the ointment I can see is the religious angle. He's Catholic."

Jerry smiled. "Maybe he'd be interested in becoming a priest. You want me to talk with him?"

"You're not funny, Jerome Soric. I want some advice on how to handle this."

"That's a pretty tall order, Steph. I'm not sure I can be totally objective. About you and another man. Can you understand my position?"

"Sure, I understand. But don't leave me out in the cold."

"You probably don't need to do anything right now. Just keep the communication channels open. Discuss everything with Tim. And I mean

CHAPTER THIRTY-TWO

everything. If you get to the point of talking marriage, then be sure that both of you are in *total* agreement about what happens after marriage. Now I'm not suggesting you convert to Catholicism—that's something you have to examine within your own conscience and religious framework. It would probably be best to talk with a priest in Tim's parish if it comes to that."

She nodded her head and rested her folded hands on top of the table. "You know, Jerry, I don't want to wind up like your mother."

"My mom? What's she got to do with this?"

"I had a long talk with her several months ago and the subject of Mark Holloway came up. I think she still harbors some regrets about not being able to reconcile her religious differences with him. In fact, I think she still loves him in some small way."

Jerry's face took on a mildly embarrassed look. "Well, I can't talk to her about something like that. It's more woman-to-woman talk than a friendly mother and son chat." After several moments of silence, Jerry had another suggestion. "Why don't you have another talk with mom? Tell her everything you've told me. Get the benefit of her experience and see what kind of advice she might have. It should be more objective and valuable than what I can offer you right now."

She got up to leave and said, "I'll do that. And I'll let you know what happens."

He looked up at her and noticed a teary glaze over her blue eyes. "I only want the best for you, Steph."

She patted his shoulder before leaving. "I know, Jerry. I know."

Chapter Thirty-Three

Mark awoke just before six o'clock on Monday, brewed a small pot of coffee, and placed a call to Averil. "Sure glad to hear your voice again, honey. I missed you a lot."

"That's always nice to hear, luv. How are you coping without me?"

"Not very well, I'm afraid. I'll be glad when all of this is over. I want us to be together again, back in our own bed."

"I'll drink to that. So how was your weekend—many fun things to do?"

"Naw, it was pretty dull. I worked out Saturday morning, then did the tourist thing at the big arch near the river. But I did get to mass on Sunday. Then I spent the afternoon here at the hotel pool—sunning, swimming, and catching up with office work." Mark hoped that Averil believed his story enough not to dwell on it. "Any more news about Flannery?"

"Nothing at all. Even Chief Inspector Hungerford said that his trail had grown cold. They're watching carefully, hoping he'll make a mistake."

"He's probably hiding somewhere, waiting until things quiet down. Just like a rat in a hole."

"I do have some good news. Emma came over and we've found a lovely place for Mum. The Botley Manor, just a few miles from her home."

"That's wonderful. What does Charlotte think about it?"

"She called it *suitable* and that's high praise indeed, coming from Mum."

"Then you'll be coming home soon?"

"As soon as possible. We've applied for admission and she's accepted for November first."

"Ouch, I wish it was sooner."

"We need the time, luv. There's plenty for us to do now, such as disposing of a great deal of her furniture."

"I should be there with you to help out."

"You have your own work to do. I'll just have to lean harder on Emma. We'll get the job done, even if we have to hire some temporary laborers."

CHAPTER THIRTY-THREE

When their conversation ended several minutes later, Mark stepped into the bathroom, removed his shorts and undershirt, and held them close to his nose. He inhaled deeply before tossing them into a corner, thinking that he could detect the aroma of Joan's perfume, oozing from his body and permeating his clothing. He took a long hot shower, hoping to rinse away all traces of his Saturday afternoon interlude with her.

Later in his office, Mark was having a cup of coffee while reviewing a user operations manual for the simulator when his phone rang.

"Hi, it's me. I need to talk. Do you have a minute?"

Mark could tell Joan was upset. "Let me close my door." When he sat down again, he said, "You sound like you're mad about something. Are you all right?"

"No, I'm not. Jerry came over to the house for dinner last night and told us a very interesting story. How some man who looked just like that Mark Holloway fellow appeared in his line for holy communion yesterday."

Mark cleared his throat while his mind started spinning. *Oh, shit. Guess I didn't pull it off after all.* "What did you say?"

"What did I say? That's beside the point. Was it you?"

Mark sighed. "Yes, but I didn't plan to see Jerry. I just wanted to go to mass."

"You idiot!" she screamed. "I thought we talked about this. We had an agreement that you weren't going to contact him. You promised. And then you go and pull a dumb stunt like this."

"I'm sorry, Joan, but it was an accident. I was in another communion line and got forced into Jerry's line. I had no choice."

"You made me look like an absolute fool in front of Frank and Jerry. I had to pretend that I knew nothing—nothing at all—about you being in town. I don't know if Frank believed me or not, but I think Jerry's convinced it was just another coincidence. Somebody that happened to look a lot like you."

"I left when mass was over. I got out of there quick so he wouldn't see me."

"He said he looked for you after mass. It's a damn good thing you bailed out. That convinced him it wasn't you." Joan calmed down and continued, "I'm a little curious about something. You say you went to communion. Did you suddenly forget about our little love-making session Saturday afternoon? How did you manage to twist your conscience around so you could receive communion?"

This latter bit of questioning irritated Mark because it revealed Joan's knowledge of the Catholic faith, something that he had badly underestimated. "It's hard to explain," he said. "It was just something that I needed to do. Can we talk about this some other time?"

"Yeah, that's right Mark. Kick the can ahead. You're very good at dodging the serious issues."

"I'm sorry," he said again, trying to sound convincingly contrite.

"Another thing that's really unfair," she continued to rail. "I don't think you appreciate the risks I've been taking. We're doing all this fooling around here on my home turf where I could be easily recognized and found out. You, on the other hand, don't even live around here anymore and your wife is off in England. The whole setup is made to order so you can have a nice little fling for yourself."

Mark bristled. "Now wait just a damn minute. It was your idea to come out to my hotel the other night for dinner. And I sure never twisted your arm to get into my bed. You know what they say—takes two to tango, my friend."

Joan sniffled and Mark sensed that she was on the verge of tears. "I think we should take a break and not see each other for a while. I need to do some serious thinking about my marriage and my relationship with Jerry."

Mark felt a huge sense of relief with her suggestion. "I'll go you even one better. Let's make it permanent and not see each other again. Ever."

Joan paused for a moment on hearing this unexpected reaction. "Just like that, huh? Don't you have any feelings for me at all?"

"Of course I do. But if we continued with this, we'd both get torn apart eventually. Neither of us is free to make a commitment right now. And what if your husband or my wife found out about us? Two marriages would go up in smoke and a lot of lives would be ruined."

"Can we still be friends?"

"I don't think we can be *just* friends anymore. We both made some choices during the last couple of weeks—we did things together that we can't pretend never happened."

Joan started crying again. "Damn it all, Mark, I hate it whenever you leave."

CHAPTER THIRTY-THREE

Mark became sad and felt a strong urge to take her in his arms and hold her tightly. After a long silence, he tried to console her. "I'm sorry it didn't work out. I really am. Maybe in a different time and place, we could have . . ."

After another long silence, Joan managed a faint response. "Then it's good-bye again. I'll never forget you and there will always be that special place in my heart for you."

After she hung up, Mark swiveled his chair around so he could look out the window. *So this is the way an affair ends. It's probably for the best anyway; it wasn't going anywhere and most of the risk was on her side, just like she said. Too bad she didn't think of that when she called me and suggested coming out to my hotel. No, that's not fair. Why did I have to send her those roses? Or invite her to have lunch with me? Or even take this job when I should have kept on my flight schedule?*

Mark shivered as he rose from his chair, opened his office door, and went to Nancy's cubicle in search of more coffee.

At three o'clock that afternoon, Mark walked to the simulator at the rear of the SIMFLIGHT facility. The room containing the system was two stories high. The simulator cabin, a rectangular box about the size of a large bathroom, was at the upper level and connected to its control room by a metal catwalk. The cabin itself was supported by a dozen telescoping metal rods that were hydraulically operated. Power and computer cables hung down from its bottom like umbilicals and were connected to the machinery below. In Mark's view, the entire system resembled some kind of super daddy-long-legs, a mutated form that could have been copied from any of the Star Wars movies.

Mark was welcomed to the control room by Tom Campbell, Dick Hightower, Fritz Delano, and a half dozen additional engineers. "Ready to give our baby a spin?" asked Tom.

"Ready as I'll ever be," said Mark.

Dick gave him a quick briefing on the flight scenario. "I'll be here in the control room and Fritz will be in the co-pilot's seat. If that's all right with you."

Mark smiled at Fritz and cautioned, "Glad to have you, podner, as long as you don't touch any of the controls."

"No danger of that," said Fritz. "I'm just coming along for the ride."

Dick continued, "OK then, let's get started. You know the routine, Mark. And be alert for any unusual events."

Mark looked intently at Dick, trying to find some meaning behind his last statement, but brushed it off as techno-macho small talk.

Mark and Fritz went into the simulator cabin and took their respective seats. Mark looked around and marveled at how closely the cabin's interior resembled and even smelled like an actual aircraft cockpit. Mark exercised the flight controls and both put on intercom headsets. After Mark checked all the display readouts, he spoke into his microphone. "All systems are looking good in here."

"Standby, Mark," said Dick. "We're going to crank her up."

Mark and Fritz felt a jolt as the simulator jumped and came to life. The apparatus supporting the cabin had been designed to allow the cabin to move among six different spatial axes, either one at a time or several simultaneously.

The instruments registered a flight heading of ninety degrees, an altitude of 34,000 feet, and a current position somewhere over northwestern New Mexico. The cabin bucked and rocked as they 'flew' east, giving Mark and Fritz the realistic sensation of mild clear air turbulence. Mark even noticed a faint hum in his earphones, a noise that sounded like the engines on the Trans-Global aircraft that he was used to flying. The sky-blue display at the front of the cockpit was also computer-controlled and gave them a view that an actual plane would encounter in daylight at the same altitude.

After only five minutes of 'flight,' Mark's mind involuntarily wandered as he recalled Joan's telephone call. *Why did she have to get so defensive when Jerry told her he'd seen somebody that looked like me? Surely she's a better actress than that. She's not stupid; she could have easily faked innocence. Don't all women have that gift for artful deception?*

I wonder just how long she and Frank have gone without sex? Did she mention that it had been years? That night in my hotel room—it seemed so easy for her—like she'd done this kind of thing before. Have I been fooling myself here, thinking that I'm the only guy she's been sleeping with? Well, sure it was good, I can't deny that. Like we were long-time

CHAPTER THIRTY-THREE

lovers and had been doing it for years. But then again, maybe she faked her orgasms.

"You're coming up on a VORTAC," said Dick over the intercom. "Get ready for a course change."

Mark snapped out of his reverie. "Roger, VORTAC approaching." A few minutes later, Mark 'banked the aircraft' slowly to the left on a new heading of sixty-five degrees that would take him over Alamosa, Colorado.

"Everything's looking good in here," said Dick. "How is she handling?"

"Very smooth," answered Mark, "just like the real thing."

After another five minutes of 'cruising,' Mark's thoughts drifted again, but this time toward Averil. *I'm glad that she and Emma found a nice place for Charlotte. About two more weeks and Averil will be ready and able to come home. I should probably take some vacation time when she returns. Get to know my wife again. Man, I sure hope the police nail this Flannery scumbag soon. She won't be safe again until he's caught and returned to prison, and I won't stop worrying about her until that happens.*

Bam! The cabin suddenly bucked hard to the left, causing Mark to snap out of his daydream in a mild panic. He gripped the control yoke firmly and struggled to return the cabin to its normal attitude. A red light above the cockpit windshield flashed on and off, accompanied by a blaring noise that stopped and started in synchronism with the red light.

"Oh shit," said Mark. "We've got a fire in number one engine."

"Understand fire in number one," Dick echoed.

Mark reached up to a bank of switches with his right hand and said, "Feathering number one."

To Mark's astonishment and slowly mounting horror, the simulator cabin collapsed on its support rods, the windshield display turned black, and the auxiliary lighting came on. Mark looked at Fritz and asked, "What happened? What the hell's going on?"

Fritz replied sheepishly, "I think Dick just shut us down."

"How come?" asked a wide-eyed Mark.

The cabin door opened and an agitated Dick Hightower entered as Mark got out of his seat. "You know what you did?" asked Dick. "You shut down the wrong damned engine. You were flying with one dead and one burning out of control."

Mark turned around and stared in disbelief at the switch panel. He turned back to Dick and said in a low voice, "By God, you're right. I did." Mark started trembling and continued, "I've never made a mistake like that before. Thank God it wasn't a real situation—at night over the Atlantic."

Dick placed a hand on Mark's shoulder. "Are you OK? You want to call it quits for today?"

Mark jerked his head up. "Hell no. Just give me a couple of minutes. After I take a pee break, let's do it again. Different scenario this time— one where I don't screw it up."

Fritz offered a few consoling words. "Maybe those switches aren't labeled as well as they could be. Or maybe they should be in different positions."

"Nice try, Fritz," said Mark, "but there's nothing wrong with those switches. It was just a full-blown case of pilot error."

As Mark stood in front of the urinal, another thought crossed his mind. *If I can stop thinking about pussy for an hour, I just might be able to fly the son-of-a-bitch correctly.*

Chapter Thirty-Four

Sean Flannery talked with his landlady just after Tuesday's dinner. She had inquired whether he'd be staying another week. If so, she said she would very much appreciate another fifty pounds which would continue to make him a most welcome guest.

Flannery politely declined and told her that he'd be leaving the next morning for Liverpool where he was certain to find work. He had left the rooming house every morning since his arrival, presumably on a job hunting quest, a story that he faithfully repeated whenever she asked if he was having any luck. The truth of the matter involved something completely different. Instead, he went daily to a local library where he spent hours pouring over newspapers and reference materials concerning other countries.

The newspapers featured less and less about Flannery's escape as each day passed. This gave him not only more confidence, but a certain boldness for the formulation of his next move. The research he did in the library's reference section was more extensive. His aim was to find a country where he could live openly without fear of extradition, with or without Averil, even if his true identity became known by the local law enforcement authorities. His preference was South America but he didn't rule out either the Middle East or Central America. A more pressing concern, however, dealt with entering the United States. Before settling anywhere as a permanent resident, he would have to enter the U.S., find Averil, and then make another successful escape. It could be done, he reasoned; he would just have to find a clever way to make it happen.

The next morning, after eating a large breakfast, Flannery packed all his belongings into a brand new suitcase he bought at Marks & Spencer the day before. He'd also purchased shoes, a suit, and several shirts and was now dressed in his new finery. The suit was a rather common looking brown wool fabric, the shirt a pale green cotton, and the tie a dark green with muted red and gold stripes. He was pleased with his appearance because it looked so ordinary; a black pin-striped suit, a white shirt, and a regimental tie would have looked and felt out of place. He looked in the bathroom mirror, adjusted his tie, and tried to critically examine his appearance. His mustache was now full and matched his dark hair.

Flannery quietly left the rooming house, intentionally not saying goodbye to his landlady. He didn't want her to remember what he was wearing as he left, just in case the police came around and made inquiries about a Mr. Sullivan. He took a bus to the railroad station and, instead of buying a ticket to Liverpool, bought a one-way coach fare to London.

He arrived at Euston station several hours later. As he debarked the train and made his way through the terminal, he recalled the many times he passed through years ago when he was courting Averil. He found a small rundown hotel nearby and rented a room for a week at a price that was almost double what he paid in Birmingham.

After unpacking his belongings, Flannery left the hotel and took the underground to the Marble Arch at the corner of Oxford Street and Park Lane. He walked down Oxford Street and entered the Selfridge Department Store, leisurely moving from one section of the store to the next like a casual shopper with a great deal of time on his hands. When he came to the department that offered women's gloves and purses, the same one that Averil had worked in, he recognized a familiar face. He could barely control his excitement.

Claire Blackwell had changed little since he had last seen her sixteen long years ago. Her hair was longer now, well below her shoulders, and he thought she was probably coloring it a lighter shade of brown than it had been before. Although she had obviously gained a few pounds over the years, she was still an attractive woman. Flannery was quite pleased with her overall appearance because it would make the next part of his mission even that much more enjoyable.

He wanted to move in closer, but he wasn't completely sure that his disguise would fool her. If she recognized him, she might scream for help and that was the last thing he wanted, so he left the store.

That evening, Flannery sat alone at a small table in the Hogshead, the same pub where he'd met Averil and Claire long ago. He had just finished his third pint of beer and a large order of fish and chips and was now enjoying a cigarette. He chuckled to himself as he looked around the pub,

CHAPTER THIRTY-FOUR

thinking that little had changed over the years. Apparently the management didn't want to spend much money to spruce up the place.

He ordered another pint and, after the waitress left, he patted the large wad of twenty pound notes tucked away in his suit coat, reassuring himself that it was still there. He had visited a bank that afternoon, one that specialized in off-shore accounts and foreign exchange. After presenting his bogus identification papers, the teller completed the necessary work to close out his account, the one that had been holding his money since his capture. Flannery scooped up just over 3100 pounds in cash and quickly left the bank.

He watched and waited, slowly sipping his beer, hoping that Claire would come to the pub this evening. As time passed, however, he decided that she had gone elsewhere for her customary after-work drink. He wondered if she still lived in the apartment near the one where he and Averil had lived together. *It's worth a gamble,* he thought. *I'll just take meself over that way and see if me hunch is correct.* Flannery finished his pint, walked to a nearby underground station, and was in South Kensington in a matter of minutes.

He found the familiar three story apartment building and walked confidently up to the front entrance as if he were an expected visitor. He examined the nameplates next to the front door, each with its associated doorbell button, and saw the lettering C. BLACKWELL printed on a card in one of the six slots. He walked half-way around the block to the rear of Claire's apartment building; it was quiet all around as he stood silently, pondering his next move.

Once his eyes became accustomed to the darkness, he noticed that the only way to reach the rear of her second story apartment was up a rickety fire escape ladder. While thinking about how noisy his climb might be, a train thundered by, close enough so that Flannery could feel a vibration through his shoes. *That's the answer. I'll make me move when the next train comes along.*

He didn't have long to wait. When the next train rumbled by minutes later, Flannery scrambled up the ladder and rested against the apartment's rear door. Once he regained his breath, he tried opening the door but no amount of jimmying would make it yield. Finally, he wrapped his handkerchief around his right hand and, when the next train passed by, smashed in the window immediately next to the door. Reaching his other hand through the window, he was able to unbolt the door and enter the apartment's kitchen.

He stood still in the center of the room, listening for any sounds, and moved his head around from right to left, trying to gain an appreciation for the size and shape of the room. Satisfied that he was alone, he rummaged through several cabinet drawers until he found a small flashlight.

Flannery made a quick inspection of the entire apartment, pausing only to look at a number of framed photographs displayed on a table in the living room. Two photos in particular caught his eye: one showing Claire and Malachy O'Brien seated closely at a night club table; and the other, Claire and Averil standing in front of a carnival entrance with their arms around each other's waist. Flannery became angry and was seriously tempted to destroy the latter one, however, he gently returned the picture to its original position.

He returned to the kitchen, found a half-full bottle of cheap whiskey, and poured himself a generous portion in a small tumbler. He took the flashlight and whiskey into the darkened living room, removed his jacket, and settled into a large overstuffed chair turned to face the front door. The whiskey warmed and relaxed him as he waited for Claire's eventual arrival.

Several hours later, a dozing Flannery was awakened by the front door being unlocked. He sat motionless as Claire entered the apartment, locked the door behind her, and tossed her coat at a nearby chair. She walked quickly to her bathroom, turned on the light, and sat on the toilet for a minute in obvious relief.

She made her way directly to the kitchen, turned on the light, and put a kettle of water on the stove for tea. She stopped suddenly when she realized that the room was colder than normal. A mounting sense of terror came over her as she looked about and noticed the broken window and whiskey bottle on the counter.

Someone's broken into my apartment. Someone wants to rob me—although God knows I haven't anything valuable enough to steal. Have I been robbed? Could the burglar still be here in the apartment?

She reached into a drawer and quietly pulled out a large butcher knife.

CHAPTER THIRTY-FOUR

She headed slowly down the hallway to the living room, intending to get far enough into the room so she could turn on a light. As she stepped through the doorway, a waiting Flannery swung a candlestick holder against her hand, sending the knife skittering across the wooden floor.

Claire was too startled to cry out, but Flannery, not wanting to risk her screams, came up behind and placed a hand over her mouth. Her survival instincts kicked in and she started struggling, but Flannery moved her over to the couch and forced her to lie on her side while he lay on top of her, his mouth next to her ear.

"Now, Claire," he spoke soothingly, "be a good girl. It's just an old friend who's come to pay a visit. After you give me some information, I'll be on me way."

A few sounds came from her mouth but he couldn't understand what she was saying. He continued talking softly to her, repeating the things he had just said.

Flannery took his hand away from her mouth and she spat out, "Who are you and what do you want?"

"You don't remember? I can't fault you on that. It's been so many years since we've all been together. Averil and me. You and that bastard Malachy."

Claire stiffened in recognition and tried to turn her face around. "Oh, dear God," she said. "Oh, my dear God."

"I'd fancy a prayer to me," he said. "I don't believe your God's in a position to help you much."

"Please don't hurt me," she whimpered.

"Ah, that's much better now. First, you can tell me something about Averil. Surely you must be in contact with her. Where does she live?"

"You can go to bloody hell," she screamed.

Flannery returned his hand to her face and gave her head a sudden jerk, causing her to cry out in pain. "Best you cooperate," he said. "I can always search your apartment. Maybe find a letter or two."

Claire slumped and Flannery relaxed his hand. "She lives in New York—Long Island. Now let me go."

"You learn very quickly," he said. "But I'm not quite finished. Tell me about Malachy. Is he living close by?"

"Him? Why do you want to know that?"

"I've got a score to settle. He testified against me and got himself a light sentence for that Brighton business. And me rotting away in Full Sutton while he's roaming about, enjoying his freedom."

Claire managed a slight laugh. "You won't find him around here anymore. He's living in Cork—afraid to show his face for fear of being locked up."

Both became silent and each became acutely aware of the other's heavy breathing. Claire prayed that Flannery would be satisfied and leave so she would not be further harmed. Flannery was actually enjoying the physical contact with a woman, albeit an uncooperative one, and deeply inhaled the scent of her perfume and perspiration. He brought his free hand around to her stomach, slid it under her sweater, and fondled her breasts, trying to get his fingers under her bra.

"Get your filthy hands off me," she snapped.

"Ah, tis a pity Malachy is so far away and not able to enjoy these fine tits."

Flannery became so engrossed with his unwelcome caresses that he failed to notice Claire twisting her head around toward his free hand. When she was able to touch his thumb with her lips, she opened her mouth and bit as hard as she could. Flannery yelped in pain and rolled onto the floor.

Sensing that it was an opportunity to defend herself, she sprang from the couch and began searching for the butcher knife. There was just enough light filtering in from the kitchen to show her where the knife had landed.

Flannery saw what she was trying to do and tackled her just as she picked up the knife. They struggled briefly but he overpowered her again, struck her on the side of her head with his fist, and knocked her unconscious.

When he caught his breath, he dragged her into the bedroom and plopped her on the bed. The light from the bathroom was enough for him to find a pair of hiking boots in her closet and take out one of the laces. He rolled her body over to one side and tied both hands behind her at the wrists. He stuffed his handkerchief into her mouth and, with some white adhesive tape from the bathroom, taped her mouth shut.

He stood next to the bed for a few moments pondering his next move. He went to the living room, withdrew his own switchblade from a coat pocket, and returned to the bedroom. He slowly and carefully began stripping all the clothing from her, cutting away fabric with his knife when it became difficult to remove in the usual manner.

CHAPTER THIRTY-FOUR

When she was totally naked, he gathered up her clothes and tossed them into the corner. Then he sat back on the bed next to her and began rubbing his hands over various parts of her body.

As Claire regained consciousness and realized her dire situation, she began squirming and trying to scream, attempting to get air into her lungs through her nose, her large eyes clearly showing her deep and terrible fear.

Flannery brushed the hair away from her face and spoke to her as a father might lecture an errant daughter. "That was a very stupid thing you did back there, going for the knife. But I'm pleased you've come around now. I want you fully awake so you can properly enjoy this."

He stood next to the bed and smiled down on her as he unbuckled his belt.

Chapter Thirty-Five

An hour after Selfridge opened for business on Thursday morning, Claire's friend, Pauline Templeton, walked from the cosmetics counter to Claire's work area and was surprised to discover her absence.

Just before noon, when Claire had still not appeared, Pauline checked with Claire's supervisor, Agnes Lassiter, regarding Claire's whereabouts. Agnes had made several phone calls to Claire's apartment without success, prompting Pauline to go to her apartment during the lunch hour to make sure Claire was all right.

Pauline rang the doorbell several times but received no answer. When another tenant came out of the building, Pauline seized the opportunity to walk briskly through the front door to the second floor. She knocked hard on Claire's door several times and, after getting no answer, turned to leave. But she had second thoughts and tried the door, very surprised to find it unlocked. After hesitating for a moment, Pauline slowly entered the dimly lit living room, not knowing what to expect. She called out Claire's name several times but received no response.

Pauline turned on a floor lamp and was shocked to see the living room in total disarray. Books had been yanked from their shelves, drawers had been pulled from cabinets, their contents dumped on the floor, and several sofa cushions had been slashed open leaving stuffing tufts everywhere.

She moved slowly about the room feeling a terrible dread; she feared discovering something too horrible to imagine. She forced herself to keep walking. When she reached the kitchen, she felt cold air coming from the broken window.

Pauline knew only one other room remained to be checked. At the bedroom door, she peeked inside cautiously and could barely make out Claire's body lying on the bed, faintly illuminated by the light filtering in from the bathroom. She screamed and bolted for the telephone in the living room.

She dialed 999, the British emergency number, told the duty dispatcher

CHAPTER THIRTY-FIVE

what she had just found, and begged him to send an ambulance as soon as possible. The dispatcher tried to calm her down and asked several more pertinent questions, including her name and the address and phone number of the apartment from which she was calling.

A sobbing Pauline returned to the bedroom where she turned on a table lamp. She fought back the choking nausea when she saw Claire's body caked with blood and the reddish-black stain of dried blood all about the beige bed spread. "Oh you poor dear," she cried, "what cruel bastard could have done this to you?"

She brushed the tears out of her eyes with one hand and reached down with the other, brushing the hair away from Claire's cool forehead, letting her hand slide down to her neck. When she felt a faint pulse with her finger tips, she cried out with joy, "She's alive. She's alive."

Pauline ran out of the apartment and down the stairs to the front entrance. She waited inside impatiently, pacing back and forth, until the ambulance arrived a few minutes later. Two burly male paramedics in blue uniforms ran up to the front door carrying large bags of equipment. One asked, "Are you the lady that called?"

"Yes, please hurry. I believe she's still alive."

The men entered the bedroom and went right to work while a trembling Pauline hovered nearby. They cut the boot laces on her wrists, started an IV, placed several blankets over her body, slowly removed the tape from her mouth as gently as possible, and pried the handkerchief from her mouth. "We're going down for the gurney, miss," said one of the paramedics to Pauline. "You watch her real close now."

Both men left the bedroom and returned quickly with the stretcher and gurney apparatus. While they were wrapping Claire in more blankets and strapping her in, two police officers entered the room. One policeman had bushy white hair and looked like the father of the other officer. They stood mute as the paramedics wheeled Claire down to the ambulance.

The older officer removed a notebook from his coat pocket and looked at Pauline. "I'm Sergeant Barnes, miss, and my colleague here is Constable Tilden. Can we move into the living room for a bit? After we get some information, one of us will take you over to the hospital so you can look after your friend."

On Friday morning, Chief Inspector Hungerford sat at his office desk reading a summary of London police reports covering the previous twenty-four hours, a ritual he performed almost every morning. It not only gave him a snapshot of the city's crime, but occasionally yielded valuable information on cases he was working.

When he read the short paragraph about Claire Blackwell, he hesitated briefly but went on to finish the rest of the summary. He left his office to refill his coffee cup but when he returned, he went to the sole office window instead of his desk. Something was nagging his brain, some snippet tugged at his memory.

He continued staring out the window at nothing in particular. When he finished his coffee, he returned to his desk and began riffling through all the papers in his Sean Flannery file, starting at the beginning many years ago. He found and read his own memo detailing Averil's assault and Claire Blackwell's assistance. He smiled, closed the folder, and placed a call to Sergeant Barnes' precinct. Ten minutes later, Barnes returned his call.

"Good morning, Sergeant Barnes. So good of you to promptly return my call. I've just read your report on the Claire Blackwell incident yesterday. Any information about her current condition?"

"In a manner of speaking, Inspector. I just rang the hospital and she's expected to pull through. They've downgraded her condition from critical to serious, but she's still sedated and not able to speak coherently. I hope to visit her this afternoon and perhaps get some type of statement."

"Very good, Sergeant. I would like to have a look at Miss Blackwell's apartment. Can you and Constable Tilden meet me there later this morning?"

"Certainly, Inspector. Would eleven-thirty be suitable?"

"Eleven-thirty it is," said Hungerford.

Sergeant Barnes met Chief Inspector Hungerford at the apartment building's front door and escorted him to the second floor where Constable Tilden stood guard in the living room. Tilden had opened the blinds in all the rooms so that the Chief Inspector could have a good look.

Hungerford moved about the living room slowly, his hands joined behind his back, pausing occasionally to look at something but otherwise

CHAPTER THIRTY-FIVE

remaining silent. "Nothing unusual here," volunteered Tilden. "Looks like just another burglary."

Sergeant Barnes guided Hungerford to the kitchen and pointed out the broken window. "This is the way he obviously entered," said Barnes. "Stuck his hand through the hole and unlocked the door."

"Did the laboratory people check for fingerprints?"

"Yes, they did, Inspector, but the door knob and the lot were wiped clean." Barnes pointed to the counter and added, "The bloke evidently helped himself to some whiskey while he was here. No prints on either the glass or bottle. It seems he knew what he was doing."

"Quite so," muttered Hungerford. "Let's have a look at the bedroom, eh?"

A window had been opened in the bedroom to allow the awful stench to dissipate. Sergeant Barnes pointed to the bed, "You can see the outline of her body and all the blood around it. She must have lost a lot during the night."

"What did the hospital have to say about this?" asked Hungerford.

"He cut her in different places. Not deep stab wounds, mind you, but slashes and nicks in just the right places to make her bleed a lot. He probably wasn't trying to kill her outright—just torture her. A bloody sadist if you ask me."

"Anything else?"

"The man had intercourse with her. The hospital confirmed that. But we don't know if it was before or after he cut her up."

"Where are her clothes?"

"The lab blokes took them," said Barnes, "along with the boot lace and the handkerchief that was in her mouth."

"Your report stated that her clothing was slashed."

"Right you are, Inspector. My theory is that he used the same knife to cut everything away from her body."

"Any luck finding the knife?"

"No, sir. I believe he took it with him. Probably ditched it somewhere after he left the premises."

Hungerford went back to the living room, followed by Barnes and Tilden. As he looked about the room again, he asked the officers for their opinions about the case. Tilden was the first to speak. "There's something not quite right about all this. At first glance, it *looks* like a routine burglary. But the assault on Miss Blackwell doesn't line up very well with that type of crime."

Sergeant Barnes added, "There's no clear evidence that anything was taken from the apartment. I'm thinking the perpetrator intended all along to assault her and then make his breaking and entering appear a burglary. Like she surprised him during his search for anything valuable."

Hungerford said, "I think you men are on to something. My feeling is that Miss Blackwell knew her assailant and that may be the very reason she was hurt so badly. Now if you would please, talk with her as soon as the hospital allows and let me know what she says. Meanwhile, I'd like to have one more look about the place. I shouldn't be too long."

Barnes and Tilden went outside while Hungerford moved about the apartment in what seemed to be a random walk, trying to get the feel of the place. When he came back to the living room, he walked over to the table on which Claire's photographs were displayed. He picked up the one of Averil and Claire, the same one that Flannery had observed just hours before, and stared hard at their happy faces. He placed the photograph back on the table, said a brief goodbye to Barnes and Tilden outside, and went directly to his office.

Chapter Thirty-Six

*E*arly Friday morning, Mark's telephone roused him from a deep sleep. "Mark, oh Mark," sobbed Averil. "Wake up dear, I desperately need to talk to you."

Mark bolted upright. "I'm here. What's wrong?"

"It's Claire. She's in the hospital and she's unconscious. He did it to her and all because of me. I just know it."

"Av, calm down and tell me what happened." While Averil wiped her tears and blew her nose, Mark glanced at his bedside clock. It was 4:30 A.M.

"I've just had a long chat with Chief Inspector Hungerford. He told me some alarming news about Claire Blackwell."

"What happened?"

"She was brutally attacked and raped, right in her own apartment. Pauline found her yesterday afternoon and miraculously, she was still alive. They rushed her to the hospital and gave her several blood transfusions. The inspector believes she'll pull through."

"My God, that is terrible. Why did they have to give her blood?"

"It's almost too horrible to imagine. The inspector said that she had many knife wounds and lost a lot of blood during the night. He didn't care to share the gory details with me."

"So this happened Wednesday night?"

"That's right. The inspector went to her apartment this morning to have a look around for himself, along with the two officers who were first on the scene."

"What did he say about that?"

"Her apartment was all topsy turvy, just like the place had been robbed by a burglar. He evidently broke a window in the kitchen and unlocked the back door from the inside. Pauline and Claire had a few drinks after work and the police think the man was inside the apartment when she came home."

"Has Claire been able to tell the police anything?"

"No, she hasn't. She was in shock when they got her to the hospital and she's still heavily sedated. The inspector hopes they can talk with her later today."

"Damn, that's pretty bad luck, walking into a burglary in progress."

"The inspector thinks it may be more than that." Averil paused and a tremor shook Mark, as if he'd seen somebody walked across his own grave. She continued, "That's why he called. He thinks it's possible that Sean is the one who did it."

Mark broke out in a cold sweat. "So he's using Claire to find you."

"I'm afraid so. She may have told him something about me."

"What do you mean?"

"I talked with Claire last Sunday. Rang her up to chat about old times. Maybe get together for lunch later in the week."

"My God—she might have told him you're in Southampton."

"That's what the inspector thinks."

"Then you're in greater danger than ever before. You need more protection, round-the-clock, until they can track down that miserable son of a bitch."

"Inspector Hungerford is going to call the Southampton police and have them increase their presence around Mum's house."

"This whole damned business is getting out of hand. I'm coming over there, just as soon as I can."

Averil started crying again. "I was hoping you would, but I didn't feel right asking you to come across. Just after your trip to San Francisco."

"Don't worry about that. This is much more important. I'll try to get a flight this morning to New York. I should get there tomorrow morning sometime."

"I want to go up to the hospital and see Claire, but I'll wait until you get here. Maybe we can do that together."

"Good idea. They'll probably want her to regain consciousness first and talk to the police before they allow any visitors."

After he finally hung up, Mark turned on the light and got out of bed. He entered the shower stall and pounded on the tile walls, yelling at the top of his voice, "Shit—shit—shit."

Mark dressed casually, checked out of the hotel, and drove directly to the airport where he turned in his rental car. His next stop was the Trans-

CHAPTER THIRTY-SIX

Global ticket counter. He booked a non-revenue seat on the 9:45 A.M. flight to New York, however, the computer system showed the connecting flight to London's Heathrow airport was full so he was placed on standby.

He had time to kill before the flight departed so he found a restaurant in the terminal, bought a newspaper, and ordered breakfast. He was in such a state of worry and guilt that he only nibbled at his food and scanned the paper.

At nine o'clock, he telephoned the SIMFLIGHT plant and asked for Tom Campbell. When Tom came on the line, Mark gave him the details of Averil's situation and the necessity for leaving St. Louis on such short notice. "Don't worry about it," said Tom. "Being with your wife right now is the right thing to do. Why don't you bring her back to St. Louis with you?"

"I've already been thinking about that," said Mark. "First, we've got to find her jailbird ex-husband and get his ass back into prison."

The flight from St. Louis was on schedule and uneventful. When Mark reached the JFK terminal he checked in with the head of passenger reservations and explained the nature of his emergency. She assured him that he would get a seat on the London flight, even if it was the worst one in economy class.

Mark's seat on the 747 was at the absolute rear of the plane. As he entered the cabin and walked toward the tail, several flight attendants recognized him and greeted him with a warm "welcome aboard." The flight pushed back about 7:30 P.M., thirty minutes behind schedule, and was airborne by eight o'clock. The long day was catching up with him so he reluctantly decided to take a nap and forfeit dinner. He wasn't very hungry anyway and, if necessary, could cadge something later from one of those smiling flight attendants.

Before he fell asleep, his mind wandered back to his and Averil's wedding just over ten years ago. She and Emma had made all the arrangements for a simple ceremony and reception at a country club on the outskirts of Portsmouth. Claire came alone and managed to catch Averil's bridal bouquet, prompting knowing onlookers to cluck that this should finally turn the trick and get her wedded soon to Mr. Right. *How wrong did that turn out to be?*

Three years after the wedding, Claire came to America for the first time on a summer holiday and stayed with Mark and Averil for two weeks. Averil took time off from her job and the two women explored beaches and antique stores at the Hamptons, shopped in Manhattan, and got spray-soaked at Niagara Falls.

Claire and Averil made an attractive and compatible pair. Claire was about an inch taller than Averil, had a slightly fuller figure, and wore her long brown hair straight down her back. Mark recalled with amusement her large brown eyes that seemed to widen threefold when shown the many excesses of America.

He recalled Claire's humorous personality and generosity of spirit; he winced at the thought of a man forcing her to have sex. The very idea of anyone cutting her body put a sour substance in his mouth that tasted like vomit. If it was Flannery, and from all that Mark had been told it did fit his character, then Averil had been right all along and Mark had seriously underestimated the man's cruelty. *Maybe I should have told Averil to hire a temporary bodyguard.*

Mark eventually fell asleep; not a deep slumber, but a sequence of short naps. The jerky side-to-side and up-and-down movements of the aircraft's tail in the dark turbulence over the Atlantic woke him more than once.

During one of these short dozes, he had a dream fragment, one that he could not grasp completely after he awoke. He saw himself in a large circus tent on a high wire many feet above the ground. He wore a clown's costume with oversize floppy shoes. At the other end of the wire was a red-haired man dressed in pink tights, and behind him was Averil, her arms tightly folded around one of the tent's main poles, wearing a revealing set of purple tights covered with sparkling sequins.

The red-haired man moved in Mark's direction, hopping and skipping on the wire like he'd been doing it all his life. Mark moved cautiously towards the red-haired man as the raucous crowd urged him on. He looked down and noticed there was no safety net below, but somehow he kept moving, knowing that he needed to get to the other side and rescue Averil. When he got only a few feet away from the red-haired man, the man reached behind his back and pulled a long knife from his belt. As the man kept moving forward, waving and slashing his knife in the air, Mark lost his balance and felt himself falling off the wire.

CHAPTER THIRTY-SIX

He woke suddenly and, for a brief moment, forgot where he was. He left his aisle seat, walked forward to one of the galleys, and asked a flight attendant for coffee. He talked for a few minutes with two attendants and, after finishing his coffee, returned to his seat. He took a paperback novel from the seat-back pocket in front. Unable to concentrate, he closed the book and returned it to the pocket.

He leaned back and thought of Averil and how unfair it was that she should experience all this pain. *I'm the one who should be suffering because of my unfaithfulness. How could I do this to her?* As tears began to well, he said a silent prayer of contrition and asked God to bless and protect her.

Mark's reverie was interrupted by something happening to the aircraft. He could tell by the subtle changes in the sounds and movements of the plane that something was not quite right. Whether it was unusual turbulence, hydraulic malfunction, or electronic component failure, he had a growing suspicion that this 747 was not operating as it should.

The plane went into a steep right bank and began losing altitude. Mark first thought the pilot had been cleared for a new course and elevation to avoid either bad weather or another aircraft. But as the plane kept turning, Mark realized they were making a 180 degree turn and completely reversing course. *What the hell is going on here? Is he going to tell us?*

A minute later the captain came on the speaker system and made an announcement. "Ladies and gentlemen, we've just had a problem with one of our engines so we had to shut it down. Now the 747 is capable of flying safely on three engines so I want to assure you there is no danger. However, just to be on the safe side, we've taken the precaution of altering our course to make an unscheduled stop so we can have the engine repaired. We'll be landing in Gander, Newfoundland in about an hour, so please sit back and relax. I'll have more information for you prior to our landing."

Those passengers who were awake grumbled at this latest piece of news. Mark stood up suddenly in protest but then sank back into his seat when he realized he was just one helpless passenger among many. After several minutes of stewing over his fate, he flagged a passing flight attendant. "Tell the captain that I'm aboard, would you please? Ask him if I can come up to the cockpit. Maybe I can help out in some way."

Chapter Thirty-Seven

"Where in the devil are you?" asked Averil.

"Newfoundland. One of our engines crapped out so we diverted to Gander. They've got mechanics swarming all over the damned thing."

"What a bloody nuisance. When might you arrive at Heathrow?"

"I'll get there when I get there."

"I need you here now."

"Don't be upset, Av. It's just one of those things. If I'd been the pilot, I would have done the same thing. What's the latest on Claire?"

"I called the hospital earlier this morning. She still hasn't come to, but the staff are hopeful that something will happen soon."

"I'll bet the police want her to wake up too."

"Mark, I've decided to go up this afternoon. I'd like to be there when she regains consciousness."

"Do you think that's a good idea with Flannery still on the loose?"

"I shouldn't think that he'd be coming to the hospital to look in on Claire. It should be safe with police all about the place."

"Be very careful," he said. "I'll call you when I get into Heathrow. I'll try the house first, then the hospital."

While Averil gazed out the train's coach window on her way to London, Claire woke up, much to the relief of the intensive care unit's attending staff. Sergeant Barnes was notified and came immediately to the hospital with Constable Tilden. When they arrived, the duty nurse told them, "I know you have a number of questions for our girl, but please make it brief. She does need her rest."

"Right you are, matron. We'll just be a few minutes."

The officers were ushered into a cubicle formed by two white cinder block walls and a large blue wrap-around curtain that could be closed to form the other two virtual walls. Claire's head was slightly elevated and her eyes were only half open. Her pale face was clean and bore few traces of her savage attack. A light-weight blanket covered her torso while a single plastic tube was connected to her arm and numerous wires were attached to her other body parts.

Barnes walked up to the left side of her bed while Tilden stood on the right. After Barnes introduced himself and Tilden he said, "I'm very sorry to bother you at a time like this, Miss Blackwell, but we'd like to ask a few questions about your assailant. Can you remember anything at all?"

Claire tilted her head slightly to look up at Barnes. "Yes, I know the man. It was Flannery, the escaped convict."

"Are you sure of that, miss?"

"Oh yes, I'm quite sure. He was after some information about my friends, Averil and Malachy."

"And who would they be?" Tilden scribbled furiously in his notebook.

"Averil is my dearest friend. She used to be married to him, before he was sent to prison. I used to date Malachy but he lives in Ireland now. He and Flannery ran around together in that bloody terrorist gang."

"What did Flannery want to know about these people?" asked Barnes.

"He wanted to know where they live. He's looking for revenge against Averil because she divorced him while he was in prison. And Malachy testified against him in court so he could get a lighter sentence."

Tilden asked, "Did you get a look at Flannery?"

"The light wasn't very good but I did notice that he looked different. He has a mustache and a full head of black hair. It was always red before."

Barnes and Tilden made several motions as if to leave. Claire raised a hand and grasped Barnes's arm. "You've got to warn Averil. She's in Southampton now and she's in grave danger."

"Did you tell Flannery that she's in Southampton?" asked Barnes.

"No, I didn't. I told him she was living in New York. But if he takes a fancy to look up her mother . . ." Claire closed her eyes and heaved a deep sigh.

Barnes disentangled himself from her and said, "I believe that's enough for now. Try to get some rest."

Barnes and Tilden walked to the nearby nurse's station, whereupon Barnes telephoned Chief Inspector Hungerford and gave him a full report.

Averil arrived at the hospital almost two hours after Claire awakened. When she entered the intensive care unit cubicle and saw Claire, she lost her reserved English composure and burst into tears.

"Come over here, you twit," said Claire faintly.

Averil walked over to the side of her bed, knelt down, and buried her head against the blankets. "I'm so sorry," she sobbed. "You didn't deserve this and it's all because of me."

"You mustn't blame yourself for this," said Claire as she stroked Averil's hair. "The man is an animal."

"Then it *was* Sean who did this to you."

"Yes, it was. I just told the police a short time ago."

"Why on earth would he do such a horrible thing? It's me that he's after."

"I wasn't very cooperative. I had a butcher knife but he knocked it out of my hand. When I broke free, I went after it and that's when he knocked me about." Averil got up, found a nearby chair, and pulled it to the side of the bed. "He asked about you, Av. He wanted to know where you were living."

Averil shivered with fear. "What did you tell him? Did you mention my being in Southampton?"

"Of course not. I told him you lived in New York." Averil's shoulders slumped forward and she closed her eyes briefly. Claire continued, "It won't be easy for him to leave England and enter America. He'll need money, a passport."

"The authorities shouldn't underestimate this man," cautioned Averil. "He's clever, cruel, and utterly ruthless when it comes to righting a situation where he feels wronged. He'll do almost anything to achieve his goals."

"He also wanted to know about Malachy. He evidently wants to settle some old score with him about their prison sentences."

"That proves my point," said Averil. "The man is so full of hatred that he thinks only of hurting others. I'd wager he doesn't care a fig about his own safety. What a totally loathsome person. What did I ever see in him?"

The attending nurse came into the cubicle and spoke to Averil, "Would you mind stepping out into the waiting room for a bit? I need to change her dressings and give her some medication. It shouldn't take long."

Averil got up and squeezed Claire's hand. "I'll not be far away. We still have some catching up to do."

Averil returned to Claire's bedside ten minutes later. They held hands

CHAPTER THIRTY-SEVEN

again and talked of things unrelated to Claire's attack. Averil mentioned that Mark was on his way to London but temporarily stranded in Newfoundland while the plane's engine was being repaired.

Claire eventually succumbed to the painkillers she'd been given and dozed off into a light sleep. Averil relaxed in her chair and watched her deep breathing, content to know that she was safe and would survive.

Unexpectedly, Chief Inspector Hungerford entered the room. Averil rose and extended her hand. "Hello Inspector. I'm so relieved to see you again."

"I thought you might be here. I've very sorry we have to meet again under such circumstances. How is Miss Blackwell doing?"

"Quite well, considering all that she's been through. But she's a brave soul—I know she'll pull through with flying colors."

"I'd like to have a word with her," said Hungerford, "but I don't want to disturb her rest. Can we step outside, perhaps, and have a coffee?"

"Of course."

They walked to a nearby lounge and Hungerford exercised his influence by getting two cups of coffee, a refreshment not available to the general public. As they sat in a corner sipping their coffee, Hungerford gave Averil a report of all the information gathered by the police. Toward the end, he summarized the situation. "We know her assailant was Flannery, that he's probably hiding somewhere in London, and we have a description—the way he looks now. It's difficult to predict his next move, but based on what Miss Blackwell told him about you, I should think he'd be trying to leave England and somehow reach New York."

"That presents a new problem," she said. "I hope to return to New York in several weeks. After my sister and I get mother settled into the Botley Manor."

"We'd like to prevent him from leaving the country," he said. "If we could apprehend him while he's still in England, that would forestall many sticky problems dealing with the Americans. Extradition proceedings and all that."

"That's all well and good, but the police haven't had much luck so far, have they?"

"That's true, but I have an idea that may flush him out of hiding. However, we will need your help if my plan is to succeed."

"My help? How can I possibly help Scotland Yard?"

"If Flannery should learn that you are in Southampton attending your mother, then he would surely travel there, hoping to find you."

"That would be terrible. Mother and I would be in serious jeopardy."

"But Scotland Yard and the Southampton police would be protecting you. We would have stakeout teams surrounding your mother's house, twenty-four hours daily and every day of the week. Our men would be invisible."

"So mother and I would be juicy targets for him."

"A well-protected bit of bait, I would say. Something to bring the rat out."

"How would you let him know of my whereabouts?"

Hungerford's eyes gleamed as he bent forward. "There's a photographer from *The Sun* who's been making a bloody nuisance of himself. Wants to take a picture of Miss Blackwell in her hospital bed and have a photo to go along with the sordid account of her attack."

"That bloody rag?"

"Mind you, I don't approve of their journalistic methods, but we've been able to use the tabloids to our advantage occasionally."

"What part would I play in this charade?"

"When the photographer comes by to take her picture, you would also be in the room by her bed. The picture would appear in tomorrow's or Monday's edition, Flannery sees it and recognizes you, and deduces that you are currently in England. When he travels to your mother's place, we spring the trap and haul him back to prison. What do you think?"

Averil got up, paced nervously back and forth in deep thought, and returned to face Hungerford. "I'm afraid, Inspector. If he manages to slip through your trap, more innocent people could be hurt. I would dearly love to discuss this first with my husband."

"Where is he?"

"Unfortunately, he's in Newfoundland, delayed by a faulty aircraft engine. I can't say exactly when he should arrive in London."

"I understand your concern, Mrs. Holloway. But time is of the essence here. We have to catch him before his trail goes cold. And, as you put it so well, before he hurts more innocent people."

Averil hesitated and looked out the window at the fading afternoon sunlight.

CHAPTER THIRTY-SEVEN

"Very well, Inspector. I'll agree to your plan. But I have one stipulation."

"Good show, Mrs. Holloway. And what is that?"

"I will not allow that newspaper to feature either Claire or me as their Page Two Girl."

A quizzical look came over Hungerford's face. "Page Two Girl?"

"Those well-endowed young women they show without any clothes."

He burst out laughing, "Oh, that's very good indeed, Mrs. Holloway. I'm so pleased to see you haven't lost your sense of humor."

Chapter Thirty-Eight

Shortly after seven o'clock the next morning, a hungry Sean Flannery emerged from his hotel. He walked briskly in the thick damp fog searching for an open restaurant. He stopped briefly at a corner newsstand, bought a copy of *The Sun*, tucked it under his arm, and continued walking. He eventually found a small cafe and took a seat in a corner booth at the rear.

He ordered scrambled eggs, bangers, mash, and coffee from a sullen waitress. She brought him a white china cup filled with hot black coffee, a small pitcher of cream, and carelessly dropped both on the table top before returning to the kitchen. He would have complained about her poor attitude but, not wanting to draw attention to himself, let the matter slide.

Flannery casually flipped through the pages of the newspaper while sipping his coffee, stopping occasionally to read something that attracted his interest. When he reached page seven and saw the article about Claire with the photo, he sat up suddenly and smiled.

Here now, what's this? She didn't die after all. Evidently me cuts weren't deep enough to do any serious damage. And who's this woman beside her? She resembles Averil but the caption doesn't identify her. It must be her. Who else would be visiting Claire in the hospital but her best friend? Yes, it is definitely Averil. Which means she's somewhere in England right now. Of course, she'd look different. It's been a long time since I last laid eyes on her.

Flannery finally stopped staring at the photo long enough to read the article. He was impressed by both the depth and accuracy of the report. The article told of Claire's rape and knife attack in lurid detail which caused Flannery to reflect on his actions during the experience and give him a mild erection. Sergeant Barnes was also quoted, confirming that Claire had recognized her attacker as the escaped convict, Sean Flannery, and had provided police with a physical description.

An excited Flannery quickly devoured his breakfast. Over his second

CHAPTER THIRTY-EIGHT

cup of coffee, he went back to the photo and slowly reread the entire article. *The cat's out of the bag, isn't it? They know it was me that done it so now I'll get me the respect I truly deserve. What fools they must be, making my work so much easier, now that I know Averil's back in England. Why didn't Claire tell me about Averil when I was with her the other night? Perhaps she just came across when she found out that Claire had been hospitalized. I'll have to be a bit more careful now. There's sure to be police watching Averil's movements.*

Flannery drained his cup, rolled up his paper, and stuck it in his coat pocket. As he left the cafe, he pulled down the flaps of his cap and lifted the collar of his coat. He walked back to his hotel in a fine drizzle, stopping again at the same newsstand to buy a copy of *The Sunday Times*.

Mark's plane landed at Heathrow just before two o'clock that afternoon, thirty hours behind schedule. After he cleared customs and immigration, he called Charlotte's home and spoke briefly with a greatly relieved Averil. He took a train from the terminal into downtown London, another train to Southampton, and finally, a taxi to Charlotte's house in the northeast part of the city. It was after dark when he arrived.

Averil, looking anxiously out the living room window, saw the taxi pull up and rushed to the front door, greeting Mark with a warm hug and a long kiss. "Thank God you're here," was all she could manage.

"For a while, I was sure they'd make us honorary Newfies."

Averil took his coat and hung it in a hall closet. Charlotte came out from the kitchen when she heard the commotion. "Welcome back, Mark. Did you have a nice flight?"

Mark kissed her on the cheek and gave her a gentle hug. "Not my idea of a fun-filled holiday, Charlotte. But I made it and that's what counts."

"Averil's fixed a lovely dinner for us. Pot roast and mashed potatoes. I do hope you're hungry."

"I'm starving. But I feel pretty grubby. Do I have time to get cleaned up?"

"Certainly, luv," said Averil. "I'll run the bath water for you."

"Shall we say seven o'clock for dinner?" asked Charlotte.

"Fine with me," said Mark. "It won't take me long to scrape off the top layer of dirt."

Mark took his suitcase into the guest bedroom and laid it flat across one of the twin beds. "We'll be sleeping in here," said Averil. "I hope you don't mind."

"Not at all. Any port in a storm."

The bathtub was a small metal container on feet, not lush by modern standards, but enough to allow Mark a quick dunk and scrub. He toweled off and put on a heavy pair of black sweat pants and a white turtleneck shirt. When he came into the living room, Averil kissed him again and handed him a large glass of red wine. "Feeling human again, luv?"

"Oh yeah, that was a good bath. A nice dinner and this wine ought to make me a new man again."

When the three eventually sat down, Mark ate like a man who had just come off a seven day hunger strike. The conversation was initially light and dealt with general subjects, but eventually it came around to Claire's attack and Averil's visit to the London hospital.

"Sorry to bring all this up at the dinner table," said Mark.

"Don't worry about that," said Charlotte. "Averil's told me the whole story already, so it makes little difference."

"Claire's body wounds will heal in time," said Averil. "Most of them are superficial anyway. I'm more concerned about her internal wounds—the trauma of being raped and brutally assaulted. I hope that some day she's able to put all that behind her."

"Were the police able to get any information from her?" asked Mark.

"Oh yes, she gave a full statement to the local police and Scotland Yard. It was Sean who did it, no doubt about that. But she said he looks different. He has a mustache and he's dyed his hair black."

"Did she give any reason why he did this?"

Averil hesitated and pushed her plate away. "He wanted to know where I live. He asked her questions about me and one of his old running mates, Malachy O'Brien."

"Did she tell him you were in England?"

"No, thank God. She said I was living in New York with you, but didn't specify a city."

Mark's shoulders slumped as he finished off the last of his wine while Averil and Charlotte exchanged nervous glances. Several minutes later, Charlotte rose and started clearing the table. Averil helped take dishes to the kitchen sink while Mark retreated to the guest bedroom to unpack.

CHAPTER THIRTY-EIGHT

As he was putting away his suitcase, Averil came into the bedroom. "Mother's retiring early. Wants to give us some time to ourselves. I've turned all the lights out in the front of the house."

"Sounds good to me," said Mark. "I'm just about ready to crash myself."

Averil reached under the pillow on the other twin bed and pulled out one of her long flannel nightgowns. She undressed quickly, removed her bra, and slid the nightgown over her head and shoulders with a falling parachute-like motion. Mark sat on the edge of his bed and watched her in the soft light of a lamp between the beds. "My, that's a glamorous piece of lingerie," he said.

"This house gets cold and drafty at night. You'll see."

She pulled down the covers of her bed, got in, and lay on her side facing Mark. She patted the mattress with her palm and said, "Come join me, luv, and cuddle for a while."

Mark smiled, stripped to his underwear, and slid into her warm embrace. "Whenever a beautiful lady invites me into her bed, I can never refuse."

"Yes, I know," she said softly.

Mark took careful note of her comment but chose not to respond. Instead, he pulled her close, gently stroked her back, and kissed her neck. "You smell good. Even better than your pot roast."

"I've felt terribly alone for the last few weeks. And I've missed this—the closeness of having you next to me. Having your arms around me now gives me the safest possible feeling."

"Sir Galahad at your service, my fair lady."

"How long can you stay, Mark? You haven't said."

"As long as it takes. As far as Trans-Global and SIMFLIGHT are concerned, I'm on an indefinite leave of absence. If everything goes smoothly, we should be able to go home after we get your mother moved into the Botley Manor. Shouldn't that be about two weeks from now?"

"That's correct. The only fly in the ointment would be Sean. Predicting his next move is not the easiest thing to do."

"If he thinks you're in New York, then he'll be trying to leave England and enter the U.S. The police could catch him at some airport or trying to board a ship headed in our direction."

"I believe the police and Scotland Yard have a different strategy in mind."

"Oh, really? What do you know about that?"

Averil stiffened and moved slightly away from him. "I haven't told you everything. I agreed to cooperate with Chief Inspector Hungerford. He has a plan for getting Sean to come out of hiding and expose himself."

"And how is he going to do that?"

Averil got out of bed, went to a dresser in the corner of the bedroom, and came back with a copy of *The Sun*. "The idea is that he would see this photo, recognize me, and come looking for me in Southampton."

"That's his plan? It makes the three of us sitting ducks, waiting for him to show up and do his shit."

"But the police will be waiting for him. It's all a trap to lure him down here and catch him when he gets close. Before he can do any harm. Did you notice the white van when you came to the house?"

"No, I didn't. What van is that?"

"Go to the living room window and take a look."

Mark padded off to the living room and came back a few minutes later. "Yeah, I saw one parked out there. What about it?"

"There are two policemen inside. They intend to change vehicles occasionally but there's supposed to be someone out there watching us all the time."

Mark slid back under the covers and put his arms around her again. "I don't like this, Av. What if something goes wrong? And why did you agree to do something like this without talking to me first?"

"I wanted to, luv, but Inspector Hungerford convinced me that we must act quickly, before Sean disappears permanently or hurts more innocent people."

They both became silent and held the other close, absorbing each other's warmth, and inhaling all the familiar aromas.

Eventually, Averil rolled over to face away from Mark, but pulled his free arm around her waist so he couldn't leave. When she finally drifted off to sleep and Mark could hear her faint snoring, he disentangled himself, slid into his own bed, and turned out the lamp. Even though he was very tired, he lay awake for a long time, wondering what manner of trouble would happen next and when their lives would return to normal.

Chapter Thirty-Nine

Flannery spent the entire afternoon in his hotel room, alternating between reading the newspapers and making plans for his foray to Southampton. *The Sunday Times* had also printed an article on Claire's assault and hospitalization with the details toned down, a practice that reflected a more conservative approach to reporting such events. There was no photograph with the article but a crude drawing of Flannery's face did appear. A police artist had sketched a picture of how he might look today with a mustache and full head of black hair.

Flannery looked in the bathroom mirror several times and concluded that the drawing was a reasonably close approximation. It took him less than fifteen minutes to remove the mustache and shave his head completely bald. He had a good laugh while running his fingers over it, feeling all the bumps and depressions.

Flannery had scanned the entertainment section of *The Sunday Times* and took note of the plays and musicals being performed in London's West End. If he wasn't a fugitive from justice, he thought how much he would have enjoyed an evening at the theater, followed by several drinks and a tasty meal. He was reminded by the advertising that there were no performances on Sunday at any of the theaters and it occurred to him that this could be used to his advantage.

At ten o'clock that evening, Flannery's bedside alarm woke him from a nap. He dressed in the factory worker's clothing that he'd worn every day in Birmingham, stuffed a few small items into his black canvas bag, and added numerous pieces of balled-up newsprint to make it look full. He left his hotel, took an underground train, and was in the West End before eleven o'clock.

The streets were fairly well illuminated but there were almost no vehicles or pedestrians to be seen at that hour. He walked along the front of several theaters and when he reached a corner, turned and went around to the dark alley in back. The theater buildings extended all the way to the alley and had many doors that Flannery checked methodically until he found one open.

He removed a small flashlight from his bag and moved silently toward a light coming from an open room at the rear of the stage. As he came to the edge of the room, he saw a night watchman sitting on a stuffed chair, fast asleep and snoring loudly. Flannery was able to move to the other side of the stage without disturbing him. He kept shining his light at different doors until he found one with a sign saying 'wardrobe.'

He went inside the room and found a treasure trove of shoes, dresses, wigs—all manner of costumes for women appearing on stage. He pulled out the balled-up newspaper from his bag and replaced it with a silver gray wig, a pair of flat black pumps, a long dark blue dress, a white shawl, and several accessories including a large flowery hat and a purse. He also found a thick mahogany cane that he gripped with his free hand.

As he walked briskly down the dark alley away from the theater, he cackled, "Aye, what a clever fellow I am. They'll never recognize me in this getup."

In Monday afternoon's fading sunlight, Flannery made last minute preparations for his departure. He first put on the work shirt and trousers and tried wearing the black pumps that he stole from the West End theater. They pinched him so badly, he decided to wear his work boots instead. He put on the long blue dress and covered his neck and shoulders with the white shawl. While looking in the bathroom mirror, he fitted the silver gray wig to his bald pate and applied lipstick to his fat lips. He placed the flowered hat on top of the wig and tied it under his chin with two long ribbons attached to the sides of the hat. When he was finished, he flashed a gruesome smile and said to his reflection, "My God, you are certainly the ugliest woman I ever laid me eyes on."

He checked the purse once more to make sure that his phony identification papers, his money, and his knife were safely tucked inside. The rest of his clothing and belongings were stowed in the room's closet, the single dresser, and the bathroom. In the event that anyone came to check on him or on the room, it would appear that Mr. Paul Sullivan had left for a short time and fully intended to return for the rest of his things.

Flannery walked slowly away from the hotel, feigning a limp and

CHAPTER THIRTY-NINE

aided by the mahogany cane. He caught a taxi at the first corner he came to and, in a gravelly falsetto voice, asked the driver to take him to Victoria Station.

Flannery had an uneventful train trip to Southampton. Most people took one look at this formidable looking old lady and wanted nothing to do with her. A few kind souls offered to help her board and alight from the train, but *she* dismissed them immediately with a threatening movement of the cane.

He hailed a taxi outside the Southampton station and told the driver that he was looking for a certain pub in the northeast part of the city. This was actually somewhat of a gamble on his part. He wanted to get as close to Charlotte's home as possible and felt certain that there would be a pub or two in the neighborhood. He gave the driver a story about meeting *her* son at the pub, anticipating that the worthless bum was going to put the arm on her for some money.

The driver found such a pub and Flannery was dropped near its front door. He went inside, found a quiet booth, and asked the young waitress for a menu and a small pot of tea. He checked his watch and it was 8:30 P.M. He decided to settle in for a couple of hours before moving on to Charlotte's home.

Mark, Averil, and Charlotte had a light breakfast together that Monday morning. Averil fixed poached eggs on toast for her mother and herself, but Mark was content with just toast, orange marmalade, and coffee.

"What's the plan for today?" asked Mark.

"I want you to help me get ready for the jumble sale," said Averil.

"Jumble? What's a jumble?"

Averil laughed. "It's what Americans call a rummage sale. Or a garage sale if you held it at your own home."

Mark groaned. "Oh, that sounds like loads of fun."

"It won't be so bad, luv. Emma and I have already done much of the work."

"So what do we need to do?" asked Mark.

"Most of the items are already in the garage. We have to attach price tags and carry the lot over to the church hall."

Charlotte was silent for most of the conversation but finally spoke up.

"I do hope my things will command a good price. They've been in the family for years and are quite valuable, you know."

Averil and Mark exchanged glances and Averil patted Charlotte's hand. "We'll get the best price we can, Mum. But you must realize they've had considerable use over the years. I wouldn't call them antiques, though. Probably somewhere in between, I should think."

"What is your point, dear?" asked Charlotte.

"My point is that people won't pay much for used household items. They'd just as soon buy new if they have to spend any considerable sum at all."

Flannery guzzled four Irish whiskies after having a light meal that evening at the pub. Midnight was fast approaching so he decided it was time to get moving again before he became totally drunk.

He walked slowly along the neighborhood sidewalks toward Charlotte's house, hunched over and leaning on the cane for support. There were no other pedestrians about but several passing cars slowed down to offer this old woman assistance so she could get home safely.

Charlotte's house was totally dark when he passed, but because of his relatively slow movement, he was able to give it a fairly thorough inspection, thanks to the glow of a nearby street lamp. It seemed to be just as he remembered it. He kept walking for two more blocks until he came to a small park. He sat down on a bench and considered his next move.

He retraced his steps and passed Charlotte's house again from the other direction. When he reached the next corner, he turned and went around to the alley and came up to the house's back door. He picked at the lock with a small tool and was pleasantly surprised when he was able to open the door.

He stepped carefully into a dark kitchen and slowly closed the door, careful not to make any sounds. He stood completely still, catching his breath, and letting his vision adjust to the darkness while taking in familiar cooking aromas.

After several minutes had passed in total silence, Flannery moved down a hallway, guided by a faint night light plugged into a wall socket and a loud snoring sound coming from the bedroom. He pushed the bedroom door open all the way and stopped to look at the body hidden

CHAPTER THIRTY-NINE

by covers, the room illuminated by the orange glow of the outside street lamps.

He walked over and, dropping his body on the reclining form, placed his mouth near the woman's ear. "Averil, it's Sean," he whispered. "Wake up now. I've come to take you away."

The woman bolted out of bed on the side away from Flannery and screamed loudly. To his horror, he could tell that it was Charlotte he'd awakened, not Averil. He had mistakenly assumed that Averil would be in the main bedroom. Flannery was momentarily confused, but then realized that if she was here, Averil must be sleeping in another part of the house.

Meanwhile, Charlotte's scream had awakened Mark and Averil. Mark jumped out of bed, went to the living room, and turned on the lights. Averil switched on the bedside lamp and wrapped a robe over her nightgown.

In the brief tussle with Charlotte, Flannery's hat and wig had come off and were now lying on the bed covers. He noticed the living room lights being turned on and heard Mark's voice calling out. The presence of another male in the house alarmed and further confused Flannery, causing him to instinctively reach for his knife and toss the purse on the bed. He made his way toward the living room, his knife at the ready.

When Mark saw a grotesque and bald headed Flannery with badly smeared lipstick and dressed in woman's clothing, he was stunned. "Who the hell are you?" he eventually asked. "How did you get in here?"

"I might be asking the same about you," snarled Flannery. "Just tell me where Averil is and stay out of me way. That way, you won't get hurt."

Mark realized who the intruder was and lunged for him. "You rotten son of a bitch," he yelled. "You'll have to get through me first."

Flannery waved the knife across Mark's left side as he came forward and cut a deep gash in his upper arm. They collided noisily, knocking over an end table, and wrestled on the floor while Mark tried several times to get the knife away from him, dodging or blocking his slashing and stabbing movements. In one close embrace, Flannery stabbed Mark on his right side near the waist, causing him to cry out in pain and loosen his hold. Blood spurted and spread into Mark's white undershirt and briefs.

Charlotte and Averil came into the living room about the same time.

Averil saw Mark lying on the floor, doubled up and clutching his side, and made a sudden motion to go to him. "Not so fast," said Flannery. "Just stand where you are so I can keep me eye on you."

Averil froze in fear and stared hard at Flannery, trying to figure out just who this person was and what had happened. When she finally recognized him, she blurted out, "What happened to your head? They said you had black hair?"

Flannery waved his knife and scowled. "Is that all you can say after all these years? What happened to me head?"

Averil folded her arms across her chest and said, "I would say more if you'd put that knife away."

Flannery considered Averil's calm demeanor, let his arms drop, and took a few steps toward her. Meanwhile, Charlotte went over to Mark, knelt down, and tried to comfort him.

"That's better," said Averil. "Why are you here, Sean? Is it your plan to punish me like Claire?"

"She was stupid. If she hadn't tried some foolish tricks, I wouldn't have harmed her."

"Then what do you want?"

"I want you. I want me wife back and I want it to be like it used to be."

She wanted to laugh but suppressed it, fearing that it would only make the situation worse. "It can never be like that again. That man over there on the floor is my husband and that's where my future is. Not with you. Ever."

He moved even closer. "All the time I was in that bloody prison I never stopped thinking about you. Never stopped loving you, even after you divorced me for that Yank."

Averil looked deeply into his eyes and became even bolder. "You still don't understand, do you? I told you that day in prison years ago that we could never be together again. Nothing has changed—don't you see that?"

Flannery's eyes glazed over. "But I have money and a passport. We could go away together. South America somewhere. I'd be safe there and they couldn't haul me back to England. I'll make it all up to you and make you happy."

Averil looked at him with pity. "No, I don't think so. It's far too late for

CHAPTER THIRTY-NINE

anything like that."

Flannery closed the gap between them, grabbed the front of her robe with one hand and brought his knife's sharp edge next to her neck. "That's where you're all wrong. It's not too late at all. Now come with me and don't try anything."

He pushed her toward the front door and motioned her to unlock it and step outside. She stepped through the doorway, stopped on the cement slab, and turned back toward him. "Where are you taking me?"

Before Flannery could answer, two men dressed in tight-fitting black clothing made their presence known, one standing on each side of the doorway. One man grabbed Averil by the arm and yanked her down and away; the other man pointed a pistol at Flannery's head and shouted, "Freeze—police."

Showing extraordinary presence of mind, Flannery bolted and ran down the sidewalk to the street. He was undone, however, by his long blue dress and tripped on its hem, sending him tumbling into the gutter while the knife bounced away. For a split second, he thought of reaching for the knife, but also realized it would give the police a perfect excuse for emptying their weapons into his dying Irish carcass. The result of his short deliberation was to meekly surrender.

The policemen quickly subdued Flannery and handcuffed his wrists behind his back. While one of the officers had his knee in the small of Flannery's back and his pistol next to his temple, the other officer went inside the house to check on Mark. Averil was already there, kneeling next to him and holding a small towel next to his side wound. Two more policemen came through the front door. The one next to Mark called out to the newcomers, telling them to radio for a paddy wagon and an ambulance.

Averil looked at the closest officer. "Were all of you cooped up in the van?"

"No, miss. The officers who just arrived are my backup. I called the station for help."

"How did you know to do that?"

"Just a hunch, miss. When I saw the old lady walk by, I thought it was rather odd. The second time she passed, I noticed she was wearing army boots so I sounded the alarm."

The paddy wagon and ambulance arrived almost simultaneously. Flannery was taken away with little ceremony and physically thrown into the rear of the mobile jail. The paramedics applied compresses to Mark's wounds, gently loaded him onto a stretcher, and took him to the ambulance. "I'm going with him, Mum," said Averil. "I'll call you as soon as I have some news."

"Yes, do keep me posted," said Charlotte. "I'm putting the kettle on for tea, so I should be up. It's not possible for a poor soul to get any sleep around here with all this commotion going on."

Chapter Forty

Mark's injuries were not life threatening; Flannery's knife just missed his kidneys. He did require minor surgery, however, and was kept in the hospital nearly a week for recuperation. He returned to Charlotte's house only two days before she was scheduled to move into Botley Manor.

Averil stayed busy during this period, looking after two semi-invalids instead of just one. In true British fashion, she persevered, continually reminding herself that this was only a temporary inconvenience and would soon pass.

Flannery was returned to Full Sutton Prison two days after his capture. It took a full day for the specially-equipped bus and his considerable group of armed guards to make the journey. Chief Inspector Hungerford called Averil and said that Flannery would face many new charges, including the rape and aggravated assault of Claire Blackwell. Averil and Mark adamantly insisted on not pressing charges. They feared that doing so would only delay their return to New York and believed there was more than enough evidence to keep him in prison for many years. The day after Flannery's arrival at Full Sutton, it became a common feeling throughout the prison that before a year would pass, he would be out again; he would either escape or be a dead man. The betting line among the inmates on this happening was ten-to-one, but the odds still weren't rich enough to attract any bets.

On November first, Charlotte moved into Botley Manor and slowly began to settle in and make friends. Several pieces of her household furniture were also brought into the single room apartment. Those items that remained and not sold in the jumble sale were donated to the Salvation Army. Keys to the house were left with the real estate agent whom Averil had chosen to sell the house. Emma was also given a set of keys and promised to get the house cleaned up for showing to potential buyers.

Mark and Averil left Southampton for London one morning, checked into the Selfridge hotel, and visited Claire that afternoon. Her wounds were healing nicely and she had already begun therapy for the internal injuries caused by her emotional trauma. In a moment of juvenile humor, Mark offered to show Claire his scars if she would show hers, commenting that they were now blood relatives since both had been slashed by the same man. Claire politely but firmly declined his invitation. When the visit ended, she tearfully accepted Averil's invitation for a long return visit to Huntington in the near future.

That evening, Mark booked seats for himself and Averil on the next morning's Trans-Global flight from Heathrow to JFK. In a spontaneous gesture of appreciation for all that Averil had done and recognition of the agony she endured during the last several weeks, he paid the incremental difference to have their seats upgraded to First Class. She didn't find out about his largess until they actually boarded the aircraft.

When they reached their cruising altitude, Mark called the flight attendant and asked for two glasses of champagne. He also winked a signal to her but Averil missed it. She was taken aback at Mark ordering the champagne because it represented a break in his usual custom of not drinking on flights. She was even more surprised when the flight attendant presented her with a vase containing ten freshly cut red roses.

"They are so lovely. But what did I do to deserve such a beautiful bouquet?"

"Just by being you," he said. "The woman I love who takes good care of me and continually amazes me."

She stuck her nose down among the blooms and inhaled deeply. "I just love their fragrance." She stared intently at the flowers and then turned to Mark. "There are ten roses in the vase—is that significant?"

"Of course. One for each year we've been married."

She leaned over and gave him a long soft kiss. "You are such a dear heart. So I still amaze you, after all these years?"

"Yes, you do. I don't think I'll ever forget the way you stood up to Flannery that night. What you did took a lot of courage. Facing him down while he still had that knife in his hand. I sure wasn't much help to you, lying there on the floor. I thought I was going to bleed to death."

"Much of the strength I do have comes from you," she said. "You tried hard to save me before I even came into the room. But I'm afraid you were

CHAPTER FORTY

no match for that gangster. He's no better than a common street fighter."

"Still, you took a big risk."

"When I got a good look at his face, I could see something in his eyes. It made me realize that, at the end of the day, he wouldn't hurt me. The pathetic man still loves me. I think he harbored some demented idea that I would go waltzing off with him to some foreign country. Utterly preposterous."

Averil laughed suddenly, causing Mark to eye her curiously. "What's so funny about that?"

"I'm sure we would have made quite a stunning pair—me in my bathrobe and him in those horrid women's clothes."

"Yeah, right. But I'd rather not think about that."

"We wouldn't have gotten very far anyway. His money and identification papers were still in the purse on mum's bed." She sipped her champagne, turned to him, and took his hand. "Enough of that rubbish. How are *you* feeling, luv?"

"Me?" He paused to consider her question. "Well, in a word, *acroyali*."

"What was that?"

Mark chuckled before elaborating. "I have to tell you a little story. You know how I like Yanni's music. One of my favorites is a piece called *Acroyali*. I had a conversation once with an Olympic pilot, a Greek fellow, and I asked him what the word meant. He said it was a feeling. He told me to picture walking with my sweetheart on a moonlit beach—our arms around each other's waist. We've just had a wonderful dinner with a bottle of fine wine and we're heading back to our hotel. We both know that once we get there, we'll make love. That combined feeling of anticipation and contentment is called *acroyali*."

"My goodness, I hadn't expected such a romantic answer." She squeezed his hand. "But I'm very happy you feel that way."

"Content but not complacent," he added.

"So we're about to enjoy a nice lunch and a suitable wine, courtesy of Trans-Global's flying sommelier. But we don't have that moonlit beach at hand, nor do we have a nearby hotel to provide us with a comfortable bed. What a pity."

"Hey, Mrs. Holloway," he said with an impish gleam in his eye. "Have you ever heard about the mile high club?"

A look of mock horror came over her face. "Are you thinking about having sex right here on the plane?"

"Sure, it's doable. After lunch, I'll get a couple of blankets from the flight attendant, we'll push up the arm rest, and snuggle up under the blankets. The cabin will be dark anyway for the movie. We'll be each other's dessert."

"But what about your wounds?"

"I'll give you some moans and groans at the right time."

She shook her head. "You're incorrigible."

Mark reached over with his left hand, slid it under her sweater, and hooked his little finger in her navel. She returned his hand to his lap and giggled, "You'll just have to be patient, Mr. Holloway. I promise you, however, that when we get in our own bed again, I'll take *very good care* of you indeed."

"You've got a date."

The flight attendant arrived with hot appetizers which signaled the start of lunch. One hour and four courses later, they relaxed over coffee.

"What happens after we get back home?" she asked. You haven't talked much about that."

"Monday, I need to check in with the airline's flight surgeon. He'll probably want to examine me before I'm returned to full duty."

"Do you want to start flying right away?"

"Not really. I want to go back and finish the simulator project."

"Ah yes, St. Louis beckons once again," she said, her smile fading.

"But it's going to be different this time. I want you to come with me. I don't want us living apart while I wrap up this job."

"Why do you want me there—for protection?"

Mark's face turned a light shade of red and he hesitated. "I just need you. I don't sleep well without you. I get terribly lonely and I work better when you're close by."

Averil laughed. "What balderdash. All right, I'll do it, but I won't live there. I'll still commute to Long Island some of the time."

She excused herself to go to the bathroom while Mark stared out the window at the white clouds below. He thought about the conversation they just had, in particular the business about going back to St. Louis. Given enough rope, he would have figuratively hung himself. That is, if

CHAPTER FORTY

Averil had let the talk about St. Louis go further, he would have been inclined to confess his brief affair with Joan and get it all off his chest. But he remembered something he'd once read in a Dear Abby column; while confession might be good for the confessor's soul, it would only hurt and anger the one who had been betrayed. Very often, the ultimate outcome of the confession just made the confessor's life a living hell, negating entirely the original purpose of his delayed and guilt-induced honesty.

Then it all became clear. He recalled the comment she made the night he arrived from Newfoundland; how she knew he couldn't resist the invitation of a beautiful woman to join her in bed. There was also her remark earlier this morning—about coming to St. Louis for *his* protection.

There is only one conclusion to be drawn from the little she had said and the sheer volume of what had not been said. She knows about my affair with Joan and she also knows it's over. Convincing her to forgive and forget will be the most important thing I'll ever do during the rest of my life. I'd better get it right this time.

About the Author

Richard C. ("Dick") Reynolds was born in 1934 in East St. Louis, IL and raised mainly in St. Louis, MO. In 1953, he enlisted in the Marine Corps Reserve as a private, and retired twenty-four years later as a Lieutenant Colonel, serving in infantry and communications-electronics assignments. During his military career, he earned college degrees in Mathematics and Electronics as well as a Master of Science in Computer Engineering from the University of Michigan. At the end of his military career, he also taught computer science and programming courses for two years at the George Washington University.

From 1977 to 1994, Dick was a System Engineer for Hughes Aircraft Company in Fullerton, CA and Brussels, Belgium. During this time, he worked on command and control system programs for Greece, Norway and Denmark, and on air defense projects for NATO, the Arab Republic of Egypt and the Kingdom of Saudi Arabia.

Shortly after moving to Santa Fe, NM in the summer of 1994, Dick began a fourth career—short story fiction writing. His thirty stories have appeared in such publications as *Potpourri, Timber Creek Review, The Roswell Literary Review, Satire* magazine, *Sweet Annie & Sweet Pea Review, Words of Wisdom,* and *Affair of the Mind.* One of his stories was nominated for a Pushcart Prize in 1998 and, in addition, he has had poems published in *New Mexico PRIME TIME* and the *Millennium Science Fiction & Fantasy* magazines. Dick is currently writing his second novel, *Mayhem in Mazatlan.*

When not at his word processor, Dick might be found at the bridge table, singing with the St. Francis Cathedral Choir, or tromping the local mountains with his colleagues in the Santa Fe Search and Rescue Group.

Dick is married to the former Maureen Duffy of Des Moines, IA. Together they have ten children and thirteen grandchildren scattered all about the U.S.